Mitakuye oyasin
(We all are relatives)

Wicahpi Win
(Star Woman)

Bonnie Jo Hunt
Love, Bonnie J. Hunt

THE LONE WOLF CLAN

AN AWESOME VISION LAUNCHES THE LONE WOLF CLAN ON A JOURNEY WHICH CHANGES THEIR LIVES FOREVER

---

by

Bonnie Jo Hunt and Lawrence J. Hunt

We have always been here. We would rather die here. Our fathers did. We cannot leave them here. Our children were born here — how can we go away? If you give us the best place in the world, it is not so good for us as this . . . . This is our home.

Weinock, Yakama

A Lone Wolf Clan Book, Vol I
(Third Edition)

A special thanks to our fine editorial staff for their detailed
and tireless efforts to make this book right.

The authors wish to express their deepest appreciation to
all who support ARTISTS OF INDIAN AMERICA, INC. (A.I.A.)
in its work with Indian youth. All proceeds from the sale of THE
LONE WOLF CLAN go to further the work of A.I.A.. For infor-
mation concerning A.I.A. contact Mad Bear Press. Contributions
to A.I.A. are tax deductible and most gratefully received.

Cover art work, "Together We Are One," is through courtesy
of talented Cherokee Nation artist, William E. Rabbit,
Pryor, Oklahoma

Revised cover designed by CYBERDESK Solutions,
Ricardo Chavez-Mendez & Michelle Marin-Chavez.

Published by Mad Bear Press
6636 Mossman Place NE
Albuquerque, NM 87110
Tel. & FAX 505 - 881- 4093

A NOTE FROM THE AUTHORS

In olden times our people gathered around lodge fires to listen to Storyteller; fascinated by his tales, we learned our way of life. Religion, legends, history, philosophy, ethics — what today we learn from books and in school, we learned from Storyteller's lips.

John Stands in The Timber recorded in his book, Cheyenne Memories, how Storyteller worked his trade: "An old storyteller would smooth the ground in front of him with his hand and made two marks on it with his right thumb, two marks with his left, and a double mark with both hands together. . . . Then he touched the marks on the ground with both hands and rubbed them together and passed them over his head and all over his body. That meant the Creator had made human beings . . . as he had made the earth, and that the Creator was witness to what was to be told."

The tradition has been lost in the changing way of life but the desire for storytelling remains. In writing of bygone days we attempt in a small way to keep this wonderful tradition alive. THE LONE WOLF CLAN is a story the whole family can enjoy.

It is a tale of lives told in the tradition of Storyteller, to entertain, at the same time to pass along bits of history, wit and wisdom. Drama, humor, tragedy, love, hate — all ingredients that are part of living are present, set against the backdrop of days when fur trappers and Indian people first met and attempted to coexist — a period of our history that makes one cringe, cry and laugh. We know you will enjoy sharing these sentiments with us. As our people say,"Mitakuye oyasin." We all are related.

Wicahpi Win (Star Woman)   Lawrence J. Hunt

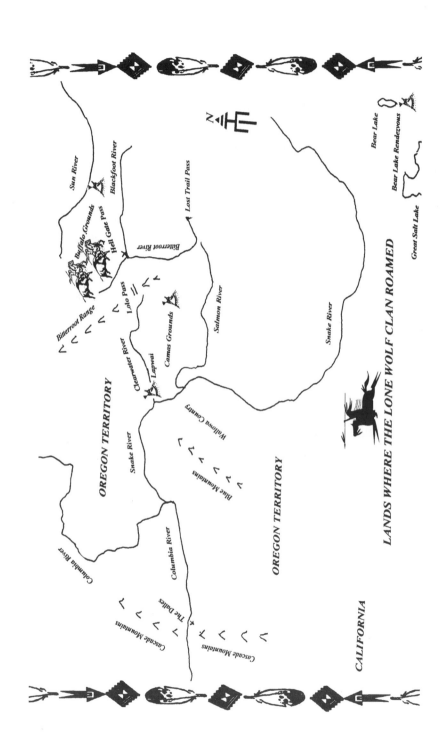

LANDS WHERE THE LONE WOLF CLAN ROAMED

THE LONE WOLF CLAN

*We are part fire, and part dream. We are the physical mirroring
of Miaheyyun, the Total Universe . . .*

Fire Dog, Cheyenne

The sound of hoofbeats came to him softly, a distant roll
of thunder. Like a dry weed before a twisting wind, the pounding
noise became louder only to fade away, and return louder and
louder and louder. His fingers trembled. Then he remembered
his instructions. He was to remain out of sight, to wait, not do
anything until they reached the last rise, not until they began to
labor up the final approach.

They swept over a distant ridge. His mouth went dry.
The host of galloping bodies spread out to cover the plain like a
brown hairy blanket. The bright sun glittered on row after row of
shiny pointed objects. The dark wave rolled over the next hillock
and then over another, engulfing everything in its path. The flash
of the shiny objects became brighter, more sinister, deadly, like
tips of lances thrust forward to engage an enemy in battle. The
awesome sight and sound made him cringe. He backed away
until he was up against a rocky ledge. The noise was overpowering. Clouds of dust filled the air. A pair of jack rabbits, caught in
the path of the explosive charge, darted for safety. One failed to
escape. Its terrified death squeal was lost in the thunderous roar
of the advancing horde. Nothing could survive the lines of surging beasts. The high grass and brush over which they passed lay
flattened on the prairie floor. Like the sharpened teeth of a har-
row, the thousands of cloven hooves churned the skin of Mother
Earth to bits.

They were so near he could single out the bobbing heads,
spikelike horns, wild eyes, nostrils flaring and red as if snorting
smoke and fire. An enormous shaggy bull broke free from the
galloping line and made straight for the spot where he stood. The

animals behind turned to follow. His legs had suddenly turned to
water. He would suffer the same fate as the jack rabbit. Again,
he remembered his father's instructions. They were coming up
the last slope. In one quick motion, he snatched up the bleached
deerskin at his feet and scrambled up on the ledge of rocks. He
began to wave the deerskin with all his might. The startled animals in the lead veered toward the deadly cliff. The dark brown
line thundered by, the sound deafening, the air thick with the smell
of dust, musk and fear. The big bull, its wild eyes flecked with
blood, took no notice of the flapping deerskin. It kept galloping
straight for him. He could see every hair on the bull's big shaggy
head, every drop of moisture on the big flared nose. He dropped
the deerskin, jumped back and screamed. . . .

For a long moment Lone Wolf lay stunned. Where was
he? What had happened? The snorting, hairy bull had gotten
him. He had been trampled to death and had gone to the other
side. No! There still came the pounding; the choking smells of
thick air surrounded him. He sat bolt upright and looked wildly
about. Instead of the face and head of a mad bull, it was the face
and head of his mate, Quiet Woman, who loomed before him.
The pounding came from pestles and mortars. The women of the
long lodge were beating kouse roots into flour. The dust and
smell he tasted came from the smoke of twenty lodge fires and
the cooking of twenty evening meals.

Lone Wolf sighed with such relief Quiet Woman rose on
her knees to inspect his face. She grasped him by the shoulders.

"Bad sleep?" she queried, her eyes filled with concern.

Lone Wolf pushed her away. Bad sleep! No! He had
been wide awake. He saw everything as clearly as he had that
day on the plains. He had just relived his first big hunt. He had
been twelve years old. His father had put him on the point to flag
the herd of great beasts over the cliff to their deaths. He had
played only a small part, yet the event was imprinted on his mind
like the carving on a tree. It had been the most successful buffalo
hunt in the history of the Nimpau. Elders repeated the tale so oft-

ten it had become a legend.

Slowly, Lone Wolf got to his feet, ignoring the curious glances of lodge occupants. He made for the doorway and stepped outside. The experience had been so vivid and real he felt weak. A sharp breeze blew up the valley off the cold waters of the Kooskooskie, the river the hairy faces called Clearwater. The clean, fresh air was like a tonic. Increasingly refreshed, he strolled toward the river. Quiet Woman would soon have the meal prepared but he needed to be alone.

A squirrel, gathering seeds and nuts, flipped its tail and dashed up a tree trunk. On the hillside a pair of deer bounded away, their black tails twitching. Geese glided over the bluff and down Lapwai Valley. "We're going south, we're going south," their wings whispered. The call of the wild birds was so strong Lone Wolf looked up. Mother Earth was changing seasons. It was the Season of Falling Leaves. Soon it would be the Season of Falling Snow.

"Ah!" Lone Wolf uttered to himself. Where had the time gone? What had he done with his life? Fifty winters had passed since that first buffalo hunt. Hunts in those days required careful planning and great cunning. With only bows and arrows and lances, it took skill and clever mounts to slaughter sufficient bison to satisfy even the needs of a small village. The big kills came by driving the shaggy animals over a cliff where, by the hundreds, they fell to their deaths. Women and children waited on the canyon floor below to attack the fallen game with knives and hatchets, making certain the pain of the wounded was ended quickly.

They butchered the carcasses; dried the meat, froze it, and made pemmican. The hides were cleaned, cured, and became robes, clothing, bags, tether lines, halters, and tipi coverings. The horns and bones were collected and made into tools, awls, knives, spoons, cups, pins, tipi stakes, cradle boards, medicines, and dozens of other useful things. The hair was woven into ropes, stuffed into pillows, cradle boards and saddle pads. The hooves were ground into glue. The padded neck pelt went to make shields. Bladders became medicine bags and water containers, the stomachs cooking pots, tendons and sinew, thread and bowstrings, skulls headdresses and ceremonial masks; scrotums were turned into rattles for religious purposes. Intestines were cleaned, roasted, and eaten. Nothing was wasted.

Lone Wolf stared at the darkening sky. How many moons had come and gone since the great hunt? He rubbed his head where the hair was beginning to thin. How many more moons would the Great Mystery grant him? If only he could lead a great hunt before he passed to the other side . . . He walked back toward the lodge only to stop dead still, stunned by a startling thought. He knew what happened. The Great Mystery had visited him -- taken him back in time to relive the glorious Big Hunt. Why did the Great One so honor him? It was a message.

Inflamed by the wondrous discovery, Lone Wolf hurried to the long lodge. The excitement that gripped him quickly faded. He paused outside the place he called home. The semisubterranean structure was over thirty paces in length covered with mats of reeds and grasses. Twenty families existed side by side, most of them related to him by blood or marriage. He took a deep breath and went inside. It was meal time. The lodge interior remained thick with smoke. The odor of roasted meat, aroma of baked camas cakes, and penetrating smell of smoked salmon, hung heavy in the air. Yellow Fawn, who was always late in preparing her meal, savagely pounded dried kouse roots into flour. The clang and clatter of pestle against mortar rapped on Lone Wolf's ears like the rat-a-tat of a woodpecker's beak.

Lone Wolf glanced down the long lodge and grimaced. "I have spent most of my life living like this, why does it upset me now?" he asked himself. These were his people. Left Hand, who had taken his sister, Camas Blossom, for his mate, had the next fire. Red Bull and his other sister, Little Bird, had the one beyond. Spring Robin, Tall Elk, Running Deer . . . The list went on and on. There were so many youngsters he could not remember their names. Usually he loved to have family around. It was a poor man who had no relatives. Now, enclosed with them in the long lodge, he felt trapped. He wanted to shout, order everyone to be quiet. When he had their attention he would announce the news. Instead, ignoring Quiet Woman's sharp, inquiring glance, he stepped outside again.

A grating voice from the shadows made Lone Wolf jump. "Hoh! The old bear is not hungry? He does not eat the evening meal?"

Lone Wolf scowled. Weasel Face, who with his family lived in the next lodge, was like a pesky deer fly stinging him when he was least prepared. Why did he put up with this sly neighbor? Of course he had to; he was a member of the same band. Unless he left Lapwai Valley there was no way to avoid him. Weasel Face's daughter, Small Goat, was the best friend of his own daughter, Raven Wing. They always were up to mischief, buzzing around annoying everybody like mosquitoes in a closed tipi. Weasel Face's second daughter, The Weaver, was Grandmother's constant companion. They sat for hours whispering, giggling, rustling in the corner of the lodge like pack rats, always doing something with their hands: pleating reed mats, making baskets, hemp pouches and, when mountain sheep were killed, spinning thread and weaving articles of wool.

"Restless friend, you wish to fly south like the geese but have no wings?" Weasel Face moved near, his teasing, close-set eyes glittering like lively, shiny black bugs.

"One who has horses needs no wings," Lone Wolf retorted.

"Oh, you will ride after the birds?" Weasel Face's voice dripped with sarcasm. "Patience, old bear. Your old bones need the sun when you take to the trail."

The snide reference to his mounting years made Lone Wolf's blood boil. "I leave tomorrow for buffalo country," he snapped.

"Hey-hey!" Weasel Face, who desired to replace Lone

Wolf as leader of the Lapwai band, stepped back in mock surprise. "My good friend, you wish for the good things buffalo
brings? Too late, old bear. It is not the season for travel. The
trail is bad. It is best you keep your bones safe and warm in the
home lodge."

Weasel Face's words pricked Lone Wolf's skin like wasp
stings. The annoying, squint-eyed, two-legged pest always found
a way to belittle him. Lone Wolf abruptly turned away. Now
nothing would keep him from making the trip to buffalo country.
If he dared, he would take only his immediate family. He wanted
to get away from people, especially Weasel Face and all of his
bothersome offspring. At every move he made there was a member of the Weasel Face family waiting to torment him.

#

Lone Wolf's eldest son, Many Horses, who came in from
seeing to the herd, was the first family member to hear Lone Wolf's
plan. His father caught him outside the lodge. "We travel tomorrow to buffalo country. Bring the herd close to the long lodge
tonight. Have the pack animals ready to load at first light."

Many Horses gave his father a questioning look. Yesterday Lone Wolf had instructed him to prepare a sheltered area
where the herd would be protected from storms during the Season of Blowing Snow. The stoic, expressionless face revealed
nothing. Many Horses kept his thoughts to himself. As usual, he
would do as his father asked.

While they sat watching Quiet Woman set the belated meal
before them, Lone Wolf announced his plans for the hunting trip
to the other members of the family. He glanced uneasily at his
mate. Would Quiet Woman object? He did not think so. During
their life together, she had accepted his decisions without comment. However, this time she uttered a groan.

Grandmother, almost hidden in the corner, chuckled. She
had told her son the mate he chose was weak and had waited
twenty-six winters to prove she was right. She pulled the shawl
up to hide her toothless mouth. "It is good," she said in a voice

that quavered. "We pack tonight and sharpen skinning knives in the morning. Think of the many carcasses to butcher and hides to clean."

Quiet Woman took the pots of food from the fire and slammed them down before the men. She sidled back into the shadows and glanced around the long lodge for their eighteen year-old daughter, Raven Wing. The lazy one had escaped again. When it came to work she was as worthless as a camp dog. What was she to do with this girl? Raven Wing shunned work even more than she did the hapless suitors who came to seek her hand. When it came time to pack for the trip she and that Small Goat companion of hers would giggle and play -- nothing would get done.

Eldest son, Many Horses, glanced at his mother. He knew how she felt. He also looked forward to the trip with dread. The herd was his main concern. He feared the summer foals were not sufficiently strong to make the mountain crossing. Even if they safely arrived in buffalo country, they faced the Season of Falling Snow in a land where wolves and other predators could hamstring them or worse. His father's stern visage told him any objections he made would be ignored.

Running Turtle, the youngest son, clapped his chubby hands in glee. His round face was all smiles. The excitement of the buffalo hunt outweighed all thought of danger and hardship. He searched for his bow and arrows. He must make certain the bow string was strong, the arrow shafts straight and arrow heads sharp. It was shameful for a hunter not to be properly prepared. Vision Seeker, serious-minded middle son, was the only one to openly question Lone Wolf's decision. "The Season of Falling Snow is upon us. Is it not late to make the journey to buffalo country?" he asked.

"You are more timid than an old woman. Look at Grandmother; she is ready to go. Of course there will be snow. Bring your robe so you do not fall ill from the cold." Lone Wolf's words cut sharply through the din and smoke-thickened air.

"Remember the last crossing of the mountains?" Vision Seeker persisted. "Did we not lose a pack animal and all it carried? It is more dangerous now. I see storms . . ."

"I do not want to hear about your signs," Lone Wolf angrily interrupted. "We go to the buffalo grounds."

Vision Seeker fell silent. From past experience he knew once Lone Wolf made up his mind no argument, however sensible, would sway him. He glanced at Many Horses. As eldest son why did he not speak up? The last time Lone Wolf hurried them off on a trip it was to the Chinook trading center at the falls of the Great River. Lone Wolf wasted days bargaining for things they did not need. But this decision was far worse. Not only was the trip across the mountains dangerous, but spending the Season of Deep Snow in buffalo country courted disaster. Storms descended without warning, dealing death to man and animal. When he finished eating Vision Seeker took his sleeping robe and slipped away, ignoring his father's disapproving scowl.

"Should you not listen to Second Son?" Quiet Woman asked hopefully when Vision Seeker had gone. "The signs he sees are often true."

Lone Wolf stared at his mate. What was the matter with his family? They were like a bunch of timid rabbits. He got up and stomped around the fire. He could not speak of the Great Mystery's visitation. The experience was sacred, not to be spoken of lightly. He glanced down the line of lodge fires. Who should he select to go? It did not have to be a large hunting party. Of course he had to ask every family in the long lodge. To overlook anyone would cause trouble. He spoke to Left Hand first. His brother was eager to go. Next he approached Red Bull. He could not wait to leave. Lone Wolf went the length of the lodge. The response pleased him. Everyone except a few elders wanted to go along. He returned to report the news to Quiet Woman.

Hardly did he speak when a flash of lightening, so bright it lit up the darkened corners of the lodge, arced across the valley. A thunderclap followed, so loud it made small children cry. Lone

Wolf frowned. Vision Seeker was right about the storms. It was the season for drenching rains. Swollen creeks and water pouring down the hillsides could create havoc on the trail. Another bolt of lightening and clap of thunder made the lodge shake and creak. Flecks of debris fell from the ceiling made of tree limbs, leaves, bulrushes and dirt.

Quiet Woman glanced fearfully around. All she saw was Grandmother's bright eyes peering out from her shawl. "Where are our children?"

"I do not know, woman," Lone Wolf retorted testily. She was beginning to get on his nerves. When they first met she hardly said a word. Now, in her middle years, she carried on like a talkative child. He supposed Raven Wing and Many Horses were with the herd. Running Turtle probably had gone into the hills to be with Vision Seeker. That was where the two youngest sons went to stare at the stars and gabble about the mysteries of Father Sky.

What strange offspring he had sired. The only one with any worth was Many Horses. First Son was slow but he always was obedient and willing to help. He was good with horses. He watched over the herd, caring for the animals as though they were his own. Raven Wing! His only daughter had given him trouble from the start. She was willful, disobedient . . . It distressed him to think about her. Youngest son, Running Turtle? He was fat, lazy, bumbling about like a village clown. It was too early to tell what he would amount to, but he had not started well.

Vision Seeker! There was the worrisome one. At his age most Nimpau youth had found their supernatural guardian, *Wyakin* -- the powerful spirit that guided them through life. Before puberty all Nimpau males went alone without food or water into the high mountains on vision quests seeking this guardian. Sometimes they stayed a day and a night, sometimes three days and three nights. Second Son remained in the mountains a fortnight and still returned without *Wyakin*.

A second vision quest also failed. After the two failed

quests people began to call him Vision Seeker. Second Son adopted the name. It was right for him, he said. The name did not please Lone Wolf. It was not one that struck fear in the heart of the enemy nor did it command respect of his own people. Instead, Lapwai villagers eyed Vision Seeker uneasily. Thunder Eyes, the medicine man, avoided him. Vision Seeker was a man without *Wyakin.* He had no spirit to guide him.

Lone Wolf gave Quiet Woman a suspicious glance. Had Second Son properly been carried in the womb? Were evil spirits at the birthing place? Lone Wolf suddenly found his mate's busyness irksome. "Sit, woman. Rest yourself," he ordered. "I do not understand Second Son. Why does he not take pleasure in the hunt? Why does he find fault with what I do? Why is he not like other young men who bring pride to their family?"

Quiet Woman put aside her work. Seldom did Lone Wolf seek her advice on anything, least of all on the rearing of their children. Now that he did, she had none to give. "He is little more than a child," Quiet Woman finally said. "In time he is certain to do the things he should."

"Time!" Lone Wolf snapped. "I do not wish to wait until I'm toothless and white-headed as the bald eagle." It was just like a woman to stand up for her cub. He ordered her to throw more wood on the fire and reached for his sleeping robe. But who could sleep when the brain was so alive? Besides worries over Second Son, his mind went over every step of the trail to buffalo country. He had to admit Vision Seeker and Weasel Face were right. It was not the season to cross the mountains. Even sure-footed ponies found the trail hard-going. On the last hunting trip, as Vision Seeker grimly reminded him, a pack horse slipped down the mountain to its death.

Lone Wolf scowled. Why was he fearful? If the hunt was not to be why did the Great Mysterious send so powerful a message? It had to be a warning. The winters remaining to him were few. If ever he was to lead a big hunt it had to be soon -- why not now? Nevertheless, that night Lone Wolf did not sleep well.

II

Nature goes her own way, and all that to us seems an exception is really according to order.

Goethe

As Vision Seeker left the long lodge, he paused outside to sniff and embrace the cool evening air. It did not please him. Everything smelled of the lodge. The river breezes that kept the valley air clean were gone. A layer of lodge fire smoke hung below the treetops thick as morning fog, its acrid odor was so strong it hurt his eyes. He could understand his father's desire to leave. Until the warm winds that ushered in the Season of Melting Snow this stifling atmosphere could cloak the village for days on end.

Vision Seeker hurried by the next lodge and the next. A dog came out to sniff. A baby cried. One woman crooned a lullaby, another scolded. A man coughed. Everything appeared normal, yet there was an uneasy stillness like that which precedes a storm. Always alert to the sights and sounds of Mother Earth, Vision Seeker felt a prickle of alarm. He attempted to shake it off. Was it fear of the coming journey that made him feel this way or did he merely imagine that disaster was in the offing? He could not decide.

Away from the village, Vision Seeker crossed the creek to follow the rocky trail that wound up to the heights of the valley's eastern bluffs. Under the willows that cloaked the creek banks he encountered the usual smothering cloud of gnats and mosquitoes. Throwing the sleeping robe over his head and shoulders, Vision Seeker increased his gait to a lope. The darkness deepened but he kept up the pace. Companions who accompanied him on overnight hikes complained he had legs of an antelope and eyes of an owl; he could jump the height of a sixteen-hand horse and see in the dark of night almost as well as in the broad light of day.

When he got above the layer of smoke, Vision Seeker took a deep breath and glanced at the star-studded sky. Some of the brightest orbs of light were so near it seemed he could reach out and pick them like fruit from a tree. The friendly twinkling lights were comforting, yet left him with a feeling of awe.

Never did he study the canopy of brilliance without marveling how the dots of light remained fixed in place. What kept them from falling through space? Why did some stars shine so early and others come out in the darkest hours of night? Why did stars shine brightest near the horizon and those high overhead shed less light? Why was it stars in the north could be seen all night and stars to the south rose and set like the moon and sun? "Ah!" he sighed. There were so many mysteries surrounding Mother Earth he could not understand. The lack of knowledge made him feel as insignificant as a speck of dust.

In a clearing high above the valley floor, Vision Seeker laid out the sleeping robe. This was his favorite spot to watch the comings and goings in the valley below. He had cut down the brush, removed loose rocks and built a circle of stones to contain a campfire. On cold nights he warmed himself by fire. Tonight he was too troubled to bother. He sank down to stare at the dots of light overhead. Perhaps a sign of what was to come would appear in the stars.

He searched the sky in vain. It was the same display of brilliant particles that twinkled like rays of the sun on icy crystals of snow. He singled out old friends. There was the cluster that resembled a running fox, not far away was the flying horse, then almost straight up were the dove, the fish and the hawk. Off to the south was the serpent entwined around the figure of a man. Sometimes it was so clear, bright and alive it turned his blood cold. Tonight the snake rippled, slithering and groping around the man's body. The sight became so real he could feel the serpent clutching at his skin. The sensation was worse than ever before. Cold clammy scales creeping and crawling made goose bumps rise. "Ah!" he groaned, what a terrible imagination he possessed.

A twig snapped to break the spell. Running Turtle, who was supposed to be in the long lodge helping his mother pack for the trail, had slipped away. He was far too excited to busy himself at such a mundane task. Now that he had eleven winters behind him he hoped to ride the hunt along with the men. He had to share the thrilling prospect with someone. Vision Seeker was the only one who would understand. Bubbling with enthusiasm, he plopped down beside his brother and began to jabber in a shrill voice that had a tendency to squeak.

"Father's trip is good. Few hunters will be east of the mountains, the buffalo will not be afraid. Herds and herds of them, as many as trees in the forest will come. They will reach from Sun River to the hills of the Blackfeet Nation. I shall go after a bull and take his horns. When we return I will fix them to a wall of the lodge. They will remind everyone I made my first buffalo kill." Running Turtle's exuberant chatter continued unabated.

"Quit chattering like the blue jay. Look to Father Sky and learn the many mysteries he tries to tell us."

Running Turtle fell silent. He glanced at Vision Seeker. His brother was troubled. It was not like him to scold. He wriggled uncomfortably. He had hoped Vision Seeker would advise him, tell him how to prepare for the trip, tell him what he should and should not do on the journey and after they arrived in buffalo country. It was important to know the ways of the trail and the proper way to conduct oneself on the hunt. This was his big chance to prove he was more than a stumbling, roly-poly child.

Running Turtle took a deep breath and attempted to compose himself. Why did he always make a mess of things? He tried to do his best but things always came out wrong. His father thought him dumb. Village boys his age would not play with him; he was not good at games. His name even caused him pain. When he first learned to toddle, he lurched and wobbled like an ungainly newborn colt. As he grew older he ran at the same awkward, slow pace. After his first foot race at the annual camas harvest festival, which he badly lost, in disgust Lone Wolf said he ran like a turtle. His fellow racers and all the spectators laughed, thought it a big joke. "Running Turtle!" they teased. "That's the name he shall be known by." No matter how hard he attempted to overcome it, the hated name stuck.

An equally humiliating experience came after returning from his *Wyakin* search. During the third night in the mountains a vivid dream came to him. Out of a snowstorm a huge bull buffalo appeared, running straight for their tipi lodge. Running Turtle quickly seized his brother's lance and threw it. The buffalo stumbled, fell and died. The dream was so real he knew *Wyakin* had visited him. He ran all the way home to tell his father. "I shall take the name Buffalo Slayer," he proudly announced.

Lone Wolf scowled. "It is not good. Everyone in the village will make fun of you. No one will take this name seriously. His father was right. The people laughed. He remained Running Turtle. He brushed at his eyes and tried to swallow the lump of disappointment that choked him. He had to do something spectacular or the name would stay with him until he made his crossing into the next world. That was why he vowed to make a good showing on the upcoming buffalo hunt.

Vision Seeker had always been the one he could talk to, the one person who understood him. He was kind. He did not make him the butt of cruel jokes like many others, and they shared much in common. They both were looked upon as being different: Running Turtle because of his unmanly stature and ungainly ways, Vision Seeker because of his lack of *Wyakin* and fascination with the stars.

Running Turtle put his troubles behind him and dutifully glanced up at the canopy overhead. A falling star caught his eye. "Vision Seeker! It falls like a spent arrow. Why does it not stay in Father Sky?"

Vision Seeker glanced in the direction the excited youth

pointed. "I am told falling stars are the spirits of earth persons returning home."

"Oh!" The tone of Running Turtle's voice was skeptical. "Why does its light go out before reaching Mother Earth?"

"The sky people are angry with the spirit. The sky people took the spirit into their midst. Now it turns against them and runs away. This spirit is like a man who is welcomed into a lodge and rudely leaves before taking part in the ceremonial smoke. When the spirit drops out of the sky world it has to give up its light and find its way home the best way it can."

"Can it find its way back to Mother Earth?"

"Yes, but it takes a big chance. It may not come to rest in a place where it is welcome or may become lost. The spirit can fall into the forest, on the plains or even into the big water which has no end."

"Why does it not go back into the sky world?"

"Once a spirit leaves the sky world it can never return. If it does not find its former home on Mother Earth it wanders around searching and searching to find a place to live. Some say the whisper and moan of the wind in the trees are lost souls trying to find their way home," Vision Seeker patiently explained.

Running Turtle fell silent again. Conversations with Vision Seeker always left him confused. His brother had the strangest beliefs. Little wonder Thunder Eyes, the medicine man, avoided him. Thunder Eyes did not understand the things Vision Seeker said and did not want to reveal his ignorance by asking Vision Seeker to explain. Running Turtle studied the sky and tried to count the dots of light. He quickly gave up. There were more than the hairs on a camp dog. Was each one a spirit of someone who died? Surely, there never had been that many people who lived. An ominous rumbling sound came from the north. Running Turtle seized Vision Seeker's arm.

Across the Kooskooskie bluffs rolled a black cloud blocking out the stars. The same lightening bolt that had illuminated the long lodge streaked across the sky. For a moment the broth-

ers were blinded. A crash told the hillside watchers a tree had
been shattered. A bark of thunder ricocheted up the valley. Like
the hollow thump of a giant drum, the aftershock echoed back. A
second lightening bolt, more dazzling than the first, bathed the
valley with light more brilliant than a midday sun. Every object
in the valley flashed vividly before the brothers' eyes.

"Stampede! The stallions are galloping; the mares are
following. They come this way," Running Turtle shouted, his
voice rising to a piercing shriek.

The dark cloud bank rolled forward to hang suspended
above the hilltops. Flashes of lightening descended from its black
skirts to keep the valley floor illuminated. A gust of wind carried
with it the smell of rain. A curtain of dust swept up the hillside.
For a moment the valley floor was hidden from view. When the
dust cleared Running Turtle jumped to his feet.

"The stallions! The herd!" he screamed. Raven Wing,
her constant companion, Small Goat, and Many Horses were on
the valley floor, running for their lives. The thundering herd was
close on their heels. Small Goat stumbled. Many Horses jerked
her back on her feet. For a moment the runners disappeared behind a thicket. The horses galloped on, the leader, a black stallion, its long mane and tail streaming in the wind, was a length in
front of a drove of mares. From the upper valley another band of
horses appeared. Led by Lone Wolf's magnificent white and gray
stallion, the second drove pounded down upon the first. Many
Horses, leading the two girls by the hands, sprinted out of the
valley and up the hillside slope, pulling the girls after him. In a
wild melee, the two bands of racing animals rammed together to
form a mass of squealing, twisted flesh. The two stallions broke
free, like gladiators, they reared their heads and flared their nostrils in the same ancient challenge that began when animals first
appeared on Mother Earth.

Running Turtle sucked in his breath. The runners' narrow escape paralyzed him. The awesome sight and sounds of the
herd suddenly gone mad held him transfixed. The squeals, the

thump of hooves, the lunging heads with teeth bared, the pitching, crashing bodies, terrified him. Lone Wolf's big gray rose up on its hind legs. The black stallion lunged forward; the big bodies collided, stumbled, only to right themselves and renew the conflict. The mares pressed into the fighting space, forcing the stallions to swerve apart. The droves regrouped to race away, one drove following the other.

Total darkness engulfed them but the thunderous roar of hooves continued. A lightening flash revealed the horses making a wide turn at the end of the valley. They came racing back, Lone Wolf's white and gray stallion in the lead. In a desperate attempt to divert the stallions and calm the herd, Many Horses ran back into the pasture, shouting and waving his arms. The white and gray stallion bore down on him, the drove of mares close behind. The thunderous roar of hooves came nearer and nearer.

Running Turtle threw his hands over his eyes and fled.

A fork of lightening zigzagged through the dark cloud, ending in an ear-splitting crack. The gray stallion reared, almost falling over on its back, then swung about and led the mares up the valley again. Suddenly all was quiet and dark. The storm passed over the hills. The pounding hooves faded away. The stars came out. The gusty wind died to a whisper. It was almost as though the wild events of the night never had happened.

Running Turtle returned, mopping his face with the tail of his shirt. "What happened? The horses acted crazy. It was like bad spirits came from the dark cloud to make them go mad."

He sat down beside Vision Seeker. He was ashamed. He had run away like a frightened child. If he was going to be invited to ride with the hunters he had to act like a grown man. Why was he not like Vision Seeker who sat through it all without moving a muscle or uttering a word?

"I had to make water," Running Turtle lamely explained. "Tell me more about the stars. Look! After the storm they shine brighter than before. Why is that? Have the spirit people built up their campfires?"

Vision Seeker glanced at his brother but did not speak. He didn't want to talk about the stars and he did not want to talk about the horses. He had not let on but he, too, was shaken by the experience. There was something terrible about the way the herd ran wild. Running Turtle was right, it was almost as if evil spirits had possessed the animals. Where did these spirits come from? Where did they go? Would the horses return to normal, or were they bewitched forever? Vision Seeker stared into the darkness trying to make sense of what he had observed.

For Running Turtle, Vision Seeker's silence was almost as disturbing as the storm. He really did not wish to hear more talk about the stars. It was the comforting sound of his brother's voice he sought. He tugged at Vision Seeker's arm. "Tell me more about the spirit people who live in the sky."

"Yes, the star people," Vision Seeker said. "Some say these are the spirits of people who once lived on Mother Earth. Every night these sky spirits keep watch on us. When they discover someone who pleases them, they guard him from harm. When the earth person dies they send a cloud person down to invite his spirit to live in the sky world . . ."

A rustle in the bushes made Running Turtle jump. The hoot of a screech owl perched in a tree made him shiver. A distant coyote began to howl, another one answered. Running Turtle moved nearer to his brother.

"Live a good life and this cloud person may notice you and come to take you to the sky world," Vision Seeker calmly continued.

The brush rustled again. More coyotes began to howl. Camp dogs rushed from their village shelters to bark at the half moon that rose above the eastern hills. The screech owl took off from its perch and swooped down to catch a field mouse that emerged from its underground home in search of food. As the cruel talons sunk into the tiny ribs the rodent uttered a beseeching squeak. Running Turtle leapt to his feet. Unmindful of tree limbs that slapped him in the face, he ran down the trail as fast as his small feet would move. Every shadow and turn of the trail was filled with ghostly phantoms, spirits of dead people waiting to be taken to the sky world or spirits of lost people who returned from the sky world and could not find their earthly home. He hurtled through the lodge door where Quiet Woman pounced on him.

"Where have you been, naughty one? Now get busy and do your chores."

Vision Seeker listened to the patter of his brother's running feet and smiled. This was often the way nightly visits with Running Turtle ended. Mystical talk sent little brother away, sometimes frightened, usually bewildered. Tonight he was both.

Soon after Running Turtle hurried away, Many Horses, Raven Wing, and Small Goat came to sit by Vision Seeker's side. The hurried climb up the slope left the girls breathless. In between gasps they reveled in the night's adventures.

"Did you see those big teeth and eyes of that stallion?" Small Goat gasped. "I was frightened. He ran so close I thought he would bite my head off and stomp me into Mother Earth."

Raven Wing pushed her hair back and laughed. Her healthy skin, flushed with excitement, glowed in the dim light. "We were near death but I never felt so alive. I wonder if that is the way warriors feel in battle."

Many Horses was silent. Whatever his thoughts, he kept them to himself. He glanced at Vision Seeker. "What do you make of it?" he quietly asked.

Vision Seeker stared into the darkened valley. The herd hardly could be seen. Like slow moving shadows, the animals, exhausted from the monstrous run, moved about like dogs looking for places to lie down. Whatever spooked them was gone. Vision Seeker hesitated. What could he say without appearing foolish? Older Brother knew the way of horses better than anyone in the valley.

Many Horses finally answered his own question. "They

were badly disturbed. It was not a mountain cat or bear and no sign of raiders. Somehow they know about the trip to buffalo country. They sent us a message. They do not want to go"

Vision Seeker sighed. His brother was so wise in the ways of animals. Had it not always been true, animals had a better sense of danger than did humans?

THE LONE WOLF CLAN

III

When they first got horses, the people did not know what they fed on. They would offer the animals pieces of dried meat or back fat and rub their noses with it, to try to get them to eat . . .

Wolf Calf, Piegan

Vision Seeker, who stayed the night on the hillside, entered the long lodge to find the place in an uproar. All twenty lodge fires burned brightly. A dozen or more half-dressed children scampered around the fires shouting and laughing. Camp dogs let in to escape the cold, snapped and growled over scraps of food. Two young girls, uttering loud shrieks, fought over a moccasin. A small puppy scrambling to get out of the way, tumbled over its own feet. Vision Seeker's mother's brother, Left Hand, was berating his wife for her tardiness in preparing the morning meal. Red Bull and his big sons were eating, the women scurrying about at Red Bull's gruff commands. Raven Wing was hidden in the covers, still sleeping. Grandmother sat in her usual corner, combing and braiding her long, gray hair. Quiet Woman busily shoved cooking utensils around. Running Turtle sat next to the fire, yawning, scratching and rubbing sleep from his eyes. He and his father waited to be served the morning meal. The place reserved for Eldest Son was vacant. Many Horses was still in the pasture inspecting the herd and caring for animals injured in the stampede.

"Is the weather made for travel?" Lone Wolf asked his second son. He wore his special hunting shirt. The white bone beads down the front glittered in the lodge fire light, making his shadowed features appear more somber and darker than usual.

"It is clear and cold."

"Good! It will bring game down from the hills. We shall have meat and new robes before the Season of Deep Snow."

It pleased Vision Seeker to see his father in a pleasant

mood. Like a boy with his first pony, each hunting and trading excursion excited Lone Wolf. Everything else was forgotten when he had his mind on these two pleasures. This hunting trip probably excited his father more than others. It gave Lone Wolf the opportunity to test the new hunting mounts he and Many Horses had spent weeks training for the chase. Shooting bison while riding at top speed took skill of both horse and rider. The horse not only had to watch the fleeing buffalo, but also the ground. It had to be nimble with uncanny quickness to avoid stumbling over brush and rocks and instinctively shorten its stride when coming to dips and hollows. At the same time it could not ignore the buffalo that might momentarily turn on the galloping horse and gore it with its thick short, sharp horns.

Quiet Woman plunked down a bowl of kouse mush in front of the waiting males. Already she was out of sorts. She had not begun to pack. Her back ached and her breath short. She felt like this the day Lone Wolf led the trading party across the swollen Kimooenim and Baby Young Wolf slipped from the horse and was lost in the surging current. Grief over the lost son lay in her heart like a block of ice. The trip had been another one of Lone Wolf's unexpected decisions, hastily launched without regard for dangers on the trail.

Quiet Woman uttered a deep sigh. Ever since the Kimooenim tragedy she looked forward to each journey with dread. She hid her feelings from the family but as the years passed they were harder and harder to conceal. Her hands trembled; her stomach quivered. "Ah!" if only the horse had not stumbled or they had waited until the raging waters had subsided, Young Wolf would be alive. He would now be ten, the age to start his vision quest. She glanced fearfully at Vision Seeker and Running Turtle. She could not bear to lose another child. A burst of cold air made her shiver. Many Horses had come in from seeing to the herd. Quiet Woman ladled out another bowl of mush and stood aside to watch First Son dip a buffalo horn spoon into the steaming gruel.

Ignorant of the previous night's stampede, Lone Wolf impatiently waited for Many Horses to eat. "Why do you dawdle? There is no time to waste. Bring in the pack animals. Then fetch my stallion and hunters."

"Why hurry? The White Birds have not come. No packing has been done," Grandmother cackled. She grinned, making satisfied smacking noises as she rolled a spoonful of hot mush around on her toothless gums.

"White Birds?" Lone Wolf glared at his mate.

Quiet Woman did not look up. "I sent word. If they are not invited my people will never forgive us."

Lone Wolf scowled. "Do not sit there," he ordered Many Horses. "When we are ready; we leave. The White Birds can follow in their own good time."

Many Horses glanced anxiously at Vision Seeker. Who was going to tell their father the bad news? By first light he discovered the casualties. Animals were lame. Many suffered bruises and bites. Some wounds were severe with hide ripped, leaving great strips of flesh exposed. Lone Wolf's gray and white stallion was one of the most badly wounded of all.

Artless Running Turtle blurted out the news. "Last night the herd went wild. A black cloud came. It frightened the herd. The horses ran up the valley and down until they could run no more."

"What are you talking about?" Lone Wolf demanded.

"About the horses. They fought. They screamed like twoleggeds. The stallions reared, kicked and bit like wolves fighting over a carcass, then stampeded. Never have they run so hard -- faster than the wind. Nothing could stop them. It was terrible. They almost ran down Raven Wing, Small Goat and Many Horses."

"What were they doing there? The pasture at night is no place for women." The mention of Weasel Face's pesky daughter aroused Lone Wolf's ire. Small Goat! What a name to give a child! Why couldn't Raven Wing pick a more suitable companion? He gave Grandmother's corner a hasty glance. It would be just like Weasel Face's first daughter, The Weaver, to be sitting there gloating over Lone Wolf family quarrels. The thought of her put his teeth on edge. Homely, the girl was as homely as a skinned skunk, two small eyes set together so closely they looked like one. And that tongue of hers, it was as sharp as a two-edged knife. She pretended to be busy but he was wise to her tricks. She listened to every word that was said, then returned to Weasel Face's lodge to repeat and embellish everything she heard.

Why was he worrying about those Weasel Faced females? The important thing was to get on the trail and leave those squint-eyed people behind. Lone Wolf glared at his three sons. "Horses do not run up and down the valley for no good reason. What frightened them? Was it mountain cat -- a bear?"

Running Turtle glanced at Vision Seeker. His brother sat staring into the fire, his face an inscrutable mask. Running Turtle suddenly felt unwell. Once again, he had made a mess of things. He should have kept quiet. It was Many Horses' place to report on the condition of the herd. He squirmed under Lone Wolf's angry gaze. His father would not let up until he learned what happened.

"No bear, no mountain cat, only a big black cloud that came over the Kooskooskie, spitting fire. Everywhere, lightening, thunder, wind, dust . . . it was awful, like Mother Earth was angry. That was what happened. The horses knew Mother Earth was unhappy. It frightened them so, they went wild."

"Nonsense!" Lone Wolf scolded. "They have not had enough work. Once we are on the trail they will be themselves again." Lone Wolf turned away and reached for his quirt. He noticed Raven Wing still asleep. "What is the matter? Is this woman ill?"

"Raven Wing! Get up, lazy girl!" Quiet Woman pulled away the sleeping robe that covered her daughter. She slapped the last bowl of mush down and glared. "So that is where you were, in the horse pasture up to mischief with that Weasel Face girl when you should have been helping in the lodge. Shame!

Shame! I try to make you a proper woman but you never learn."

Grandmother smiled, hiding her toothless mouth behind a shawl. "Sons bring joy. Daughters bring grief."

Vision Seeker scooped up the last of his mush and pushed the bowl away. This was often the way a trip began: quarrels, arguments and Grandmother offering wise words. Raven Wing was always the last to rise, doing her best to avoid the chore of packing. Why did Raven Wing hate women's work? It was not right to leave all the camp drudgery to Quiet Woman. In a way he felt responsible for Raven Wing's behavior.

As the brother nearest her age, they had played together, joining forces in fighting childhood battles against others and hatched little schemes to outwit their mother and father. Was it his fault Raven Wing had not grown into a normal maiden? Of course, Raven Wing was not the only daughter who failed to do her duty. Her friend, Small Goat, was as rebellious as an untamed colt. The two of them were enough to upset the whole Lapwai band with their unruly ways.

The way the Lone Wolf family lived was partly to blame for Raven Wing's uncontrollable behavior. Lone Wolf's wanderlust always had the family on the move. Trading and hunting was Lone Wolf's way of life. Eagle feathers, dried salmon and salmon oil, baskets of camas and kouse cakes, hemp purses filled with bone beads, bales of mountain grown grass hemp, buckskin garments trimmed with porcupine quills and colorfully painted ponies were his stock in trade.

While still strapped to their mother's back, the youngsters began to travel with their father. Raven Wing was born on the trail. When the pains became too severe, Quiet Woman stopped, laid a robe behind a protective bush and delivered the child herself. Except for keeping a watchful eye on the whimpering bundle, Quiet Woman made camp that night as usual and kept up her daily work for the remainder of the journey. Vision Seeker remembered the event vividly. The basket containing the bright-eyed baby appeared out of nowhere. For a long while he believed his mother had found it beside the trail. Only much later, while helping his father deliver a foal, did he understand how babies arrived on Mother Earth.

Trade took the Lone Wolfs to many exciting places: west to the base of the shiny peaks where Chinooks who lived on the banks of the great endless water came to fish and trade; south to the beautiful mountains and lakes of Wallowa, the homeland of the Wellamotkin band of the Nimpau; north to the lands of the Spokan and Couer d'Alene; and, when the snows melted in the high mountain passes, Lone Wolf often took his family east to meet with peoples of the plains. A favorite trading center was the Chinook village where the waters of the Great River forced their way through the foothills of the Cascades.

All kinds of people and trade items were present at this great Chinook trading place. From the far northwest came the Haida with their strange wooden figures and masks carved from wood; the Tlingit brought Chilkat blankets, wooden battle helmets and raven heads with black obsidian eyes. From the deserts of the southwest Pima and Papago came with grass baskets woven so tightly they held water; roots of the yucca plant that created cleaning suds; rattles made from dried squash and gourds; the skins of lizards, snakes and horned toads; and pottery of every shape, color and size. The people who lived by the Endless Water brought sea shells, iridescent blue abalone and tusk-shaped dentalia that decorated dresses of Nimpau women. Trading ships with wings sailed across the Endless Water to supply prized blue glass beads used to adorn hunting shirts, moccasins, belts, hair pieces, bridles, cradle boards and many other things.

The Chinook trading camps, alive with children, barking dogs and reeking with the smell of rotting fish offal and campfire smoke, were places to make new friends, visit old friends, learn new skills, tell stories and recount myths and legends. It was at a Chinook camp Vision Seeker first heard of the sky world and its people. A half-blood from the lands of the Great Lakes took a liking to him and told him many fascinating tales of distant peoples: Cree, Ojibwa, Osage, Cherokee, Wyandot, Assiniboine and others Vision Seeker could not remember.

On one trading excursion Lone Wolf took his troupe to the mouth of the Great River to camp on the shores of the Endless Water that stretched to the horizon and swallowed Father Sun. At first the roar and fury of the waves that pounded the rocky shore frightened the children. Unable to sleep, they sat up far into the night watching the tide march in with white crested waves luminous in the moonlight. Just when they thought the water would inundate the campsite, the incoming waves slackened and began to recede. The angry waters ebbed away.

Eleven year-old Vision Seeker never forgot the experience. What made water run up hill in one forceful wave after another? A Chinook villager explained Moon God wielded the power that pulled water high up on sandy beaches and rocky shorelines. It was Moon God's way of telling people She had the power to flood Mother Earth as She did when the first two-leggeds came to live on the lands that bordered the great water. But now Moon God was a kindhearted God. She held the water in check. She had made an agreement with Mother Earth, never again would She turn this mighty power loose to cover the land, destroying plants, animals, two-leggeds -- everything that lived and breathed. From that day on Vision Seeker viewed the moon with awe. The great power it wielded equaled that of the power that held stars suspended in Father Sky.

Trade with peoples of the plains especially fascinated Lone Wolf. He loved the products of the Blackfeet, Crow, Cheyenne, Gros Ventres and Dakota. From their homelands came richly decorated rawhide garments, feather headdresses and the coveted red pipestone. These people lived within traveling distance of the Redcoat and Boston trading posts. This gave them access to products of the hairy faced ones. Lone Wolf's traveling band traded with the plains peoples for guns, lead and powder, axes, knives, cooking utensils, brightly colored cloth, beads, mirrors, trinkets and other items made in the far away factories of the

Bostons and Redcoats.

Under the impatient gaze of Lone Wolf, Many Horses finished his porridge and made his painful report of the previous night's stampede, carefully listing the names and injuries of the lame and wounded animals. Lone Wolf stared at him in disbelief. His face turned the color of the bone decorations on his shirt front. He loved these beautiful animals as much as he did his mate and children.

Lone Wolf's suffering was too terrible to watch. Even Grandmother remained silent. She suffered along with her son. Since she could remember, the Nimpau had been famous for breeding great horses. White horses with spots like daubs of paint on the rumps were the favorites. The Nimpau horsemen kept these animals apart and interbred them. The original breeding stock came from the Mexican state of Chihuahua, passing through the hands of the Apache, Navajo, Ute and Shoshoni before arriving in the Nimpau homeland. These oddly marked horses were raised in large numbers on the Great River plateau. They became known as Appaloosa horses, named after the Palouse River. The Nimpau were soon recognized as the premier breeders of this remarkable creature. The Nimpau Appaloosa was not only spectacularly marked, but tough. These exceptional animals could travel all day without tiring and were as sure-footed as mountain sheep. They were coveted by horsemen everywhere. Half a dozen lowland horses were often given in trade for one Nimpau-bred Appaloosa.

Lone Wolf hurried to the pasture fields to see for himself the harm that had befallen his four-legged friends. He was appalled by what he found. He walked around his prize stallion and groaned. Healing herbs had been applied, but the wounds looked mean and painful. The horse would not be ready to ride for days.

"Wha-what happened?" Lone Wolf stuttered in his concern. The handsome stallion was more than a riding mount; he was a dependable companion. They had been together since before Running Turtle was born. The big gray nervously jerked against the halter line Many Horses held; the big eyes expressed such misery Lone Wolf reached out to pat the silky, white-gray neck. "Do not worry friend, we will soon make you well."

He turned on First Son. "Thunder and lightening did not do this. It has the look of an attack by grizzly or mountain cat. You did not . . ." The pained expression on his son's face made him choke back bitter words of blame.

Lone Wolf examined one animal after another. None were as badly injured as his stallion. Why was that? He glanced around the pasture to see Weasel Face and his eldest son, Toohool, inspecting their herd. "Weasel Face!" Lone Wolf spit the name out like a curse. "Did harm come to his horses?" he added, trying to subdue shrillness in his voice.

"Everyone's animals suffered."

"Hmph!" Lone Wolf grunted. "Sort out the sound mounts and pack mares."

"You will go on the hunt?" Many Horses queried, astonished his father would consider leaving his favorite mounts in Lapwai. Obviously many were not fit to travel.

"Of course we go on the hunt. A lost day does not matter. Now the White Birds have time to arrive. Do not stand there. Get busy with the lame and hurt. We want them healed by the time we return."

Many Horses led the big stallion away, his heart heavy. It was not right to leave the wounded animals. He did not trust any hands but his own to care for his four-legged friends, but it was futile to attempt to change Lone Wolf's mind. When his father launched a trip it expanded like a spring flood. It began small but became a torrent. Now Quiet Woman's White Bird relatives would swell the hunting party. They were the kind of folk who could not stand to see any of the family embark on a venture without tagging along for fear they would miss out.

"Silly fools!" Many Horses said to himself. Most of them did not know what they faced. A Lone Wolf hunt could last a year. It meant leaving comfortable winter lodges, bounteous fishing streams and fertile camas grounds. It meant taking the hazardous trail up the Kooskooskie, then across the snow covered heights of Lolo Pass before descending into Bitterroot Valley. From there they would pass through Hellgate Gap and encounter the gales that whistled through the canyons and swirled down the draws beyond. Arriving in buffalo country did not bring safety. When the Season of Deep Snow was at its worst, blinding blizzards caught even wild animals unawares. Creatures of all kinds froze to death before finding shelter.

Many Horses groaned. He did not want this to happen to his precious four-legged friends.

IV

He who goeth far hath many encounters
Outlandish Proverbs

Preparations to leave camp began slowly, then rapidly deteriorated into mass confusion. Vision Seeker watched the goings-on from his hillside lookout. He knew the habits of his people and wanted to avoid the turmoil. He especially wished to stay clear of his father. The first day of a trip made Lone Wolf as snippy as a snapping turtle.

At first sleepy-eyed youths dribbled out of the village and went toward the pasture to round up the horses. Gradually more and more lodge inhabitants emerged to do various chores. When the pack animals were brought in, bags and bundles were taken out to load. The horses, unaccustomed to work, bucked and crow-hopped, avoiding their handlers, and when loaded, attempted to shake the annoying burdens from their backs. People streamed in from all over the valley to help, offer advice, bring gifts, say good-byes or merely share in the excitement. At this point everyone in Lapwai Valley appeared to be involved in the chaotic effort to get the hunting party on its way.

Activity within the long lodge was not much different than on the outside. Children, dogs and hunters milled about smoldering fires, getting in each other's way. Women scolded and shouted orders. Departing on a journey was especially hard on them. They had to deal with the maddening matter of deciding what to take and what to leave. Up and down the long lodge each family mother went through the same indecision. Their mates urged them to hurry but they still could not bring themselves to break away. The precious possessions they had to leave behind were ever-so-hard to part with -- would they ever see them again?

Other wrenching fears made leave-taking a torture. Winter was not far off. If they dawdled on the trail the high passes could fill with snow. Hellgate was certain to greet them with freezing winds that neither animal nor human could long endure. They had to keep their wits about them, pack the right bedding and clothes. Living in tipi lodges through a buffalo country winter was a test of human endurance. The prospect of adventure was exciting, at the same time minds were clouded by painful memories of friends and relatives who lost their lives on either the Kooskooskie Trail or on Sun River hunting grounds.

Lone Wolf paced back and forth, snapping a braided rawhide quirt on the leg of his fringed leather britches, his expression grim. The day had started badly and did not look as if it would get better. The White Bird families arrived before dawn. Quiet Woman's sisters and mother had rushed into the long lodge before the Lone Wolf family was fully awake. A swarm of children scrambled in after them to romp and play. Chattering like magpies, they scattered bed clothes, pummeled Running Turtle, rousted out Raven Wing, causing such turmoil Grandmother seized a child and gave her a resounding swat on the seat, something no one had ever seen her do. The shocking action caused a row, the child's mother shrieked at Grandmother and child in the same breath.

Lone Wolf, who waited for his breakfast, was fit to be tied. When he demanded something to eat the women scurried around only to run into each other and burst into fits of giggles. They tipped over a basket of meal, slopped water all over, soaked the reed matting that covered the dirt floor and burned the mush until it had the texture and smell of horse droppings. Lone Wolf sniffed the concoction and shoved the bowl away.

"What is the matter with you people? Can you not do anything right? Why have you not packed? This is not a gossip meet. This is a hunting trip," Lone Wolf raged. No one paid him the least bit of attention. Quiet Woman's mother gave him a sharp glance. It told him to run along as if he was an unruly child. "What good is a hunting trip if the women do not have time to chitter-chatter?" Quiet Woman's mother asked. Lone Wolf seized his quirt and stomped outside where Lame Horse, Quite Woman's father and leader of the White Birds, sat on a rock quietly smoking his pipe.

"Nice morning for travel," the White Bird observed.

Lone Wolf exploded. "What good is the weather if we never get started? These women . . ." He grimaced. "Look at them! 'We are rushing as fast as we can,' they say. I have seen snails move quicker. The way they fool about it will be nightfall before they are ready to leave, if at all."

"Patience! Patience!" Lame Horse said in the tone of voice he used to soothe skittish horses. "You should know by now, women cannot be hurried. They get ready in their own good time."

Lone Wolf looked at his relative by marriage in disgust. What a slipshod family the White Bird man had reared. It was little wonder Raven Wing and Quiet Woman were forever late. They took after their White Bird relatives. Time did not matter; if they did not complete a job today there was always tomorrow. How did he ever get mixed up with such shilly-shallying people anyway? He sent a hand signal to Many Horses to hurry with the pack animals. At least these four-legged creatures would not give him an argument.

Many Horses had spent much of the night in the pasture deciding which horses to ride, which would bear the packs and which would draw the travois. Naturally, the stallions would not do as pack animals; the prized buffalo hunters were much too valuable to carry packs and too frisky to be entrusted to women or children. Then there were all of the injured. He could not take them. Finally, he separated a few old mares and led them to the long lodge.

"Why do you linger?" Lone Wolf demanded. "Are you waiting for the Season of Falling Snow?" That was the trouble with First Son; he also took after his White Bird relatives. Slow! He was as slow as a centipede trapped in a spider web. He did his chores well, but so methodically. Nothing anyone could say or do would ever hurry First Son.

Many Horses wisely held his tongue. His father had been impatient all morning. It was the White Bird families who arrived so early that had him upset. Visits of the White Birds were always the same. They descended like a swarm of grasshoppers. They settled in and made themselves at home as if they owned the lodge. They talked incessantly about nothing at all. They joked, laughed and poked fun regardless of who it might offend. They were not exactly lazy but only did work when it was impossible to avoid it. Many Horses could never understand why Lone Wolf had chosen a member of the Lame Horse family for a mate. They were so unlike him. What a shock it must have been for Quiet Woman when she came to Lapwai and was thrust into the Lone Wolf lodge where everyone was expected to be industrious and get things done quickly.

After delivering the pack mares to his father, Many Horses returned to the pasture and began to cut out the horses that would remain behind. His heart was heavy. Like Lone Wolf, he loved every one. Most of the animals he had known since they were foaled. As he passed through the pasture he rubbed the nose of a mare and patted the side of a frisky colt. He stooped to lift the leg of a lame gelding to inspect its hoof. He released the hoof and gave the horse a pat on the back. He groaned, how he hated to leave his four-legged friends when they were not well.

#

The hunting party finally got underway. Heads of families pranced out of camp and up the Kooskooskie Trail on spirited mounts. Sedate pack animals, loaded with camp paraphernalia and small children strapped to their backs, followed. In their midst was Grandmother. With her shawl wrapped tightly around her neck and shoulders, she sat sprightly on the broad back of a slow plodding mare. She clutched a great-grandchild in front, another clung to her from the back, both offspring of a granddaughter who had taken a White Bird mate. At the end of the column came another cluster of pack animals driven by women and children. Loose, extra stock, came last, herded by Many

Horses and a group of youths.

Lone Wolf, Vision Seeker, Left Hand, Red Bull, Lame Horse and heads of families stood by the creek bank watching the column form. When the last straggler fell into place, Lone Wolf lifted his eyes skyward, grateful the frustrating delay was finally at an end. "Grandfather, thank you for safely getting us on our journey," he uttered in silent thanksgiving.

The day passed pleasantly. The pack mares set an easy pace. Except to adjust a pack that had slipped or to answer a call of nature, no one stopped. Warmed by the morning sun, children drowsed and fell asleep, their little heads bobbing along with the steps of the plodding horses.

The party arrived at the first campsite by late afternoon. Women and children scurried to unpack. Men led their mounts and the pack animals away to water in the Kooskooskie and feed on the rich forage that grew along the river bank. The loose stock was herded to a grassy open space some distance away. A bevy of youngsters walked up and down the trail side scrounging for dry firewood. Young girls fetched water from a nearby creek. A group of boys went exploring. Another group cut fishing poles to try their luck at a likely looking pool. Shelters went up. Fires were built. Within the hour the smell of cottonwood smoke and cooking food filled the air.

Lone Wolf, Lame Horse and family heads watched the activity from a rise above the campsite. When the herd was pastured and the guards set, they handed their horses over to herders and hunkered down to rest and discuss the day's trip. Their watchful eyes roved back and forth over the outreaches of the camp. When the meal was ready they descended to sit on buffalo robes carefully laid out by the women.

At the Lone Wolf camp Quiet Woman waited for her mate to say a prayer of thanksgiving, then she served him and each son in order of his birth. When the males finished eating, Raven Wing, Grandmother and Quiet Woman sat down to scrape the pot and partake of what was left.

After they had eaten, Lone Wolf and his sons walked toward the pasture grounds to inspect the grazing horses. At the edge of camp dogs began to bark. A guard ran along the river bank shouting. A body of horsemen had been sighted coming up the trail. Shortly, a tall rider on a bay rounded a bend. Lone Wolf stared and stopped so abruptly Running Turtle ran into him. Following the lead rider was a string of pack mares with trailing travois.

"It's Weasel Face and his family!" Running Turtle exclaimed.

"I can see who it is!" Lone Wolf snapped.

Riding behind Weasel Face and his oldest son, Toohool, was Small Goat. She gaily waved and shouted a greeting. "We could not stand to see everyone leave," she called out. "When the Lone Wolf lodge is empty Lapwai Village is no more. Where is Raven Wing?" She galloped ahead of her father, passing close to Lone Wolf, blithely unaware of the consternation the arrival of the Weasel Face family caused.

Weasel Face's first daughter, The Weaver, trailed closely behind her sister. Perched on a tall horse, she resembled a bird ready to take flight. Her narrow face, sharp pointed nose and chin gave her a sparrowlike appearance. Her beady dark eyes glanced at Lone Wolf and his sons without a sign of recognition.

"Woman Who Rides with Head in Sky, that is the name you should have," Running Turtle jeered. "Come down from the clouds and walk on two legs like everybody else!"

"Never mind," Vision Seeker admonished. "It is not good to cause trouble on the trail." He said the words for his father's benefit. It was clear from Lone Wolf's dark expression he was ready to explode.

Weasel Face, as slender and tall as a tipi lodgepole, stood in the stirrups and bowed as he passed, his arm so long it almost touched the ground. "Hoh!" he greeted, smiling broadly at Lone Wolf. "The old bear did not travel far. What is the matter? Did the old bones give out?"

Lone Wolf retorted. "What brings you here? I thought you said the best place to spend the Season of Falling Snow was in your warm, snug lodge."

"Ah, yes, that is best, but if the old bear should fall apart on the trail someone should be along to pick up the pieces," Weasel Face answered, chuckling to himself. He led his entourage to a clearing where he curtly motioned for his two wives to unpack and set up camp.

Lone Wolf turned away. He felt as though he would take sick. Weasel Face had plagued him since childhood. The narrow splinter of a man did everything he could to annoy him. When they were barely out of cradle boards Weasel Face stole and broke his play things. When they were old enough to ride Weasel Face lamed his pony so badly it had to be killed. When they went on their first vision quest, Weasel Face started the night before so he would return with a guardian spirit first. When Lone Wolf looked on Quiet Woman as a mate Weasel Face begged his father to bargain for her. Then, for months after Quiet Woman came to live in Lapwai, Weasel Face took every opportunity to remind her she had made a mistake in accepting Lone Wolf as her mate. Only after taking a wife of his own, a jealous woman, did Weasel Face quit pestering.

Lone Wolf muttered in disgust. He had half a notion to return to the long lodge, but that was no answer. Weasel Face would only follow and make life miserable all winter. The thought made him furious. He kicked at stone in his path, then grabbed his bruised moccasined toe and uttered a howl of pain. A startled owl perched on a limb awakened and fluttered away to disappear in the trees. Running Turtle sucked in his breath. Night owls flying during daylight hours carried messages of death.

#

At the pasture grounds the sight of the grazing horses soothed Lone Wolf's ruffled feelings. The pain in his toe was momentarily forgotten. He missed his prized stallion terribly but loved all of his horses. He spoke to each animal, rubbed his hand against the soft, velvety muzzles and patted them on the rump where the colorful Appaloosa markings rose above the silky smooth hides like dashes of paint. He never should have worried about making it across the mountains. Nimpau bred horses were ideal for the narrow, steep mountain trails of the high country. Their forelegs were spaced close together, making them sure-footed on the most hazardous terrain.

Satisfied the herd had adequate pasture and was safely guarded, Lone Wolf gave the order to fetch the hunting mounts. On the trail it was wise to tether them within the camp for the night. Raiders might descend, a violent storm break or the herd spook and run wild. Without mounts on hand to ride, the wealth of the camp could be lost in the blink of an eye.

After bringing the special mounts into camp, Many Horses went back to spend the night near the herd. They were still far from enemy territory but if another storm occurred he wanted to be on hand. Vision Seeker and Rabbit Skin Leggings of the White Birds went along. Each of the men would take a turn standing guard. The White Bird man carried a Redcoat musket. Running Turtle skipped alongside to put a hand on the cold steel. Would he ever possess one of these iron sticks that spit fire and lead? He wanted to ask Rabbit Skin Leggings if he would show him how it made fire. His father had an iron stick but never allowed him to do any more than hold it and polish it. If he was going to be a great hunter he had to have one and know how to use it.

Covertly, Vision Seeker studied Rabbit Skin Leggings. It was obvious the White Bird thought well of himself and took pride in his dress. Rabbit Skin Leggings wore a neat, clean hunting shirt artistically decorated with beads and porcupine quills. His long black hair was carefully combed and swept back from a broad forehead. Two long braids fastened by buckskin ties framed a large, square face. A string of round bone beads circled his neck. From the top of his head four feathers stood out like a fan. Yet, his eyes, nose and mouth were the features that attracted one's attention. His eyes were dark, alert and set wide apart. The nose was broad, long and strong. His mouth was wide and expressive. The lips were curved as if just waiting to smile.

It was not only Rabbit Skin Leggings' neat and unusual appearance that Vision Seeker found attractive. He also admired his knowledge. The White Bird, who was related to him in some obscure way, spoke with authority on many interesting topics. He had a wealth of stories and legends of the ancients. He knew much about barks, leaves, roots and seeds that healed. He had studied the hairy faces' Great Spirit Book and told of the strange words it contained. Rabbit Skin Leggings claimed his greatest desire was to learn the ways of the Great Spirit Book and teach them to his people.

When they arrived at the pasture grounds Vision Seeker and Rabbit Skin Leggings rolled out their sleeping robes. Rabbit Skin Leggings stood first guard. For a while Vision Seeker watched with him, his keen eyes examining the pasture grounds. Like Many Horses, he worried about another mysterious stampede. It would be disastrous to have the herd run amuck in the narrow canyon, choked with trees, brush and boulders. Shattered hooves, broken limbs, death by drowning in the river -- any number of accidents could occur to decimate the herd.

Vision Seeker glanced at his placid White Bird companion, Rabbit Skin Leggings. Was he oblivious to the hazards that faced the hunting party? Even their campsite had its hidden dangers. Should raiders attack the canyon was a perfect trap. A heavy rain quickly could fill the canyon and sweep them away. Vision Seeker shook himself. What was the matter with him? One potential disaster after another flitted through his mind. He threw himself on the sleeping robe and closed his eyes.

"All is well," Rabbit Skin Leggings said when he shook Vision Seeker awake to take his turn standing watch. The White Bird hunter rolled up in his robe and was soon fast asleep. To keep himself awake, Vision Seeker looked to the stars. As always, their twinkling nearness gave him comfort. He attempted to locate his friends. The dove, hawk and running fox were almost directly overhead but his other friends he could not find. The high walls of the narrow canyon cut off much of the sky. He would be glad when the hunting party arrived in buffalo country. There, the stars were bright and close and stretched from one distant horizon to the other.

A horse uttered a shrill whinny. Another snorted, wheeled around and pawed the earth. The entire herd began to stomp and mill about. Vision Seeker's sharp eyes searched the shadows. Something was amiss. "Oh-ha!" Near the base of the trees crouched a mountain cat. Vision Seeker reached for his bow and an arrow and then put them aside. The bow string did not have the strength or resilience to send an arrow accurately that distance. He glanced at Rabbit Skin Leggings' long-barreled flintlock. Would the fire stick send a missile that distance and kill? "Ah, yes!" It was good. If it did not kill, the noise would frighten the cat away. He seized his companion and shook him awake.

"Your gun. Hurry! There's a cat near the herd. See it? It is in the fringe of trees."

Rabbit Skin Leggings rubbed the sleep from his eyes and fumbled with the rifle. "I do not see a thing."

"Right there! Near your horse. He's stalking your horse!"

"Take the gun. You are the one who sees in the dark. The rifle is cocked. All you do is aim and pull the trigger. Quick! Shoot! Shoot!"

Vision Seeker hesitated. He never had fired a gun, only watched Lone Wolf and others. They simply pointed the barrel at the target and set the iron stick afire by pulling a twig at the bottom of the wooden handle. The big cat was ready to pounce. He swung the rifle up, sighted down the long barrel and pulled the trigger. The recoil knocked him backwards. The muzzle blast blinded him.

"Eee -- yeh!" Rabbit Skin Leggings chortled. "A kill!"

V

Never trouble trouble till trouble troubles you.

English Proverb

The single rifle shot aroused the camp. Shouts of alarm, screams of fright, whimpers of half-awake children and the wild barking of dogs, created bedlam. Running Turtle popped out of the bed covers like a startled prairie dog emerging from its underground home. He had not slept well. He could not erase the sight of the night owl and its message of death. Gunfire! Someone had been killed. He hurriedly slipped into his leggings, seized the nearest weapon he could lay his hands on, and ran outside.

For a moment he could not get his bearings. Where did the deadly sound come from? More sleepy-eyed, half-dressed men were having the same trouble. They ran through the tipi encampment shouting and pointing. At the height of the confusion a guard rushed down the hill, waving frantically toward the pasture grounds. "The herd! Raiders! Save the horses!"

Hunters grabbed for weapons, fumbled for tether lines, seized halter ropes, mounted up and thundered up the slope in the direction of the grazing grounds. Weeping women and children ran to see them off, fearing that their fathers and brothers might never return. Hooting and shrieking war whoops, the riders stormed over the hill and into the pasture field.

Many Horses ran forward, waving his arms, trying to keep the arriving riders from spooking the herd. "It is all right. It is all right. No harm done. It was only a mountain cat. It has been killed." Already skittish, the horses in the pasture threw up their heads; snorting, they swerved about and headed straight into the thickest part of the forest.

"Hiya! Turn them! Head them off!" Many Horses jumped on a bare back. Guiding the pony only by the pressure of his legs, he raced to turn the runaway herd. He ducked his head just in time to escape a low hanging limb. Into the thick woods he disappeared. The mounted herders followed. The armed riders from the camp quickly joined in the chase. Watchers could hear the horsemen crashing through the brush. They only could speculate on what was taking place.

Lone Wolf, who had been in a deep sleep, belatedly shook himself awake. He heard the confusion and shout of the guard. He reached for his rifle. He could not find it. He dug through the bed clothes thinking he had laid the weapon by his side. Then he remembered, Running Turtle had been polishing it. Where was he? The bed covers where the boy slept were empty. Lone Wolf shouted for Third Son.

"This is no time to fuss over the fire stick," Grandmother scolded. "Take your bow and arrows. The raiders will be gone with the herd before you get out of the lodge."

Lone Wolf arrived at the pasture site fuming. He saw Vision Seeker and Rabbit Skin Leggings and reined toward them. "Where is everybody? What has happened? Where is the herd?"

"In the woods," Vision Seeker answered, pointing with his lips and chin. "Listen! They return."

"Hi yi! Hi yi!" It was the cry of the herders. Two horses burst into the clearing, then two more. A herder emerged from the trees driving a drove of mares. Many Horses, still riding without bridle or saddle, followed, chasing a second drove. Lone Wolf grunted his approval. No one could deal with livestock better than First Son. This talent he inherited from his father, Lone Wolf told himself.

"What was the cause of all this?" Lone Wolf asked. "There was a shot . . ."

Rabbit Skin Leggings lifted the barrel of his Hudson's Bay musket and pointed toward the dead mountain cat.

Lone Wolf rode over and swung down to examine the predator. The great cat measured two long strides from tufted tail to black muzzle and rounded ears. The size amazed him. He looked for the death wound. Except for the staring eyes, the mountain lion looked as if it merely had fallen asleep.

"You made a fine kill." Lone Wolf said to Rabbit Skin Leggings.

"It is your son, Vision Seeker, who made the kill. My eyes were blinded by sleep. I gave him the iron stick. Boom! The big cat is on the other side."

"Hmm!" Lone Wolf grunted. Maybe this son who stared at the stars and talked of sky people would come down to Mother Earth and become a respected member of the tribe after all. He gave the cat a push with his still sore toe. The fur was heavy and thick, the coloring good. The bullet barely had damaged the skin. He was not only immensely pleased with Second Son's shooting skill, but the pelt would have much value in trade.

"This is a good omen," he said. "A kill the first day on the trail means a plentiful hunt." The sight of Toohool, Weasel Face's eldest son who came up to admire the dead predator, did not dampen Lone Wolf's spirits. "See what a fine kill my son made," he said proudly.

Lone Wolf spied Running Turtle who came out of the woods carrying his rifle. Running Turtle quickly turned back into the trees and attempted to hide the gun but it was too late. His father was on top of him. He was trapped. He came forward with the rifle, that stood taller than he did. He handed it to his father. "The camp was in danger. I needed a weapon. The iron stick was the first one I could find."

For a moment Lone Wolf silently studied this rotund creature he had sired. Perhaps he also had misjudged Third Son. He had shown more alertness than his father. "Next time take a weapon that's your own size," he said not unkindly. "Now, let us cut out a pack mare and take the big cat Second Son killed back to camp. Its skin will make a fine fur."

It took two men, with Running Turtle holding the pack mare, to load the big cat. After the campers finished admiring the kill, Lone Wolf ordered the women to skin the cat and keep the claws. "Make them into a necklace for Second Son. It will remind everyone of his great coup," he told Quiet Woman.

Vision Seeker had no desire to display evidence of his coup. In his eyes, the fuss over counting coups was childish and a waste of time. Unlike most men his age, he never had the urge to prove himself on hunts, in raids or on the battlefield. Besides, the early morning drama seemed unreal. He had done nothing special. He merely had pointed the iron stick at the big cat and pulled the trigger.

Many Horses did not understand his brother's lack of exuberance. Vision Seeker had saved a valuable horse's life. "Why are you not happy? You made a coup every man in camp would give his best horse to claim."

"It is nothing. Anybody who saw the big cat would have done the same."

"Why do you belittle yourself?" Many Horses persisted. "Rabbit Skin Leggings, the great White Bird hunter, could not see a thing. In one quick movement you pick up the gun, you point it, make it spit fire. The big cat is gone to the next world. You should take pride in such things. M-m-m . . . !" He could not find words to express his dismay.

Vision Seeker took his sleeping robe and shook out the dust and twigs. He put a halter on his spotted mount and led it away. He wanted to leave this place behind and not be reminded of this night again. The Great Spirit put the big cat on Mother Earth to breathe the air, feel the warmth of the sun and enjoy all the other things Mother Earth provided both man and beast. Why should he, with one tug of the finger, deprive it of all these good things? He should have aimed over its head and let it live.

After the first wave of enthusiasm Lone Wolf, too, had second thoughts about the kill. It took the women longer to skin the cat than he planned. Small Goat came to help Raven Wing. Instead of scraping and cleaning the hide, they whispered and giggled. Grandmother cut a finger. Quiet Woman did not feel well. She pulled the hide from the slender carcass and ran into the brush to be sick. Lone Wolf looked on, impatiently snapping his quirt against his leggings. Drawn by the smell of fresh blood, dogs gathered to sniff and whine. With a lash of his quirt, Lone Wolf sent them scooting away yipping. Lone Wolf scowled. The skinning of the big cat should have been completed quickly. Instead, it had already turned into the loss of a half day's travel.

Irked by the delay and envious of Vision Seeker's prized kill, Weasel Face ordered The Weaver to fetch Small Goat. "Why does Second Daughter spend all her time with that Raven Wing woman?" he peevishly asked Wife Number One. "Why do you not keep her busy in our own lodge?" With his family finally together, Weasel Face and his entourage moved out. Others followed until the entire camp had gone ahead leaving the Lone Wolf family to bring up the rear.

"Why do they not wait for us?" Running Turtle anxiously asked. "Are you not their leader?"

Lone Wolf fumed. If it wasn't for that narrow-eyed Weasel Face no one would have left until he gave the word.

To hurry their departure, Many Horses drove the pack mares in and started to load. The smell of blood and the acrid odor of the fresh hide made the animals shy away and skitter in circles. Many Horses' soothing talk did little good. The mares drew back their ears, bared their teeth and nipped at their handlers like angry dogs. A loosely cinched load slid under the belly of a mare. The startled animal started to run only to trip and fall. After struggling upright she began to buck and kick. An errant hoof lamed another pack mare and caused yet another to bolt into the brush.

"What has come over you?" Lone Wolf scolded First Son. "Can you not handle these animals? At this rate we will never arrive in buffalo country."

There was no need for Lone Wolf to get upset. Half an hour on the trail and they caught up with the column. A brace of fallen trees blocked the path. In attempting to leap the obstacle, the front legs of one of Weasel Face's pack mares became wedged between two limbs. Weasel Face, his wives, sons and daughters tugged and hauled but the mare was stuck fast.

Lone Wolf immediately swung down. The situation gave him satisfaction. Weasel Face was as helpless as a turned-over beetle. Lone Wolf signaled to Many Horses. "Calm that mare. Pull her legs free when we pry away this log."

Weasel Face, his long neck as red as a turkey gobbler's, mounted his big bay and sat glaring at Small Goat. "This is all your fault," he accused. "You wanted to come on this trip. You put the mare in this fix. You frightened her or she would not have jumped. Toohool, where were you? You should have handled the mare. You know your sister is no good with horses. This mess is all your fault."

Lone Wolf paid the quarreling Weasel Faces no heed. He pointed to a limb to use as a pry pole. Vision Seeker inserted it between the two tree trunks. With Running Turtle's help, he was able to open a space large enough to free the mare's legs.

Weasel Face was not appeased. "The mare is all right but the trail is not. We only have started. Who knows what greater dangers lie ahead?" The Weaver came and took her father by the hand.

"You are right, Father. The trail is bad. We never should have come. Shall we turn around and go home?"

Weasel Face put a long arm around The Weaver and pulled her close. "Your words are good, daughter, but what will people think if we desert them? We must stay and help as best we can." The two narrow sets of eyes flicked rapidly back and forth around the circle of onlookers. Father and daughter, the one short and plump the other slender and tall, looked so comical Running Turtle ducked behind a log and hooted with laughter.

Lone Wolf scowled. Weasel Face was working on the column. In his sly way he was telling the people their leader was not to be trusted; he was risking their lives. Lone Wolf could see by their expressions Weasel Face's words were hitting the mark. If he wanted to stay in command of the party he had to act and do it fast. He quickly examined the barrier. The only way to get by the fallen trees was to follow the river bed. That meant wading in the icy, turbulent, boulder-strewn stream. It was dangerous but could be done.

Lone Wolf took Many Horses aside and explained his plan. "We can manage this with a safety line. People can make the crossing if they have something to hold on to -- something to keep them from slipping and falling."

Many Horses did not like the idea but he understood the situation. His father was in a fix. He needed help. He signaled Left Hand and explained the plan. The two men quickly linked several rawhide strands together. Left Hand fastened one end to the nearest fallen tree trunk. Many Horses took the other end and urged his horse into the river. The horse stumbled and nearly fell, then regained its footing. On the far side of the tree barrier the horse again lost its footing and dropped to its knees. Many Horses jumped down and jerked the horse's head above water. By tugging and shouting encouragement, he managed to get the animal up the slippery bank.

"This is no good," Weasel Face blustered. "We cannot cross here. We will lose everything we have."

Lone Wolf gave him a withering look. "There is little danger. My small son, Running Turtle, can make this crossing. Show them, son. Lead a pack mare across."

Running Turtle pulled the reluctant mare to him. This was his chance to prove his worth, make up for taking his father's rifle. He gripped the halter line tightly and took a step forward. In his excitement he forgot the safety line. He plunged into the icy water and tripped over a boulder. The current cut his short legs from under him. He let go of the pack mare's lead. The swift water picked him up and swept him away; over and over he tumbled. The turbulent current tossed him to the surface like a cork, then slammed him down like a rock. His head struck the boulder strewn river bottom. For a moment all he could see were flashes of light against a blanket of black. He came to the surface and sucked in a torturous breath. He tried to yell for help but couldn't. The water closed over him again.

Toohool, who quickly recognized Running Turtle's predicament, grabbed a coil of rope and ran along the river bank. The current was carrying Running Turtle so fast he barely could catch up. Finally he threw out the rope. Running Turtle grabbed for it and missed. Toohool quickly coiled the rope and ran farther down river. A whirling eddy caught Running Turtle, swirling him around in a circle. Toohool flung the rope again. This time his aim was true. The rope end nearly struck Running Turtle on the head. The struggling lad clutched it for dear life. For a moment Running Turtle was too exhausted to do more than hang on. He had swallowed so much water he hardly could catch his breath. The current twisted him around, pulling him under again.

Toohool tugged on the line keeping it tight. "Hang on!" he ordered. Vision Seeker and a dozen other men ran to help. Working together the men pulled the battered boy into shallow water where Toohool and Vision Seeker caught him by the shirt collar and dragged him onto the river bank.

"Safety line! Safety line! What do you think we put it there for?" Lone Wolf thundered. He was so frightened by the close call he did not take offense when Weasel Face hooted, "I told you the trail is not good."

VI

It is not good for people to have an easy life. They become weak and inefficient when they cease to struggle.

Victorio, Mimbres Apache

The near disaster sobered the hunting party. For a while there was a dispute over whether they should continue or return to their Lapwai home. Although shaken by the near drowning, Lone Wolf's pride would not permit him to accept defeat.

"We are the Lapwai band. We have courage. We can not let a small thing like this to upset our hunt."

Weasel Face started to speak, then hesitated. Wife Number One had glanced at him and frowned. "Remember your wish to become leader of the band," the frown said. "You won't get that way by looking a coward."

Lone Wolf easily prevailed. Most of the people were related to him. They knew he would take it ill if they did not stand behind him. Another line was stretched across the rushing waters. With protective lines on either side of them the travelers managed to make the crossing. Except for getting drenched to the knees, the hunters suffered no injury and lost no possessions.

Because of the delay, that night the hunting party was forced to camp on a stretch of trail so narrow there barely was room to bed down. Lone Wolf camped away from the others. There was a rumble of grumbling late into the night. "Silence!" a shrill voice finally cried out. Quiet fell over the camp but few were able to sleep.

The following morning the travelers were up and around before daylight. Grousing and mumbling to themselves, they took to the steep trail, wondering if the summit would ever appear. Late in the day two horses were swept away by an avalanche of rocks. Many Horses, who was in charge of the loose stock, took the blame.

"Why is it when a member of the Lone Wolf clan does a task it ends up badly?" Weasel Face was heard to ask loudly of Wife Number One at the evening campsite.

The charge made Many Horses' ears burn but he did not attempt to defend himself. The loss struck him far worse than it did Weasel Face. One of the lost animals was from the Lone Wolf herd, one of his special friends. Anyway, there was little he could have done to prevent the tragedy. From behind a tree trunk that had fallen beside the trail, a fisher popped up to chase violently after a squirrel. The rodent's sudden appearance, startled the horses. They shied, jumping back into those that followed. The narrow trail did not provide room to maneuver. To avoid tumbling down the mountain side, the horses pawed up the slope.

Rocks and dirt began to slide. In a wild panic, the animals clawed at the mountain side like badgers digging burrows. A boulder gave way, hurtling down upon them. Two geldings were knocked off their feet and went rolling head over heels to pitch off a cliff and into the rocky canyon, dropping hundreds of feet straight down. The sickening thud that echoed back made the travelers cringe; a mother shrieked and a child cried.

The third night on the trail was the worst. The party camped in a tree surrounded cove. Below the campsite the Kooskooskie hurtled by, its cold clear water surging over and around a string of boulders, thundering like a runaway herd of bison. Hardly were shelters erected and campfires started when the trees began to moan and sigh. No one became alarmed. Blustery zephyrs were common on this stretch of trail. Toward evening the wind kept rising, a fine mist began to fall. A guard came to report it was raining ice pellets on the hill that overlooked camp. The wind continued to increase in strength. Icy rain soon enveloped the campsite. Women and boys tightened the pegs that held the tipis and brought in all possessions that had been left outside.

Many Horses, fearing for the herd, put on a protective cap and ran towards the grazing grounds. He was still on the edge of camp when the icy gusts turned into a ferocious gale. Many Horses clutched for his cap only to see it fly across the river and into the trees. To avoid getting blown away, he laid down, clutching at an exposed cottonwood root. Treetops whipped back and forth like creatures in torment. Tipis collapsed, loose clothes and bedding sailed into the river bank brush. Women clutched at their skirts. Frightened children ran screaming to their mothers. Camp dogs scurried for shelter. Vision Seeker glanced at his father. This was the type of weather he had feared they would encounter. Lone Wolf was too busy trying to keep his possessions from blowing away to pay Second Son any attention.

Grandmother, her toothless mouth agape, grasped her shawl tightly around her streaming gray hair and stared up at the frothing treetops. "Oh-hah! Father Sky is angry. He has turned his bag of winds loose. See! They come in every direction. Someone should catch the winds before they do great harm."

"Grandmother! No one can catch the wind," Running Turtle said sharply. He was frightened. This was more terrifying than the storm that turned the horses into uncontrollable demons. If the horses went crazy here and ran away . . . The thought of being left afoot high in the mountains made goose bumps rise on his skin.

"Oh, yes, the wind can be captured," Grandmother insisted. "Have you not heard the story of the young man who set a snare for the wind?"

Running Turtle grunted. Grandmother was off on one of her many tales again.

"Yes, you see, once long ago Wind became angry with the two-leggeds -- killed many people, blew down many lodges. A young man saw the terrible things Wind did and vowed to catch and tame him. He set snares. Wind was clever and blew the snares away. One night while Wind rested the young man sneaked up on him. He seized Wind and locked him in a cave where he kept him for many days. The people were happy. Everything was good. They went about their work without being afraid of being blown away. Then slowly campfire smoke, cinders, bugs and things began to fill the air. It grew hot and uncomfortable. People barely could breathe. Wind was not there to blow away the bad things, keep the air clean and cool. The people begged the young man to turn Wind loose. The young man did, but not before Wind promised never again to do harmful things."

"Maybe Wind forgot his promise," Running Turtle muttered as a gust tore at his clothes and a shower of stinging pellets of icy rain struck his face.

Suddenly as it sprung up, the wind and rain ceased. Only the thunder of the river could be heard. Believing the storm was over, the travelers emerged to search for lost possessions. Downed tipis were set straight. Fires were built and meals cooked. Just as the campers sat down to eat, the wind rose again, hurtling down the canyon. A tree top snapped. Two tall evergreens moaned and creaked. A second gust, stronger than the first, struck. The two evergreens slowly tipped. The dirt around their roots split open.

Slowly, then gaining speed, the tall heavy trunks came crashing to the ground. A pack horse was trapped. Men with hand axes frantically chopped at the limbs that crushed the mare. The poor animal screamed like a human in great pain. The terrifying sound rose above the roar of the wind and the thunder of the river. Vision Seeker ran to help. In the trees that remained standing, a big limb broke loose. It fell to knock the running Vision Seeker off his feet.

Rabbit Skin Leggings was the first to get to the dying horse. He placed the muzzle of the rifle next to the wounded animal's ear and pulled the trigger. The rifle report and death cry of the horse was lost in the roar of the wind and thunder of the river.

Women and children ran for an open space where they huddled together, fearfully watching the fury of the storm. It was as if the gods were angry. Someone said they had camped on an old burial ground. The spirits of the dead had risen to drive the intruders away. Suddenly the storm was over. The wind died to a whisper. Even the river seemed to have calmed. The stunned campers began to move, searching for belongings, some of them deposited miles away by the wind.

It was a long, cold night. Everything dripped with water. People were soaked to the skin. Bedding that had not blown away was wet through. The tipis that remained erect, stood in puddles. Fires were impossible to start. People stumbled around, stomping their feet and flinging their arms back and forth trying to keep warm. While searching for shelter, Toohool discovered a cave. It smelled of skunk but was filled with precious dry brush and debris. The hunters vied with each other trying to start a fire.

Much to everyone's surprise, Toohool again came to the rescue. He wrapped his bow string around a slender length of wood. After carefully placing an end of the stick on a dry mossy log, he began to pull the bow string quickly back and forth. The friction of the spinning stick created sufficient heat to start the dry moss smoking. Soon, out of the smoke burst a flame. A cheer went up. Even Lone Wolf grudgingly admitted the young lad's efforts were good.

#

Finally, the column arrived at the summit. The travelers paused by an eight-foot stone mound which the ancients had built. Here it was customary to give thanks to the gods for safe passage. Family leaders gathered in a circle for the ceremonial smoke. All around them the dark, heavily forested slopes looked down. There was little to give thanks for. The superstitious believed the terrible wind and screaming horse were omens: even more terrifying events awaited down the trail. Although many wished they had not come, it was too late to turn back. After the ceremonial smoke the men quickly disbanded and hurried to their families.

Weasel Face and Lone Wolf were the last to leave. The tall lean man glanced at Lone Wolf and shook his head. "Old bear, I warned you this trail was no good. You led us into this mess for a bit of buffalo meat. Was all we have been through worth it to satisfy your stomach?"

Lone Wolf scowled. "We are safely here, that's what matters."

"True, true. We are all safe because my boy pulled yours out of the river like a hooked fish." Weasel Face bared his teeth in a mirthless grin.

Below the summit the cool mountain breeze died away. At a broad grassy meadow Lone Wolf pulled his mount to a halt. "We will camp here for the night," he announced. The campers took cheer. The terrible Kooskooskie was left behind. The air was unbelievably warm. This was the best campsite since they started. Perhaps their troubles were over. The only disagreeable feature of the campsite was, like the dry cave, it smelled strongly of skunk. The warmth came from steaming pools of water.

The temperature of one pool was so great it burned the hand of Weasel Face's youngest son. His howls brought his mother running to see what the commotion was all about. She picked up her child who continued to scream. "A mad skunk has bit my precious son!" the mother shouted. There was pandemonium until Toohool reported, "Mother, Little Son is not badly hurt; he burned his hand. Put a little grease on the burn. He will forget his pain and be all right."

The pools of hot water intrigued Toohool. As Weasel Face's oldest son, Toohool was kept under close watch by his father. He had little opportunity to do anything on his own. All of his life Weasel Face had instructed him on every task he tackled. Toohool dutifully obeyed his father but still had an inquiring mind. He tested each pool of water until he came to one that pleased him. Someone in the past had built a dam to form a pond. Elders said the hairy faced explorers, Lewis and Clark, had camped nearby and bathed in these same waters.

Toohool dipped his hand in, then removed his moccasin and thrust his foot in. The water was extremely warm but felt good. He quickly stripped down and jumped into the pool. When he became uncomfortably hot, his skin the color of red pipestone, he ran across the trail to the rushing creek that drained the snowy mountain slopes. With a mighty shout, he dove head first into the crystal cold water; sputtering and shivering, he scrambled out to dash back into the hot pool. Soon every youth in camp joined in the fun. Raven Wing, modestly watching from the Lone Wolf shelter, took note of Toohool's slender, naked form. "Hmm!" she thoughtfully uttered. Perhaps she and Small Goat should start including Toohool in their daily escapades.

The next day the column moved down the trail to the floor of Bitterroot Valley. The descent followed a noisy creek that tumbled over boulders and cascaded down rocky drop-offs at the bottom of which were quiet pools thick with trout. Before the creek met the Bitterroot River, the trail turned north. A stiff wind blew down the valley, stinging the travelers' faces. It had the feel and smell of snow.

Lone Wolf urged the column onward. Many Horses drove the herd ahead as fast as it would go. Bands of elk, deer and a black bear bounded out of the way. When Mother Earth's creatures descended to the lowlands in such great numbers it meant a change in the weather was near. Lone Wolf, Left Hand, Red Bear and a number of others went hunting, bringing back seven carcasses of deer, a bear and two elk. The fresh meat was greeted with joy. What the travelers did not roast and boil they saved for drying and for making pemmican.

The party of hunting families entered Hellgate Pass where the winds whipped their clothes and made noses and eyes water. Up the river called Blackfoot the column meandered and then zigzagged over a steep range of hills. On all sides beautiful dark evergreens like tall sentinels marked the way. They struggled up a slope to reach a summit to see white-topped mountains so near they could feel the coldness of the snow. Into a forested gorge they descended. Through a rocky canyon the trail wound, a place so dark and foreboding children whimpered, horses shied and riders cocked their rifles for fear of ambush.

Finally, they broke out to see treeless grasslands. Before them stretched the golden rolling hills where buffalo came to spend the fall and winter. Lone Wolf galloped wildly back and forth shouting the good news. "Buffalo country! We are here! This is our hunting grounds!" On the top of a hill he reined his mount to a stop and gazed across the endless horizon, awed by its immensity. He dismounted. It was a proper place and time to give thanks to the Great Mystery. He muttered a silent prayer of gratitude. If the Great One had not come to him, he still would be trapped in the stifling, noisy long lodge.

VII

The Great Spirit, in placing men on the earth desired them to take good care of the ground and to do each other no harm . . .
                                   Young Chief, Cayuse

Lone Wolf leisurely went about selecting a permanent campsite. He saddled up and rode away from the temporary camp in a lighthearted mood. His family was safely across the mountains. They had run into difficulty; three horses and a handful of possessions were lost. There was no use to worry about that. All and all it could have been far worse. He breathed deeply of the cool crisp air. He felt so vibrant and alive he urged the horse into a gallop and raced to the top of a ridge. It was good to be a member of the Nimpau. Their homeland lay between the Endless Water and the Shiny Mountains, the high peaks that carried snow all four seasons of the year. In a few days travel the Nimpau could overlook the ceaseless waves of the ocean or camp on the rolling plains of buffalo country.

For a while Lone Wolf savored the feeling of contentment. It was a brilliant late fall day. The canopy above was azure blue. Not a cloud was in sight. A sliver of moon hung over a faraway stand of gray-green evergreens. A pair of high flying hawks floated like circling dots of black against the sun. The terrain in all directions was wild yet beautiful. Grass-covered hills rose one after another to merge into the distant horizon. Skunk cabbage lay in brown piles in the hollows. A covey of grouse ran through the grass to take off in a flurry of beating wings. A family of prairie dogs popped their heads out of their holes to utter scolding chirps and quickly disappear again. A rabbit dashed along a well worn path to vanish in a swale where bulrushes thrust their brown heads above the grass like clusters of tipi poles.

"This is good," Lone Wolf thought. All of Mother Earth's creatures welcomed him. It was a perfect place to spend the Season of Falling Snow. He gave himself a pat on the back for his perseverance in insisting on completing the trip. On a still morning like this, Lapwai Valley would be gloomy with lodge smoke and damp with fog that rose from the river and creek. Here the sky was open and clear. One could see to the horizon in any direction. Unlike the long lodge, shared by nineteen other families, in buffalo country each family had its own separate tipi. If the family became too irksome, a few steps away all outdoors was there in which to lose one's self. The annoying Weasel Faces and lazy White Bird relatives would not always be underfoot. The thought pleased Lone Wolf so much his stoic countenance broke into a pleasant smile.

Lone Wolf selected a protected spot near the river to set up camp. Everything needed was at hand. Water, crystal clear and cold as ice, swept over rocks, silt and shifting sands that formed the river bed. Great mounds of driftwood left by spring floods would provide fuel for tipi fires. Willow trees, now bare of leaves, grew along the river bank as a barrier against unexpected intruders. Back from the river, clusters of cottonwoods would break the wind. Behind the cottonwoods the land sloped upward to level out into a plain where the horses could graze and still be in sight of camp.

#

Before the column of hunters had come to a stop, Many Horses had galloped ahead to scout the grassy pasture fields. He wanted nothing but the best for the herd. He was also pleased at what he found. Knee-high grass in patches as thick as a horse's mane rose on all sides. Water was near and plentiful. When the winds of winter blew down from the north the animals could take shelter in the cottonwood groves.

Many Horses rode into a swale and dismounted. Here, where additional moisture collected, the grass rose above his waist. He pulled a stalk and chewed on it. Although dry, the grass was thick and firm, the kind buffalo preferred. Its salty, nutritious content satisfied them and gave their meat a pleasing flavor. According to village elders, who had sampled every kind of food-stuff Mother Earth offered, meat of a young bison cow raised on buffalo grass was the most satisfying and palatable of all.

As soon as tipis were erected and final unpacking completed, the hunters gathered in an opening in the trees. They formed a circle to smoke the ceremonial pipe, a tradition that had been handed down from one generation to another since the beginning of time. After everyone was seated, Lone Wolf took the long-stemmed pipe from its case and held it before him. His thoughts were solemn. Once again he counted the many reasons he had to be thankful. He looked forward to the good times ahead.

Any day the buffalo would stream down from the high country. He and his people were prepared to welcome these sacred creatures when they arrived. The Season of the Big Cold would be harsh but livable. There would be plenty of meat and hides. Everyone would be well fed and well clothed. They would forget the hardships they suffered on the trip up the Kooskooskie. From a special pouch Lone Wolf took a mixture of tobacco, the bark and leaves of willow, dogwood and petals of the wild rose. The aroma delighted him. He packed the mixture in the redstone pipe bowl and raised the pipe above his head.

"Oh, Grandfather, hear our humble words. We gather to thank you for bringing us safely to these beautiful grasslands. We look forward to the bounty they provide." Out of the corner of his eye Lone Wolf caught sight of Weasel Face. He raised the pipe higher. "We thank you for our good neighbors and our bad. We know you have placed all creatures on Mother Earth for a purpose. May their deeds never dishonor you. . . ."

Vision Seeker noticed his father's glance. Even while at prayer Weasel Face pricked him like the needles of a nettle. Vision Seeker sighed. All winter his father and Weasel Face would find one reason or another to make each other's life a trial.

After the ceremonial smoke hunters walked into the prairie and marveled at the thick nutritious grass. They all had the same thought. Soon these slopes would attract buffaloes by the thousands, turning the rolling hills as dark as night. The hunters sat down and listened to the breezes rustle through the grass. An elder announced the wind had a good sound. It whispered of bountiful buffalo harvests to come and great hunts of the past. Running Turtle, who had been allowed to join the men, hunkered down to listen to the pleasant music of the whispering wind. He found it comforting yet it carried a melancholy message. "You are still a boy of eleven, not yet a man. What makes you believe buffaloes will fall by your hand?"

Vision Seeker also sat in the grass and let the lulling, whispering sounds take over his thoughts. Since man first walked the surface of Mother Earth buffaloes had roamed these rolling plains. In numbers as countless as the stars, they had lived and died on this ground. There was little wonder the grasses whispered a melancholy tune. The spirits of those great buffalo herds made this their home. The restless spirits spoke to each other, telling tales of the long ago times when they alone ruled this land.

Vision Seeker thought of the many buffalo legends he had heard. Some Indian peoples believed before man appeared on Mother Earth buffaloes were human. They lived in a world beneath the one in which two-leggeds now lived. When people first appeared they did not know how to survive. They kept offending Mother Earth and displeasing the gods. Mother Earth and the gods got together and decided a buffalo must teach them. The buffalo teacher told the people they must live in harmony with each other, and with all things on Mother Earth. He taught them sacred mysteries and created a holy order so man could speak with the gods and do their will.

Vision Seeker knew he should not lie in the grass and dream the day away. There were many things to be done. But lying next to Mother Earth, with Father Sun warming him and the singing wind lulling him, it was too pleasant to move. He lingered and daydreamed. Did buffalo people still live in the underworld? Did they still tell humans how to live? Were these the messages the whispering grasses were sending?

Vision Seeker tried to imagine what it had been like when buffaloes were people. It was said they were happy. Each family had a lodge of its own with walls so thick the inhabitants neither felt heat nor cold. They lived in harmony and were servants to the gods. . . .

If it had not been for the strident voice of Weasel Face, Vision Seeker would have dreamed on. "Now that we are here, we should not waste time. We should make plans for when the buffalo herds arrive," the lanky squint-eyed man declared.

"Of course we should," Two Kill, an elder who had not missed a buffalo hunt since anyone could remember, agreed. "Buffaloes could come over the horizon any day."

Now, too old to ride the hunt himself, Two Kill came on hunting trips to instruct the youth. Both young and old treated him with respect. He had hunted buffaloes when guns were unknown. He received his name by dropping two buffaloes with two arrows on a single run. No one in memory had achieved such a singular feat.

The youthful hunters, including Running Turtle, gathered around Two Kill. Silently, he looked them over. His dark face, lined and lumpy as a boulder-strewn ravine, gave his features a rough, harsh appearance. The single feather, thrust at an angle in the graying hair, made him appear even more distant and unyielding. His audience waited patiently for him to speak. They had heard much about this great hunter. He was a legend; a glance from his eyes was enough to make one's spine tingle with excitement and apprehension. Were they up to the standards he expected?

"We are here to make meat for the winter," Two Kill began, taking every listener in at a glance. "Good hunters always attack the herd together. There is no place for the hunter who is out to make coups for himself. A lone horseman may make a kill but often does more harm than good. He scatters the game, sending animals running in all directions.

"When you ride after the herd, carefully select your prey.

Make it a good one. For meat, a young cow is best. Rein your horse alongside and take time to aim your weapon. Shoot behind the ribs for the heart. Have a second arrow ready. One may kill, more often it will not. Watch the buffalo's eyes. If the eyes point your way, watch out. The buffalo is waiting to turn and gore your mount. It is best to take one shot and veer away. If you wound an animal it will soon run itself out and drop."

Running Turtle, who sat near the great hunter, listened open-mouthed to every word. He tried to imagine reining his horse next to a running buffalo. How did one guide his mount and still shoot? What if the horse stumbled and fell? The thought made him shiver. Maybe hunting the bison was not as thrilling as he had thought.

Vision Seeker, listening and watching from his hideaway in the grass, waited for the hunters to disband. He got up and brushed himself off only to find Weasel Face still there. "I saw you, sleeping through the instructions of your elders," Weasel Face chided. "You take after your father. You think you have no more to learn."

"No, I was listening to what the buffalo grass has to say. Sometimes plants and trees speak more wisdom than human beings."

Weasel Face walked away muttering to himself. "I must keep my daughters safe from Lone Wolf's sons. They are not right in the head."

#

The hunters soon settled into an established routine. Life in hunting camps was different than in the home long lodge. There was always the threat of hostiles who might descend at any time to steal, plunder and murder. There was the anxious and exciting watch for the herds of game to arrive. When and from what direction would the great shaggy beasts first appear? The weather was a worry. Would it hold fair or would it descend in an onslaught of blinding white fury?

Lone Wolf and Quiet Woman also endured the pain of

watching Raven Wing act like no respectable maiden should. As on previous journeys, she was not content to cook, sew, scrape hides and do chores around the lodge. Each morning she and Small Goat rode from camp; often they did not reappear until dusk. Lone Wolf watched her come and go as he seethed with rage. He finally could stand it no longer.

"Why don't you make that daughter act like a proper female?" he queried Quiet Woman. "She should stay away from Small Goat. That offspring of Weasel Face leads Raven Wing around by the nose."

"Sh! Sh!" Quiet Woman gave Lone Wolf a warning frown.

Grandmother giggled from the back of the tipi. Alongside Grandmother sat The Weaver. A bundle of bulrushes almost hid the two women from view. They were weaving bulrush mats. Lone Wolf scowled. He should have known Slinky, The Weaver, would be in the lodge. She was like an eel, slipping in and slipping out when he was not looking. Why did he put up with it? There she sat, silent as an owl, listening, cocking her head this way and that so as not to miss a word. Now she would slip home and tell her weasel-faced parents everything he had said.

Lone Wolf grabbed his quirt and stomped outside. The camp dogs sensed his wrath and skittered away. How could he escape the tortures inflicted by his rebellious daughter? He had done everything a father should. As soon as Raven Wing had reached the age of marriage he had traveled from village to village to trade and seek her a suitable mate. Wherever Lone Wolf stopped he made secretive observations to acquaint himself with men of proper age and position. He dropped carefully worded hints to encourage a match. He was a rich man with a great herd of specially bred horses, coveted Appaloosas. A man who took Raven Wing for a wife was certain to gain stature and wealth.

Discouraged by lack of success among the Nimpau, Lone Wolf extended his searches to the Cayuse, Palouse, Umatilla, Yakama and Walla Walla. Fathers with their sons came to look but departed without taking the bait. They saw an attractive maiden with flashing eyes, bold lips and an upsweep of hair, the color and texture of a raven wing for which she was named. Aware she was on display, scrutinized like a prize mare on the trading block, Raven Wing always found some way to cause affront. Once she seized Lone Wolf's bow and shot an arrow at a Palouse suitor. It clipped off the otter tail attached to the astonished admirer's cap. At another time she pulled a Yakama youth from his horse and galloped away on his mount.

Lone Wolf sighed. Somewhere he and Quiet Woman had failed in their duty as parents. Slapping his quirt against a legging, he strode toward the pasture grounds. The sight of grazing horses always soothed him and took his mind off his troubles. He thought back to the many feats Nimpau warriors and hunters had performed. There was no doubt in his mind, he belonged to the most powerful and rich people of his time.

He topped the ridge and shaded his eyes. The herd was a brown blot against the blue/gray horizon. He could not single out one animal from another. He should saddle up and ride out to inspect his horses. Instead, he walked briskly to the top of the next rise where there was a better view. He shaded his eyes again. Two, no, three guards watched over the herd. One was the White Bird, Rabbit Skin Leggings. The other two rode so closely together they looked like one. He could not make out their features until they finally turned to face him.

"Aaah!" In his astonishment he nearly stepped into a prairie dog hole. He took a second look. Yes, it was Raven Wing and Weasel Face's oldest son, Toohool! Even as he watched, Toohool reached out to caress a lock of Raven Wing's hair. Lone Wolf gasped. His daughter did not pull away, she moved nearer. She was smiling!

VIII

In my youthful days I have seen large herds of buffalo on these prairies, and elk were found in every grove, but they are here no more, having gone towards the setting sun.

Shabonna, Potawtomi

In after years the people discussed that fateful winter as Time of the Circled Moon. Vision Seeker was one of the first to fully understand the significance of the unusual phenomenon. It was the third week in camp. The mood of the Sun River camp was glum. The buffaloes the hunters anticipated had yet to arrive. There was talk the great herds, instead of coming south, had been driven north. The dreaded Blackfeet were to blame. Their watchers had discovered the presence of the Nimpau and had vowed to keep the coveted shaggy animals from them.

As was their custom, Vision Seeker and Many Horses went to the pasture grounds to bring in the special mounts that at night they tethered close to their lodge. While Many Horses haltered the animals, Vision Seeker sat on a hilltop to watch the gauzy, almost furry silvery moon rise above the eastern horizon. At first he did not notice the circle. As the moon rose it became more defined. Like a lasso loop, it seemed to hold the moon anchored in space. The sight was so eerie it sent a chill racing up his spine. This brilliant orb that had the power to make water run uphill, awed him. What other great things could this giant star do?

Like many members of the human species, Vision Seeker had a dread of the unknown. The circled moon was an omen. Did it bode well or was it the forerunner of bad things to come? He feared it was the latter. The hunting party had received many warnings, all pointing to trouble. The violent lightening and thunder storm that struck Lapwai Valley was the first. Happenings on the trail made it doubly clear the gods did not favor the journey: an owl flying before nightfall; fallen trees that blocked the trail;

the landslide carrying two horses to their deaths; the disastrous wind below the summit. It, alone, should have alerted everyone the gods were angry. Now, the moon that should be clear and bright, came up looking like a ragged ball of fur.

Finished with his work, Many Horses let the special lodge animals stand and hunkered down beside Vision Seeker. He glanced at the moon. "Weather will change," he observed. "It is good. It will bring buffaloes down from the hills."

For a long while Vision Seeker did not speak. He chewed a blade of grass and studied the moon that gradually became more distinct. "It is so. We can expect snow. It will be some while before buffaloes arrive. Strange happenings will befall us first."

Many Horses looked at him sharply. "The people are hungry. The buffaloes must come. Make your talk straight."

Vision Seeker plucked another stem of grass. He should have remained silent. Many Horses would report his words to Lone Wolf. His father, already upset by the long wait for the hunt and antics of Toohool and Raven Wing, would be furious. Anyway, it was not good to reveal signs unless one understood them. If signs were not properly interpreted they had no value.

"Do not sit there and chew grass," Many Horses scolded. "Tell me what you see."

Vision Seeker ignored his brother. What words could he say when he, himself, did not understand? Something unexpected would happen -- something that would affect the lives of everyone in the hunting party. He knew the direction from whence the danger would come. All afternoon Mother Earth's creatures had been sounding the alarm. Three crows flapped out of a tree. Cawing loudly, they circled around and flew south. Immediately afterward a coyote came over the ridge from the north, paying no attention to barking dogs it loped right by Sun River camp on its way south. Almost on its tail a rabbit darted from the bushes. It took the same trail as the coyote; in its hurry it nearly ran its normal predator down. Now, as they sat on the hilltop with the circled moon behind them, from up river came the haunting, sinister cry of a loon. Mother Earth's creatures were speaking; but no one seemed to listen.

"Strangers come from the north. Their scent is strong -- unpleasant. Like buffaloes, they flee before the snow. . . ." Vision Seeker stopped. Were these the same signs he had seen long ago, so awesome he never dared breathe a word of them to anyone? Why was he burdened with this frightening power? It was torture peering into the future, especially when most everything that came to him was one disaster followed by another.

"A raiding party!" Many Horses exclaimed. "What about our herd? Had we not better drive all animals close to camp?"

Vision Seeker shook his head. "No, it will only make Lone Wolf angry. He will say we are foolish." Vision Seeker clamped his lips together. Long ago he had learned that even when his predictions were true, few believed him.

Many Horses knew it was futile to question his brother further. As usual, he was expected to make sense of the words already spoken. He picked up the braided elk hide halter ropes. Walking side by side, the brothers led the lodge mounts toward camp. Running Turtle came to meet them. Many Horses handed him a halter rope. They staked the animals in the cottonwood grove behind the tipi lodges. The horses were still hungry. They snuffled at the ground and pulled at tether lines to nibble tender tree bark. Many Horses handed Running Turtle his knife.

"Cut and fetch grass from the river bank," he ordered.

Third Son, who had been practicing with his bow and arrows, did not like to be given orders. Over the past fortnight he had gained confidence, actually had become proud of himself. His marksmanship had improved until he could hit a square of deer hide three times out of four. In his thoughts he was no more bumbling and awkward. Instead of resembling a ruffed grouse, he was tall and strong. He saw himself returning from a successful hunt with a string of buffalo ears taken from his kills. The rumor of Blackfeet in the region also stirred his imagination -- he had gone scouting and run into a war party that he decimated.

His pictured coups included many Blackfeet scalp locks. To make this image real, lengths of squirrel and skunk tail hung at his belt.

"Cutting grass is for women and children," he said scornfully.

"Come down to Mother Earth," Many Horses scoffed. "You think too highly of yourself. Look at you. You do not rise to the belly of a yearling pony."

Grumbling, Running Turtle took the knife and ran to do his brother's bidding.

During the evening meal Running Turtle was humbled further. Just as he was putting the last bite of a pressed berry cake into his mouth a blue jay as large as a crow, swooped down to snatch it away. It startled him so he fell over backwards and uttered a terrified yelp. His brothers laughed. It was Grandmother who took away the sting.

"You are honored, my son. Blue Jay brought you a message. Blue Jay told you the Season of Falling Snow comes soon. The Season of Deep Snow that follows will be long and cold."

Lone Wolf gave his mother a sharp glance. In her old age she was getting more and more like Second Son, turning unusual happenings into troubling signs. The next morning he had to admit Grandmother's prediction was at least partially correct. During the night a sharp wind whistled across the plain from the north. The campers awakened to see white dust sifting through tipi smoke holes. Ridges of snow lay in drifts, surrounding the tipis. The groves of cottonwoods, which took the brunt of the storm, were nearly covered with a blanket of white.

Gradually, the camp came to life. Tipi flaps pushed open. Lodge occupants crawled out. Eyes still filled with sleep, the hunters stumbled about trying to determine what should be done to make the lodges secure from the storm that was certain to follow. Wood gatherers scrounged among driftwood piles along the creek banks to fuel lodge fires. Horse herders untethered the hungry camp animals. Shivering, they led the special horses toward the main herd. Fires were lit. Smoke lazily drifted up to spill through smoke holes. The sight and smell of smoke and aroma of food cooking, brought night guards in from their posts. They entered the tipis and covered themselves with buffalo robes still warm from sleeping bodies. Silently, they watched the women prepare the morning meal. Their mood was grim. Winter had arrived but where were the buffaloes?

Many Horses and Vision Seeker were among those who trod through the snow returning special lodge mounts to the herd. Except for the knife at his belt, Vision Seeker was unarmed. Many Horses carried his bow and quiver of arrows. As the brothers approached the herd, a pair of geldings threw up their heads to stare to the north, ears pointing into the cutting morning breeze. They took a few steps and whinnied. The mount Vision Seeker led jerked on the halter line and also whinnied. An unearthly answer drifted back.

Many Horses stopped stock still. "What is it? Did the call come from a loon?"

The brothers cocked their heads to listen. The sound was repeated, somewhat louder and more insistent. Many Horses dropped the rawhide halter rope and ran behind a clump of trees. Fiercely, he motioned for Vision Seeker to do the same. He whispered, "this call is most strange. It is too strong for a bird. Can it be that of the bull moose?"

"A moose in buffalo country?"

The brothers crouched, listening intently, mystified. From early childhood they had studied the calls and ways of every bird and animal that inhabited the Nimpau homeland. This call was new, unlike anything they ever had heard. It was terrifying. Did these grasslands contain animals they knew nothing about?

"Can it be a four-legged with bad windpipe, like a horse with the heaves?" Vision Seeker queried.

"Ha! Brother, your thinking is good. This animal is not well."

The brothers cautiously edged through the pliant willows. On the far side of the thicket, Many Horses abruptly stopped. In the lee of the next ridge stood a cluster of four-leggeds, their ears pointed directly toward the clump of willows. Behind the animals, half-buried in drifts of snow, was a shelter. From its size it held no more than a few men.

"Ah!" Vision Seeker murmured. These were the strangers with the strong scent who frightened Mother Earth's creatures. From what land did they come and why? They did not show themselves; were they hiding in ambush? The brothers counted six of the strange sounding four-leggeds. The brothers stared at the beasts. They had the shape of a horse but were not as large. They had big heads, long ears, short manes, big bellies, thin legs; their tails were like fly whisks; there was no hair around the base yet the ends were bushy. The four-legged nearest them threw up its huge head, opened its big jaws and sucked in a horrifyingly loud scream of a breath. Then out its being came an ear shattering, strangling sound. The Nimpau youths recoiled into the brush and stared at each other.

Many Horses whispered in awe. "Stallions must have bred with moose to make creatures like these."

Vision Seeker motioned Many Horses forward. Reluctantly, Many Horses obeyed. The brothers slid deeper into the willow growth only to stop as a fur clad figure crawled from the small shelter. Vision Seeker sucked in his breath. Big! It was the largest two-legged he had ever seen. Many Horses gasped. Another, even larger two-legged, came to stand beside the first. A tremor of fear ran up Vision Seeker's spine. Many Horses' heart began to pound. These people were giants. The brothers pulled back, almost scrambling over each other in their hurry to get under more cover.

Through a slit in the willow branches Vision Seeker studied the strangers. Except for their huge size they looked like normal men but also resembled grizzly bears. The skin around their eyes was bare yet hair covered most of their faces. It fell from their chins and jowls like that of the mountain sheep. It was not fine hair but coarse and bristly as a porcupine's tail.

Many Horses backed farther into the trees. "Could these be the people called 'hairy faces' who came from the land beyond the River of Many Canoes? Do they mean to do us harm, or do they seek the buffalo? What are they doing here?" Many Horses looked anxiously to his younger brother. Vision Seeker was the one who could see into the future. Perhaps he knew the answers.

"I think it is not buffalo they seek. Rabbit Skin Leggings speaks of these people. He tells of men with hairy faces who go into the mountains to trap the beaver. They use the skins for trade. They send the beaver skins to the land beyond the River of Many Canoes where they are made into clothes, things that cover the head and shoulders."

"There are no beaver streams on these grass covered plains. These people either wait for the buffalo or are up to no good. Ah! The herd!" Many Horses' immediate thought was to protect the herd. Without horses the hunting party would be afoot miles from home. He would have turned back but Vision Seeker stopped him.

"There is time to care for the horses. We must learn more about these hairy faced ones. Lone Wolf will ask many questions. If these people bring danger we must know."

"My wits leave me. You are right. We cannot turn away and run like frightened hares."

Hidden by the clusters of willows, the brothers crept up until they could hear the newcomers' voices. "O-hay! Yellow hair!" Vision Seeker exclaimed as one big man removed his head covering. The hair that rose in wavy swirls, was the color of aspen trees in the Season of Falling Leaves. Sunlight glinting on it gave the wavy strands a golden glow. Vision Seeker was awed. There was something holy about this man. He had been touched by Sun God. The other big man's hair was as black as a tipi smoke hole in the spring. He resembled a big black bear, blinking in the morning sunlight like he just had emerged from the long winter's sleep.

From the low shelter came a third hairy face. He was not a big man but short and round. His head barely came up to the shoulders of the giants. In a voice that made chattering noises like that of a scolding blue jay, the short one began to chide the big men. When he raised his cap to scratch, the brothers saw the hairy face was topped by a head as slick and white as a fresh laid egg. The sight was so unexpected it made them gasp. Ducking farther back into the protection of the willows, the brothers stared at each other.

Many Horses exclaimed. "What is it? The man must have a terrible disease."

Vision Seeker was struck dumb by the awesome sight. Had this man been scalped? If that was so, the warrior was very skilled. He had left the skin as neat and smooth as if it had never known a hair.

Under cloaks of fur, the hairy faced ones wore buckskin much the same as the brothers. They carried long, heavy-barreled fire sticks. From belts around their waists hung sheathed knives and shiny bladed hand axes. Their packs, half buried in the snow, bulged with trade goods or animal pelts. Which it was the brothers could not tell. The strangers did not appear hostile or on guard. They leaned the heavy-barreled fire sticks against their packs and dug through the snow to uncover dry twigs and wood. Black Hair took a smoke smudged pot and dipped it into the river. After several attempts to strike sparks from a flint, the man with no hair on his head started a low fire. From a rawhide bag he took the makings of the morning meal.

The brothers were fascinated. The round man with no hair on his head went about women's work as deftly as did their own mother. The other two looked on as indifferently, smoking and talking, as any pair of Nimpau men waiting to be served. Suddenly No Hair On Head glanced toward the brothers' hiding place and seized one of the long heavy-barreled fire sticks.

IX

*It has been our misfortune to welcome the white man. We have
been deceived. He brought with him many shiny things that
pleased our eyes.*

Red Cloud, Oglala Sioux

The three newcomers knew they were under scrutiny.
They had made too many treks into Indian territory to be caught
off guard. In spite of their experience and skill in traversing wil-
derness trails, they just had suffered disaster. A member of their
party had been slain in cold blood. He had gone hunting and
never returned. The partners found his scalped body with a half
dozen Blackfeet arrows in his chest. They buried their companion and fled. The Blackfeet homeland was rich in beaver streams
but too dangerous to stay and work trap lines.

For three days the trio had been on the run. The blinding
snowstorm finally had stopped them. However, it also had saved
them. The wind-driven snow had obliterated their tracks. Believing they were safe from pursuit, they made camp. They awakened to face a new threat. The youth lurking behind the bank of
willows meant an Indian encampment was close by. The keen
blue eyes of the man with hair the color of aspen leaves in the
fall, spied the brothers first.

"Don't look," he warned his companions. "We have visitors, a couple of lads in yonder thicket. Perhaps Blackfeet, more
likely Nimpau, the tribe the French named Nez Perce. I am told
they often trek up the Clearwater, the river the natives call
Kooskooskie, probably here on a bison hunt."

Ignoring his partner's warning, No Hair On Head glanced
toward the willow bank. "Damn redskins. We skedaddle from
the Blackfeet then run smack dab inta another batch. I'll flush
these sneakin' critters out," he uttered, reaching for his rifle.

"Leave them be!" Yellow Hair ordered. "Keep your hands

off that firearm. Now, you see, you frightened them away. No telling what tale those young men will take back to their elders."

Yellow Hair, leader of the three men, was known among the trapping fraternity as Buck Stone. He was an oddity, not the normal rough-and-ready mountain man. By New England standards he was considered a cultured person from a long established upper-class family. He was a graduate of Harvard College. Against his parents' wishes, he had traveled west to study North American Indian culture. After a few years in Indian country his father cut off his allowance. Buck Stone accepted his change in fortunes with equanimity. He took to trapping beaver. It seemed a natural way to earn a living and still carry on his study of the American Indian.

In his travels Buck Stone had become acquainted with natives of many tribes. He could speak several of their languages and knew many of their customs. From the moment he emerged from the shelter he sensed the presence of the Indian youth. From the corner of his eyes he surveyed the willow trees, the nearest place an enemy could hide.

Immediately, he spotted the shadowy figures. He could tell they were young braves. He believed they merely were curious. When they returned to their home camp and reported the presence of strangers, that was when the situation could become serious. Although irked with his short, quick-triggered partner for the threatening act of reaching for the rifle, he did not fuss.

"No need to get flustered. Take things as they come and hope everything comes out in the wash. We're in a strange land amongst strange people. There's no need to pack up and run before we know where we are and whom we face. We'll wait a spell, see what these people do. If I remember correctly the Nez Perce were very friendly with Meriwether Lewis and William Clark. In fact the explorers lived with them for several weeks. Sergeant Patrick Gass, a member of the expedition, wrote in his journal the Nez Perce were the most friendly and most honest people they met on the entire journey."

"I hope the sarg'nt was tellin' the truth," the rotund trapper grumbled. "After thet Blackfeet mess, I ain't trustin' no Injun."

The big man with black hair remained silent. He never spoke two words when one or none would do. His companions knew little about him and no one had the courage or desire to inquire into his past. They didn't even know his given name. He simply was called Little Ned. He did his work and asked for nothing more than his fair share of the catch.

The black haired man also had been quick to spy the Indian youth. He pretended not to notice them. Of course they were curious, probably had never seen a mountain man before. He would have liked to call out to the young men, say they came as friends. Although a silent reserved person, he wanted to be friends with everyone. He enjoyed the life he led. He loved the beauty of this wild country. It made him feel alive. He loved adventure, the challenge of pitting skills against Mother Nature. He found every day exciting. To be astride the continental divide was like being on top of the world.

He looked forward to meeting these people who made this their home. He liked what he heard of them. They were great horsemen, breeders of the hardy, picturesque Appaloosa. If he had Buck Stone's easy-going demeanor and his ability to gain the confidence of Indian people, he would stay in this beautiful country, learn the language and ways of the natives. When they got to know each other he was certain they would be friends.

The short man with the bald head harbored no such amiable or optimistic feelings. His feet were killing him. His legs and back ached. The trappers had lost their riding horses to the Blackfeet. From the Yellowstone onward they had walked or taken turns riding the spare pack mule. Long-legged Buck Stone and Little Ned had set a fast pace. He barely had been able to keep up. Now, when he thought he could stop running and rest, there were Indians lurking in the bushes. To encounter another band of murderers was more than he could face.

"Buck, I ain't at all happy 'bout this business. Dad rat it, it's like bein' nailed in a coffin. Anywhichway a body turns, there's savages awaitin' ta fill yuh full of arras an' lift yer hair. Why ain't we packin'? Sure's I'm standin' in a foot of snow, those two're hightailin' it back ta their people. Before yuh kin say scat a war party'll be on top of our heads." He pulled off his fur cap to mop his bald pate. "I ain't hankerin' on some young buck carvin' this tender skin."

The speaker's name was Deacon Walton. As a young man he had attended the seminary. He knew the Bible from Genesis to Revelations. He loved to preach but lost his pulpits for quarreling with his congregations. He worked through one church after another until he wound up on the frontier. Then a bright idea struck him; he should convert and baptize the heathen redskin people. Instead, a Cheyenne maiden caught his eye and converted him to the ways of the Indian. Somewhere in Sweetwater country he had a pregnant wife and six year-old child. Only once in a great while did he mention them. He was not a family man.

"No need to get overheated," Yellow Hair admonished. "Those lads are still trying to figure whether or not we're hostiles. They're probably a lot more afraid of us than we are of them. Fix something to eat. We have time. Nothing will happen until they report to the main camp. Then it'll be either a pow-wow or a scrap. Either can be handled better on a full stomach."

#

Lone Wolf looked at his sons in amazement. "Strangers on our pasture grounds -- hostile hairy faces?"

"They are giants," Many Horses exclaimed. "Their four-leggeds are strange creatures, half moose, half horse." Many Horses' sucked in his breath and let it explode out. "Hee-haa!"

Running Turtle, who listened intently, mimicked Many Horses then rolled over and over with a fit of giggles.

Lone Wolf frowned at Third Son. The appearance of the hairy faces was a serious matter. He remembered back to when the Lewis and Clark Expedition passed through the Nimpau homeland. Three boys spied them coming down the Kooskooskie.

Frightened by their first sight of hairy faces, they ran and hid in the tall grass. Captain Clark called to them, held out shiny objects. The hairy faces wanted food. They were so hungry they gobbled the food given them like hungry dogs.

Lone Wolf, who had been with a war party fighting the Snake, returned to find the entire party of hairy faces in the village. They greeted the warriors in remarkably good sign language. One came to him saying he wanted to trade for a horse. Lone Wolf exchanged a mare for a blanket and handful of beads which he wanted to give Quiet Woman with whom he had just married. The hairy ones were agreeable and helpful. Grandmother was ill with bad eyes and a hairy face gave her medicine that relieved her pain. They also were happy people, making music with bow strings fastened to cradle boards -- things they called fiddles -- they did strange dances -- stomping up and down as if caught in a nest of red ants, then circling around and around like dogs trying to catch their tails.

Lone Wolf pondered over his sons' report. "Did you make warlike signs? Why else would the man with no hair on his head take up the fire stick?"

Lone Wolf fell silent. He should not scold his sons who did not understand these hairy faces. At first he did not understand them himself. They greeted people by grasping one by the hand, shaking it up and down fast and hard, the same way one struck sparks with flint and steel. He remembered children mimicking the strangers by shaking hands, laughing and giggling until they ran away to hide from frowning parents.

Among the hairy faces was a black man with teeth white as new fallen snow and a laugh that could be heard all over the village. He allowed curious villagers to inspect his skin, even let them attempt to wash away the color. To their astonishment he traded a hand ax for a fat bitch, then proceeded to kill it, skin it, gut it and roast it on a spit. When it was cooked to his taste, he invited them to partake of the feast. The villagers were horrified, it would have been like feasting on the flesh of a friend. Also, to everyone's dismay, the hairy faces returned the villagers' gifts of kouse and camas foodstuffs and asked for a young horse which they promptly killed and ate. But it was dog meat they liked best. They traded for dogs until hardly any canines remained in villages along the explorers' route.

After the explorers rested and ate their fill in the Nimpau homeland, they traveled on to spend the Seasons of Falling Snow and Deep Snow on the shores of the Endless Water they called ocean. In the Season of First Grass they returned. They said they were on their way back to the River of Many Canoes. Then snow blocked the mountain passes and the hairy ones were forced to remain in the land of the Nimpau for many days.

People from every band came to see the strangers who ate horses and dogs. They held council with many speeches and much gift giving, followed by a great feast. Red Bear, Cut Nose, Twisted Hair, Broken Arm, Speaking Eagle, Black Eagle -- all the important leaders of the Nimpau were present. The event still was remembered by elders as the Council of Friendship. That was a great moment. Along with his father, Great Wolf, he was among those who smoked the pipe that sealed the pact of friendship.

As Lone Wolf recalled these memories, it came to him that a fine opportunity presented itself. If he handled the coming of these three hairy faces well, it would boost his standing among the people. He glanced toward Grandmother's corner. The Weaver sat in her usual place, watching and listening. For once Lone Wolf was glad for her presence. She would take back the news to Weasel Face. The leader of the Lapwai band had the skills to make friends and conduct council with these people from beyond the River of Many Canoes.

"Hairy faces come in peace," Lone Wolf declared. "Four-leggeds with call of a strangled loon are named mules. The packs are filled with trade things." Lone Wolf rubbed his hands together in anticipation. "We must welcome them and see what they bring." He ordered Quiet Woman to lay out his elk skin robe and necklace of bear claws. He sent Running Turtle for his favorite hunter. He told Many Horses and Vision Seeker to ready themselves in their best attire. "We must not bring shame to our people. These hairy faces have traveled many sleeps. It is important we give them proper welcome." Lone Wolf turned to his mate and daughter. "Women! Busy yourselves. Make ready a feast. This is the way to show we are friends."

Raven Wing, who just had awakened and was contemplating the day ahead with Small Goat and Toohool, objected. Lodge work irked her. To prepare meals for people she did not know infuriated her. "We do not cook for strangers. Why do you ask them to our lodge? Vision Seeker says they do not act friendly. Do we feed our enemies? They may kill us and take all we have."

Lone Wolf glared at his willful daughter. Why did she rebel? She always gave trouble. If only he could find her a mate, but not that son of Weasel Face. One did not solve one problem by creating another.

Grandmother tittered behind her shawl. "The daughter does not like hairy faces. She fears one will seek her hand. Think of a hairy faced one as a mate?" She rocked with laughter.

"Enough foolish talk," Lone Wolf snapped. "This is no time to make fun. Do as I say. Prepare to receive our hairy faced guests. Their packs are heavy with trade goods. They will have many good things. They will not rob and kill. They will give gifts. That is their custom."

Raven Wing started to retort but her mother motioned her into silence. Why did her daughter make life so difficult? She was as obstinate as a she-bear with a batch of cubs, and old enough to know not to challenge her father. She hated to think of what would happen to the man who took Raven Wing for a mate. His life would be anything but pleasant.

Vision Seeker donned his best skins and favorite decorations. Since he never had met with a hairy face, he wondered what the strangers would do when approached by a band of hunters. They were heavily armed and had the look of people who would defend themselves to the last man. It was a long time since Lone Wolf had sat in council with hairy faces. Was he doing right by going into their camp?

Lone Wolf, himself, also was unsure how to deal with the situation. How should he approach these people from beyond the River of Many Canoes? He did not speak their language. He knew little of their customs. Who besides himself and his two sons should greet them? Should he call on all heads of families to welcome the hairy faces? No, a large party might frighten them. Besides himself, Left Hand and Red Bull should go. Lame Horse, the White Bird leader, could not be left out. Weasel Face? No, he was not needed. His squint eyes, pushy manner and blustery talk -- the hairy faces would find him tiresome. He would try to take over the whole meeting. He should be kept away from the hairy faces as long as possible.

Once Lone Wolf decided who should be included, he was still in a quandary. Would these people take fright by the approach of the delegation? Should he send a scout first to announce their coming? Who could he send? Rabbit Skin Leggings claimed to have knowledge of these pale faced people. Lone Wolf discarded the thought. Why should he give the White Birds this opportunity? The hairy faces were certain to have trade goods in those heavy packs. No one knew the ways of traders better than did he.

Lone Wolf again thought back to the council meeting with the explorers Lewis and Clark. They smoked and then feasted. That was the way to begin. The hairy ones enjoyed tobacco. First they would smoke. Lone Wolf took the special pipe bag from its place on the tipi lodgepole. He withdrew the long stemmed pipe and polished the red stone bowl until it gleamed. Another bag contained the mixture of sweet grass and bark of the willow and dogwood. When combined with tobacco, the mix would make smoke gratifying to the gods.

An important occasion like this also should begin with a prayer. He thought of words that would please the hairy faces. He would treat them as brothers. After all, did not The Creator place all men on Mother Earth to share and enjoy her fruits alike? Yes, he would make a prayer that said such good things. Lone Wolf motioned to Running Turtle to bring his mount close. He was ready to lead the welcoming party to meet the three trappers camped in the snow.

Within sight of the strangers' encampment Lone Wolf and his party, pulled up. It was unwise to approach a camp unannounced. To Lone Wolf's relief, almost at once the big man with hair the color of yellow aspen leaves appeared. It was a good sign. He had been expecting them. Yellow Hair held his hand high, palm forward with first two fingers thrust upward. "Says he is friend," Lone Wolf interpreted. "They lay aside weapons. Still, it is wise we approach with care. I will go. The rest wait."

Lone Wolf handed his musket to Many Horses. He rode forward, his hand outstretched. When a few steps separated the two men, he stopped. Motioning with the adeptness acquired during many years of trade, Lone Wolf's hands expressed age-old words of friendship. "Our people welcome you. Under the skin we are brothers. Our weapons sleep. They wait the coming of the bison. Stay with us. Together we make the big hunt."

The big stranger rubbed the palm of his left hand with the right clenched fist, then crossed one index finger over the other. "Let us smoke and talk," he signed. From a pouch he pulled a twist of tobacco and held it out.

Lone Wolf took the long stemmed pipe from its bag. Holding the pipe in front of him, he walked forward until tobacco and pipe touched. Watchers from both sides came to gather at the ceremony. Lone Wolf took the tobacco and rubbed it into fine flakes, combining it with the mixture of bark and sweet grass. Carefully, he tamped the mixture in the stone pipe bowl. The short man with no hair on his head brought robes to spread on the blanket of snow. As the men sat to form a circle, the sun burst through the overcast. The light, shining against the snow, was so bright the men put up hands to shield their eyes. The appearance of Father Sun pleased Lone Wolf. It was a favorable sign.

Lone Wolf held the pipe before him. It was time to say the prayer. All the good words he had prepared suddenly left him. The man with yellow hair seemed to understand. He nodded encouragement. The big silent man with black hair waited impassively. The other man, who had a roly-poly figure like Running Turtle, seemed not to see him at all. The expression of disinterest unnerved Lone Wolf. Perhaps Vision Seeker's signs were right. These people were the forerunner of trouble but it was too late; he could not hesitate in the midst of the ceremony. The gods would look on it with displeasure. He had to pray.

"Hey, hey," he quietly chanted. "Grandfather, hear the words we speak. We join with our brothers from the lands beyond the River of Many Canoes to salute you."

Grasping the pipe bowl in both hands, Lone Wolf pointed the stem toward Father Sky, then toward the east, south, west and north, then to Mother Earth. He took two puffs, paused for a moment and passed it to his left. Yellow Hair, Lame Horse and Black Hair took two puffs, so did No Hair On Head -- the pipe went to Left Hand and Red Bull . . . .

Although he was not cold, Vision Seeker shivered. Behind the brilliant scene of seated figures, outlined against the pure white snow, he saw darkness. Many Horses, who sat next to him, took the pipe and sent two puffs skyward. The white smoke mingling with condensation of his brother's breath, formed a shadow that surrounded Many Horses' head. From the shadow came the muzzle flash of a fire stick. For a moment tendrils of puffy haze obscured a battlefield. The haze lifted. A warrior lay dying.

The sign was so clear and overpowering, Vision Seeker was momentarily paralyzed. Many Horses passed the pipe. Vision Seeker refused it. Unsteadily, he got to his feet. The amazed circle of smokers watched as he mounted his horse and blindly rode toward camp. In spite of the startled look of the others he could not remain. The ominous vision was imprinted on his mind like petroglyphs on a sandstone cliff. Before the Season of Tall Grass passed, death would visit the Lone Wolf camp.

X

Covetousness is the greatest of all monsters,
as well as the root of all evil.

William Penn

Lone Wolf watched Second Son ride away from the ceremonial smoke in disbelief. His rude behavior was an insult to everyone in the gathering. Lone Wolf started to leap to his feet and call Vision Seeker back. He noticed the hairy faces glance at each other. He remained seated, his face an inscrutable mask. Now was no time to censure his son. It would make matters worse. The hairy faces were uneasy. Suspicion had replaced the good will the meeting had created. Lone Wolf was so upset when the pipe completed the circle to be put away, he burned his finger on a hot coal and nearly dropped the pipe. He was so stunned he could scarcely breathe. The pipe was a sacred object, to let it hit the ground would be a terrible thing. A special ceremony would have to be performed if that should happen.

"Did we offend your young man? Why does he refuse to smoke with strangers?" Yellow Hair asked in sign language.

Lone Wolf was so upset it took him a moment to think of a suitable reply. Finally, he held his right hand next to his body and vigorously pushed it away in a half circle, turning the palm up and fingers outward. "It is nothing. My son is young. He will learn."

Yellow Hair nodded but the expression on his face remained blank. No Hair On Head moved within arm's reach of his long barreled fire stick. Lone Wolf inwardly fumed. The meeting which began so well had turned into a disaster. With as much dignity as he could muster, Lone Wolf continued to clean the pipe bowl and put the pipe in its case.

"Peace unto you," he made the sign to the still seated hairy faces. He stood up and motioned for the hunting party members it was time to leave. In a last attempt to salvage the situation, Lone Wolf invited the trio of hairy faces to the hunting camp and made signs they eat and make trade. Black Hair nodded. Yellow Hair smiled. No Hair On Head did not respond. Lone Wolf could see he was the one who had to be won over. Sick at the way the meeting ended, Lone Wolf turned away. To remain longer would be fruitless. He had to get back to camp and quickly think of some way to erase the shame his son had brought upon himself and his people.

All the way back to the hunting camp black thoughts tortured the Lapwai band leader. The faces of Left Hand and Red Bear also were grim. They clutched their weapons and rode with an eye cocked over their shoulders to see if they were followed. They were nervous and disappointed. They had looked forward to receiving gifts and viewing trade goods. Their leader's son had spoiled things, but not a word of reproach was said. They could tell Lone Wolf was suffering. He had not seen one speck of trade goods either. His companions' silence only increased Lone Wolf's ire. By the time he arrived at his lodge he had to bite his lip to keep from shouting out loud. He flung the tipi flaps open, strode in and glowered at Second Son who sat silently by the fire.

"You behaved like a spoiled child," Lone Wolf stormed. He tossed the elk skin robe on a sleeping pallet and pulled the bear claw necklace over his head and handed it to Quiet Woman. "When will you grow up and act like a proper son? When will you stop bringing dishonor to our lodge? It would have done you no harm to smoke the pipe with these hairy faced ones. What are they to think, that we are people with no manners? Why make enemies when we can make friends?"

"Father is angry," Grandmother observed from the back of the tipi. "The hairy faces did not make trade."

The Weaver, who had been sitting with Grandmother, quickly got up. Her narrow eyes darted back and forth like a ferret searching for a way to escape. Then she skittered through the tipi flaps, stepping on a dog's tail on the way out making the poor canine howl. The furtive act doubled Lone Wolf's fury. "That squint-eyed woman! Always underfoot! Why does she not stay home and mind her own business?"

"She likes Lone Wolf lodge best," Grandmother answered. "Why be angry? She does no harm."

Lone Wolf silenced her with a glare. He glanced at Quiet Woman for support. His mate looked the other way. She did not understand his quick change of mood. He departed so pleased with himself, then returned as sour as a hound with a nose full of porcupine quills. Why did he scold Second Son? Did they have another quarrel? What could she do to keep peace in the family? She glanced around for Many Horses. Was he also in trouble with his father?

She was disgusted with the whole affair. Instead of bringing cheer and good things to the lodge, the hairy faces brought disillusionment and bitterness. For once Daughter Raven Wing was right -- they should have had nothing to do with these strangers. Coming out of the storm like they did was not good. The night guards had not done their job. If they had been raiders from the Blackfeet Nation the entire camp would have been slaughtered and their goods and herd plundered.

Vision Seeker saw his mother's troubled expression but what could he say? It would do no good to speak of the signs. Lone Wolf would get more furious, say he was no better than a frightened old woman. Silently, he ate the midday meal, his eyes averted from Lone Wolf's accusing glare. When he finished, he mounted his horse to ride to a distant hilltop that overlooked a bend in the river. He slid down to sit on a sun warmed boulder that had lost its coating of snow. He made an effort to clear his mind of all thoughts but the beauty of Mother Earth. It was useless. So strong were the dark premonitions that penetrated his mind he wondered if he suddenly had gone mad.

All morning Lone Wolf remained in the lodge, brooding over the botched meeting, going over every move that was made and every word that had been said. He groaned. Everything had gone well until the very last. It was Second Son's fault. He always had his head in the sky. It was just like him to forget where he was. What was he going to do to make him come down to Mother Earth? Since an early age Vision Seeker had not been a normal child. He took no pleasure in games or competitions where skills of strength were involved. Watching the workings of an anthill, beehive, wasp nest or the spinning of a spider web, gave him more pleasure than hunting squirrels, snaring rabbits or fishing in the creek. Lone Wolf groaned again. Why was he burdened with a family that never did anything like they should?

#

Late in the day the hairy faces entered camp escorted by Weasel Face and his sons. Running Turtle announced the arrival. "Come quickly," he said to Lone Wolf. "The hairy faces have come. They are looking for a place to stay the night."

Lone Wolf stepped outside to see Weasel Face point to a space right next to his own lodge where the hairy faces could set up a temporary shelter. Lone Wolf choked back the harsh words that came to his lips. He returned to sit and fume only to hurry out again when Running Turtle shouted the newcomers were handing out gifts. Lone Wolf watched in quiet fury. Weasel Face was getting the gifts that should have been his. He was furious with Second Son and furious with himself. He should have known better than take Vision Seeker along. He had driven the hairy faces right into Weasel Face's camp. Lone Wolf uttered an agonizing groan. Why did the Great Mystery keep torturing him with the presence of this Weasel Face family?

Lone Wolf turned back to reenter the lodge only to bump into The Weaver who had slipped in to rejoin Grandmother. "Aaah!" Lone Wolf exploded. The sight of the squint-eyed woman was the last straw. The gods were plotting against him. The Weaver had listened to him scolding his son and hurried home to report to her father the meeting with the hairy faces had gone wrong. Never one to miss an opportunity to humble his rival, Weasel Face had honey-talked the hairy faced ones into making camp alongside his tipi lodge. The thought of his hated adversary turning the situation to his advantage nearly blinded Lone Wolf with rage. He had to bite his tongue to keep from lashing out at The Weaver and tearing the lodge to bits.

Grandmother, who understood her son's moods, started to console him, then changed her mind. Silence was the best medicine to calm a tortured man's soul.

#

After a short period of shyness, curiosity brought the Sun River camp inhabitants out to inspect the newcomers. For many it was their first sight of these people who came from beyond the River of Many Canoes. They approached them quietly, eyeing them with awe. Finally, a small girl darted in and pulled the fringe on the yellow haired one's britches. Before she could scramble away, he picked her up and held her high above his head, perched her on his shoulder and laughed. His big strong teeth were a streak of white against the sunburned skin and heavy beard. Like a trapped bird, the little girl held herself still, her round brown eyes filled with amazement and fright. The big man fished in a hunting jacket pocket and pulled out a strip of red ribbon. He gave it to the girl and set her down. She ran to her mother shrieking with joy. The mother picked her up and smiled at the hairy faced trio. These strangers were huge and looked fierce but showed kindness to children. Their hearts were good.

Suddenly everybody laughed and talked at once. Fear was replaced with a feeling of good will. The gift of the tiny strip of ribbon sent a message the Nimpau understood. These men who came from beyond the River of Many Canoes desired to be friends. Youngsters of all ages surrounded the hairy faces, touching them and staring at their long beards. The man with yellow hair fascinated everyone. The women whispered among themselves. Never had they seen a head of hair like this; from one angle the color was like the hackles of a golden eagle. From another angle it was the tawny yellow of the great mountain cat. When his startling blue eyes glanced their way they covered their mouths and giggled in embarrassment.

Everybody wanted to demonstrate friendship. The men pushed up to invite the trappers to their lodges. The hairy faces were quick to respond. They spoke with their hands and said a surprising number of words in Sahaptin, the language spoken by tribes of the Columbia Plateau: Nez Perce, Cayuse, Palouse, Walla Walla, Wanapums and Yakama. They laughed and looked pleased when they were understood. Yellow Hair said his name was Buck. In English it was the same name as the male deer, he explained. Black Hair had the strange name, Little Ned. The Hairy Face with the bald head called himself Deacon. The people were half afraid of him. A man with a head as slick as a fresh laid egg was indeed strange. Had the spirits cursed him or blessed him? They could not decide. They tried to get him to remove his cap. He pretended not to understand and kept his head covered.

Running Turtle and several youth offered to help the visitors set up camp. They collected tent stakes, firewood and bedding boughs. Once the trappers' strange animals they called mules were relieved of their loads, Many Horses led them to pasture. He was interested in these strange sounding creatures with dainty hooves and jack rabbit ears. He wondered if they made good pack animals; would they be sure-footed on steep mountain trails? He wanted to learn all about them but had no wish to make friends with the hairy faced ones. Their presence troubled him. They appeared harmless but so did the poisonous black widow spider and wasp. Friendly talk and smiles often concealed evil.

The three hairy faces were tendered the treatment reserved for honored guests. Buffalo robes were spread out for a smoke. Weasel Face conducted the ritual of preparing the pipe. When the smoke finished, gifts were exchanged. Twists of tobacco, pieces of red cloth, shiny-bladed skinning knives, small tinkling bells, tiny mirrors, beads and various other trinkets came from the visitors' packs. In return members of the hunting party gave hemp pouches filled with pemmican, pressed berry cakes, dried salmon and articles made from the prized horns of the mountain sheep.

Lone Wolf remained sulking in his lodge but when Running Turtle brought word the hairy faces were displaying trade goods, he swallowed his pride and went outside. At first he watched from a distance but soon found himself caught up in the jostling crowd. The hairy faces had traveled the lands of the Crow and Dakota. They displayed feather headdresses, bone beads, pipestone and many works of rawhide decorated with elk teeth.

"I must have that!" In her excitement Raven Wing forgot she was angry with her father. She pulled at his arm and pointed at a Crow made garment colorfully decorated with beads, porcupine quills and elk teeth.

Lone Wolf shook her hand away. He had not forgotten the quarrel or the sight of her with Toohool. He was finished spoiling this obstinate, undeserving child. Besides, he had his eye on a Dakota feathered headdress.

The man with black hair noticed Raven Wing's interest in the dress. The girl with the raven hair fascinated Little Ned. She had that wild, beautiful look Mother Nature reserved for a special few. He had seen many native girls in his years on the plains and in the mountains but none had the sparkle and beauty of this graceful maiden. He took the Crow-made garment and held it up to Raven Wing. It was neither too large nor too small. The coloring set off those wondrous dark eyes and glistening black hair. It was as though this dress had been made especially for her.

The stranger's nearness made Raven Wing's nerve ends tingle. This man was so big, his shoulders so wide, his arms and hands so strong, they made her feel small. His beard was so black it looked unreal. It was the eyes that made her feel at ease. They were blue as the sky above but soft like those of a fawn. She did not understand the words he said but they had a caressing sound like the call of a mourning dove. He had a good clean smell that reminded her of campfire smoke and pine needles. She came nearer, reached out and touched the dress. The polished elk teeth shone like jewels. Someone had fastened them with great care.

The porcupine quill trim was cleverly designed and firmly attached. The dress was a treasure. "Oh! If this was only mine. I would never ask for anything else as long as I lived," she thought to herself.

Black Hair motioned she should take it. Raven Wing stepped back and sadly shook her head. She had nothing to trade. Black Hair nodded. He did not seem to mind. Early to Rise, the mate of the White Bird leader, put a hand out to feel the garment. Raven Wing held her breath. From the corner of her eyes she noticed the big man draw the dress back. He carefully folded it and placed it in his pack. Her heart beat quickened. Did he understand the dress was made especially for her? She walked thoughtfully to the tipi. Her mind buzzed like a swarm of honey bees. She had to have that dress, but how? She sat on her sleeping pallet and began to scheme.

Trade did not go well. The three mountain men insisted on beaver skins, something the hunting party did not have. After much haggling, Lone Wolf got his headdress in exchange for a horse. The hairy faces acquired two more horses, then, except for a few knives, tobacco, beads and knickknacks, trade came to an end. Lone Wolf also walked back to the tipi lodge to plot and scheme. He glanced to where The Weaver sat with Grandmother and did not care. The hairy faces paid no more attention to Weasel Face than they did to anyone else, perhaps less because he could see they did not like the manner in which Weasel Face hung over them, cackling like a mother hen. Lone Wolf's thoughts instead were on the many good things in the hairy faces' packs he would like to possess. What could he do to keep the hairy faces in camp until somehow he acquired these goods? The first thing to do was get Second Son to make peace with the hairy faces.

"Running Turtle! Fetch Vision Seeker," Lone Wolf commanded. There was no time like the present to put things right.

XI

*A good hunter watches all animals for one often
betrays the presence of another.*

Luther Standing Bear, Oglala Sioux

While the Sun River hunting camp inhabitants were busy
trading, Vision Seeker sat on a distant hilltop. The signs he had
witnessed haunted him. He wished the hairy faces had never
come. Their presence frightened him. The dark spirit of death
rode with them. He even disliked the manner in which they opened
their packs and spread out their wares for trade. They acted as
though they were doing the people a kindness when actually they
were doing them harm. The Nimpau hardly had enough possessions to keep themselves through the winter. Yet, there they were,
trading these essentials for useless gewgaws they did not need.

Weasel Face's daughter, Small Goat, took the only saddle
blanket she owned and traded it for a mirror and a shiny bell that
tinkled. Without the saddle blanket her poor horse would surely
suffer from saddle sores. This was cruel. Why should the poor
animal suffer because its owner selfishly put her impulsive de-
sires above the needs of her four-legged companion upon whom
she depended?

This was not the way of the Nimpau. They always had
been a generous people. From childhood they had been taught to
give and not to expect anything in return. When the hairy faces
gave they did it for a reason. They knew by giving trinkets and
shiny doodads the native people would think well of them. They
then would be allowed to do whatever they pleased, trap their
streams, hunt their game and set up lodges on Nimpau land. Already the hairy faced ones had moved from their poor camp to
that of the hunting party and had everyone falling over themselves to see that the hairy faces were comfortable. What would
they do next? It was impossible to tell.

Vision Seeker slid off the boulder and walked around in a circle. Perhaps if the hairy faces left right away the signs would not come true. The Lone Wolf camp would not suffer the death that had been so vividly revealed to him. What could he do to make them go? He had to be careful. Lone Wolf already was furious with him but he could not let that stand in the way. The people were the ones to worry about. If he could keep this terrible pending calamity from happening all his efforts would be worthwhile. He thought back to what he had learned about hairy faces. Rabbit Skin Leggings said the Redcoats of Hudson's Bay and Bostons who came over the Endless Water in ships with wings, erected trading posts for the sole purpose of trading for animal furs. The beaver pelt was their favorite. It was so coveted brigades of men spent the Season of Falling Snow and the Season of Deep Snow searching for them.

To snare the beaver the trappers laid deadly jaws of steel in beaver paths and in the entrance to their lodges. When the animals passed near, the cruel trap jaws leaped out to snare them. The beaver desperately tried to free themselves, twisting and turning until feet and legs were torn, sometimes the wise water rodents gnawed off their own feet to gain freedom. The clever trappers knew this. They set the steel jaws deep in the water. Before the beavers could make their escape they drowned.

It suddenly occurred to Vision Seeker how to get the hairy faces to go. Find them beaver! If they knew where the beavers lived, without fail they would rush away to set their deadly steel-jawed traps. Here on the grassy plains beaver colonies were few. The streams feeding into the Blackfoot and Bitterroot rivers -- that was where beaver abounded. Vision Seeker was so delighted with the solution of his troubles he laughed and did a little dance. The most serious of problems could be solved if one put one's mind to it.

Vision Seeker quickly returned to camp. Trade was still in progress. Everyone in camp was huddled around the goods the hairy faces displayed. Lone Wolf was inspecting a feather headdress, turning it over and over in his hand as if counting each plume. Weasel Face and his son, Toohool, were debating on which hand axe had the best weight and sharpest cutting edge. Raven Wing was admiring an elk skin dress. He could tell by her stance she wanted it badly. The big man with black hair who towered over her also could see how desperate she was to possess it. Poor Raven Wing! What did she have to trade, nothing but herself. Vision Seeker shuddered at the thought and hurried on. That was another reason to get the hairy faces away before Raven Wing made a fool of herself.

Unnoticed, Vision Seeker slipped into the lodge for a sleeping robe, a small bag of provisions and his bow and arrows. He wanted to get away while everyone was absorbed with the hairy faces trade goods but Grandmother's sharp eyes spied him from her corner. "My son, you are in a big hurry. Is something wrong?" she asked.

"No, Grandmother," Vision Seeker answered but said no more. Grandmother did not question her grandson. She knew his ways. He was leaving and did not want anyone to know. "Ah! This poor youngster," she thought, "he is so serious. What will he be like when he is as old as I?" She uttered a deep sigh and went back to her weaving. She had watched him come and go many times. Never did she pry or scold and never betrayed him to his parents. She would not begin now.

Many Horses, watching over the herd, also saw Vision Seeker leave. He, too, made no attempt to stop or question him. His brother often embarked on unexplained journeys. In the past when Vision Seeker disappeared, Lone Wolf had mounted searches. The searchers followed his trail only to find him meditating on a hilltop or deep in an isolated ravine watching tadpoles turn into frogs or magpies and blue jays building nests. "What is the matter with you?" Lone Wolf invariably asked. "Why are you here all by yourself?" "I am learning the mysteries of Mother Earth," Vision Seeker would answer. Anymore when he went away few paid any attention; Vision Seeker was off again studying the mysteries of Mother Earth.

Vision Seeker followed the trail south. A chinook breeze blew in from the west. The air was warm. The thick layer of snow melted away to leave a muddy slush. It was a good sign. Mother Earth had decided to delay the Season of Falling Snow for a few days. However, travel would be bad. Before nightfall water would be everywhere. He would be hard pressed to make dry camp.

That evening Vision Seeker stopped in a copse of slender lodgepole pine, the ground clear of snow and mud. He tethered his horse and looked around for a place to lay out the sleeping robe. A sudden noise behind him gave him a start but his heart dropped back into place. It was only Brother Porcupine clinging to the trunk of a pine tree, gnawing at the bark. Perched on a limb above the porcupine was a great horned owl, "hush wings" hunters called them. These huge owls swept down on a chick, squirrel or chipmunk so silently and with such swiftness they seldom came away with empty claws. The owl's round, yellow-circled eyes intently kept watch on the two-legged intruder. When Vision Seeker moved so did the owl's head, as if turning on a swivel. Vision Seeker laid out his sleeping robe and settled down for the night. He felt safe. No one would bother Prickly Porcupine, and Brother Owl was like a sentinel. The watchful bird was certain to sound a warning if danger threatened.

#

In the Bitterroot Valley, where streams followed rock-faced canyons and ravines down to the river, beaver signs were everywhere. The next evening among a stand of cottonwoods and aspens Vision Seeker made camp by a beaver dammed creek. Since beavers do much of their work at night, Vision Seeker waited until dusk before standing watch. He wanted to make certain beavers were present in sufficient numbers to keep the hairy faced trappers satisfied for a long, long while.

Vision Seeker ate a cold meal. A fire would frighten the animals. Beavers disliked the sight and smell of man. He found a place where light from the star-filled sky cast a mirrorlike sheen on the water's surface. He wrapped the sleeping robe around himself. Still he shivered. The damp cold from the water and chilling breezes found their way into the folds of the robe and through his clothes.

He soon forgot the discomfort as the busy beavers set to work. One flotilla after another crossed the lighted strip of water. The little black noses and broad flat tails left trails of ripples, marking their passage. Vision Seeker placed an ear to the ground and listened to the creatures scramble up the bank. Their gnawing teeth began to carve away at the trunks of young aspen trees. The rustle of limbs dragging across the ground and splashes at the water's edge, made it clear they were busy taking away their harvest. Soon branches floated through the lighted patch of water, the beavers almost hidden by the loads they propelled.

A sudden, loud popping sound, as explosive as Rabbit Skin Leggings' Hudson's Bay musket, made Vision Seeker jump. The sharp report echoed across the creek and through the trees. Another report followed and then another until the entire ravine echoed with the penetrating repercussions.

Vision Seeker became watchful. Guardian beaver had slapped their flat tails against the water to warn of danger. Something threatened the beaver colony. Vision Seeker's keen eyes searched the shadows. A waterfowl skittered out of the bulrushes flapping along the shore to disappear upstream. There was a fluttering of wings. A large bird roosting in the trees also disappeared in the same direction. An owl hooted. A dark shadow emerged from a patch of brush; the menace who had caused all the turmoil. A badger, the white marking on its face bright in the darkness, prowled the creek bank in search of prey. Unable to take the beaver or waterfowl by surprise, the badger lumbered away to more promising hunting grounds. Shortly afterward the beavers came out of hiding to continue their work.

The following morning Vision Seeker discovered other promising beaver streams. In the high forest, heavily traveled beaver trails led from one stream to another. Vision Seeker made a mental map of every stream, dam and beaver trail. Finally he said to himself, "I am ready to return and make my report to the hairy faces."

A half day's journey from the hunting camp on Sun River, Vision Seeker caught a whiff of campfire smoke. A scolding blue jay dove out of a tree and swept past, its raucous voice loudly squawking. It had been disturbed. Vision Seeker seized his bow and hurriedly dismounted. He tethered his spotted pony to an alder branch and dropped to his knees. He took an arrow from the quiver to arm his bow. He had no premonition of trouble but in these lands one did not rely on senses alone. To stumble into a camp of Blackfeet raiders was as deadly as falling into the cave of a grizzly bear.

Keeping to the shadows, Vision Seeker quickly made his way to the top of a tree covered ridge. There he dropped to his knees and soundlessly crawled forward until he could see into the ravine below. Around a campfire sat two of the hairy faces, Yellow Hair and No Hair On Head. Vision Seeker felt foolish. The hairy faces had moved on by themselves. He had not needed to search out beaver grounds to get them to leave. Lone Wolf would be angry for the way he had left Sun River to while away five days along the Bitterroot and Blackfoot looking for beaver streams.

Vision Seeker studied the two hairy faces. It appeared they had made camp for the night. A pot simmered on the fire. A pleasant aroma drifted up to tease his nostrils. His stomach growled. He had not eaten a hot meal since he had left the hunting camp. No Hair On Head took his cap off and laid it aside while he stirred the pot. The skull, as bare and shiny as polished stone, gave off light like the rays of a newly risen moon. The curious sight made Vision Seeker smile. No wonder the three trappers had traveled safely across the lands of the Dakota, Blackfeet and Crow. Only a person who had been scalped and gone to the Great Spirit Land could have a hairless head that glowed. All of sudden Vision Seeker realized something was wrong. Where was the third hairy face, the man with the black hair? Surely he had not remained in Lone Wolf's hunting camp or maybe he did. The manner in which he and Raven Wing. . . !

A rustle behind Vision Seeker made him jump. He whirled around to see a rifle barrel pointed at his heart. Black Hair had been guarding the camp. Vision Seeker dropped his bow and arrow. A faint smile touched his lips. He had made a five day journey to search out beaver for these men. Now he was threatened as though he was a member of the dreaded Gros Ventre or Blackfeet intent on raiding the hairy faces' camp.

Black Hair marched him downhill into the circle of firelight. No Hair On Head reached for his rifle. Yellow Hair placed one fist over the other and thrust them downward toward a log. "Sit!" his sign said.

Vision Seeker sat down. Calmly he studied his captors. He had a sudden urge to laugh. Yellow Hair and Black Hair had cut the hair from their faces. Their cheeks and chins where the hair had been had the pallor of a plucked goose, a badly plucked one at that. In places short tufts of hair remained, sticking out like overlooked pin feathers.

No Hair On Head looked even more comical. His bushy beard glistened with drops of tobacco juice. He resembled a marmot surprised in the act of drinking from a stream. It was a good thing Running Turtle was not here, Vision Seeker thought. Little Brother would laugh himself sick.

Instead of revealing his mirth, Vision Seeker maintained a straight face. He solemnly held out his left hand and slapped the palm with the back of his right hand to make the sound of a beaver tail slapping the water. "Many beavers," he said in sign language. With his fingers spaced apart, he made a chopping motion. He pointed south. "Two days travel."

"Hmm!" Buck Stone grunted. He liked the looks of this young man but did he tell the truth? Why should he come to them with this story of many beavers? It looked suspiciously like a trap. He could very well be trying to lure them into a cleverly planned ambush. In his twenty years in the mountains he had attempted to make friends with many Indian youths. The moment he thought he could trust them they stole or played some devilish trick.

"This is Lone Wolf's middle son," Buck said to his partners. "Vision Seeker he is called. He is the one who would not smoke with us. He left without saying good-bye or how-do-you-do; he's been missing five days. What was he doing? You found him on the hill with an armed bow. That looks bad. What do you think, Deacon?"

"Wouldn't trust him as far as I kin spit," No Hair On Head replied, shooting a sluice of tobacco juice into the fire. "Thet Lone Wolf bunch is all alike, rascals, every one of 'em. Yuh saw how the head man did his best ta hold us in camp, probably reckoned on keepin' us there long enuff ta steal our whole kit an' caboodle."

It was not hard to understand the meaning of the conversation. No Hair On Head did not like the Lone Wolf family. Yellow Hair was indifferent. Only Black Hair appeared friendly. "Where did you travel?" he asked in sign language. Vision Seeker did not answer. Did not the man know it was impolite to ask such questions? Anyway, what good would talk do now? If they were going to treat him like an enemy, why make it easy for them to find beaver grounds?

Black Hair did not take offense. "Let's escort the young man back to Lone Wolf's camp and turn him over to the chief. He was getting mighty antsy about his absence. Maybeso, he would look on it kindly. If we're going to trap these parts friendly neighbors are a good thing to have."

Yellow Hair nodded. "Might be a good thing at that."

No Hair On Head objected. "Fiddlesticks! Why waste the time? We should be settin' traps. Ain't nothin' ta be gained by gabbin' with the ol' chief. I say, give the youngster a good whack on the tail an' send him skiddlin'. These bloomin' Redskins hev gotta larn ta let us mountain men alone. It's a free country, ain't it? We ain't doin' 'em no harm. We's jest tryin' ta earn an honest livin' trappin' an' huntin', thet's all we's doin'."

#

Lone Wolf was beside himself. Vision Seeker had been gone five days. He often left unexpectedly, but not for this length of time. No one had the least idea where he went. Many Horses and Running Turtle rode in search of him but came back empty-handed. They picked up tracks leading south. They followed them for half a day only to lose them in the mud and slush that replaced the blanket of snow. "Perhaps he has gone home to the long lodge," Running Turtle volunteered.

"Why would he do that? He knows his place is here," Lone Wolf growled.

Sitting by herself in the background, Grandmother grinned but remained silent. She had watched each of her grandchildren grow up and knew them better than did their parents. Many Horses was stolid and dependable. When he did a task it was done slowly but well. Raven Wing -- impetuous, rebellious -- she was the child closest to Lone Wolf's heart and his greatest trial. Vision Seeker? He was the thinker, wise beyond his years. He saw things no one else could see. Running Turtle? He was a good lad with a lot to learn. The parents should give him more guidance -- help him find himself.

Grandmother rocked back and forth, her thoughts dwelling on her youth. When she was Running Turtle's age she had no parents to guide her yet she survived and enjoyed a satisfying life. Perhaps this lad would do the same. Her thoughts returned to Vision Seeker. Whatever he was up to she knew it was for the good of the Lone Wolf people.

"Do not fret," she said to Lone Wolf. "Second Son is fine. If he returned to Lapwai it is for a very good reason."

Lone Wolf scowled. He did not believe Second Son had returned to Lapwai. The recent snow would have made the going slow and dangerous, but where else could he have gone? Was he afraid of the hairy faces and fled to avoid meeting them again? This almost was more than he could bear. He had lost control of his family. First it was Raven Wing acting like an untamed colt, now his son had run away without saying a word. What ungrateful offspring he had sired. To make matters worse The Weaver, of course, had reported Vision Seeker's absence to her father. Weasel Face told everyone in camp Second Son was disgusted with the hunting trip. He had returned to winter in the snug, warm long lodge in Lapwai.

XII

I found that under the blanket in which the Indian shrouded himself, there was a heart and mind altogether human . . . .

Major James McLaughlin, Indian Agent

Running Turtle saw them first. He ran into camp shouting the news. "Vision Seeker and the hairy faces have come! They are here!"

The hunting families burst out of their tipis to see the Lapwai leader's son ride in, prisoner of the hairy faces. Chores were put aside. Children ran in from play. Camp dogs sensing the drama, skittered back and forth barking at nothing at all. Most of the older observers silently watched as the riders passed. The leader's second son had run away. The hairy faces had captured him and brought him back. The turn of events made them uncomfortable. They glanced at one another uneasily. Should they greet the son or should they ignore him? They did not want to do wrong and vex the boy's father. There was no such indecision on the part of the Weasel Face family.

"What have you been up to, young bear?" Toohool called out. "Caught like an ant in a honey tree, were you?"

"Of course, the young cub learned all his tricks from his old bear father," Weasel Face joined in.

Small Goat was the only Weasel Face family member to offer comfort. "Pay no attention. If you had asked, Raven Wing and I would have gone with you."

Lone Wolf strode back and forth snapping his quirt. He could not believe what was happening, Second Son brought into camp like an unbroken colt that had bolted from the herd. The shame of it made his ears burn. The taunting words of the Weasel Faces pierced his flesh like cockleburs imbedded in his buckskin clothes. He was not only ashamed for himself but for the Nimpau people. They were the most respected of all Northwest

Indian nations. He always had taken pride in upholding their
great traditions. He tried to teach these same values to his offspring. It was obvious he had failed. How could these hairy
faces have respect for his people when the son of the leader of the
Lapwai band went out of his way to make trouble?

"Why does Second Son always bring disgrace?" he demanded of Quiet Woman. "Does he have no sense of pride?"

"Ah me-oh my," Grandmother chanted in the background.
"Fathers never know how to handle their own sons. They have to
ask women and then do not listen."

The Weaver, who had been in her usual place beside
Grandmother, picked up the basket she was weaving and darted
away. "Wagh!" Lone Wolf uttered, giving the tipi covering a vicious pop with the quirt.

The hairy faces rode up to stop in front of the Lone Wolf
lodge. No Hair On Head slid off his horse and motioned for Vision Seeker to dismount. He gave back the bow and quiver of
arrows, making it plain the prisoner had been disarmed. A hiss
of disapproval swept through the crowd. This was a grave insult.
It was like flaunting a coup in the enemy's face. What would the
young man do? Vision Seeker stoically took the weapons. He
would give neither the crowd nor the hairy faces a hint to his
thoughts. Without looking right or left, he walked unhurried toward the tipi lodge. Lone Wolf gave his son a withering glance as
he passed. He then hastily composed himself and turned to face
the trappers. With the entire camp of buffalo hunters watching
he must act wisely and with dignity.

Yellow Hair, the leader of the hairy faces, paid no attention to the restless crowd. His white teeth flashed in a smile. He
lifted his hand in the sign of friendship and held out a twist of
tobacco, motioning to sit and smoke. Lone Wolf felt somewhat
better. The hairy faces wanted to smoke and talk. That was a
good sign. He lifted his hand in agreement. He snapped his fingers for Running Turtle to take the trappers' mounts. Yellow
Hair and Black Hair readily dismounted and handed over the reins.

No Hair On Head hesitated. Lone Wolf could see the little fat man did not want to give up his horse. He hated to be afoot in an Indian camp.

Lone Wolf pretended not to notice the baldheaded man's reluctance. He motioned the women away and invited the three hairy faces to enter the lodge. He did not want the inquisitive people looking on. He seated his guests on buffalo robes where they could take their ease. It was only proper to allow the visitors time to rest before they spoke. Lone Wolf took the twist of tobacco and methodically rubbed it into flakes, his mind on the coming talk. What mischief had his son done? Why did the hairy faces bring him back after they had journeyed a full day? They went to great trouble to turn about and retrace their steps. He inwardly groaned. Why had the gods afflict him with such a worrisome son?

Vision Seeker watched in silence as the pipe was prepared and passed around. Until the trouble was settled it was not proper for him to speak or take part. He did not dare look at the puffs of smoke for fear he would see more signs. Lone Wolf put the pipe away and waited for his visitors to speak. They, in turn, politely waited for Lone Wolf to say the first words.

"Has my son offended you? If this is so, what can be done to put things right?" Lone Wolf eventually asked in sign language. "It is our desire to live in peace and friendship."

Buck nodded. "That is good," he said the words in Sahaptin then continued with signs. "We are troubled by the actions of your middle son. He did not smoke the pipe with us. We find him spying on our camp with an armed bow. These things make us sad. Is the feeling in his heart good or is it bad? We believe you are good people. We want you to think of us as good people. We ask your help in making peace with your son. We want to come and go as friends, live with you as brothers in this great land."

Lone Wolf turned to face his son. "You see, their hearts are good. Why is it you do not smoke with them? Why is it you

spy on them? You leave us five days and nights, then ride home
a prisoner in the hands of these hairy faced ones? Do not tell me
you see more signs. Do you want these people to think you have
no brains?"

It was useless to speak of the ominous shadows the ceremonial smoke had cast across the sky. Neither his father nor the
three hairy faces would understand. On their return to the hunting camp No Hair On Head had ridden alongside chattering in
sign language, asking questions. Why did he ride alone? Why
did he spy on them? Had he planned an ambush? Did he want to
kill them and steal their packs? Perhaps he should have attempted
to explain to the hairy faces he had no intention of harming them,
nor did he want to possess their trade goods. What good would
they be to him? He merely had been trying to do good, to help
them, but No Hair On Head's accusing watchful eyes made him
defiant. He did not speak or make a sign all the way to the Sun
River hunting camp.

Yet, Vision Seeker knew in his heart Lone Wolf was right.
He had to swallow his pride. He had to make peace with these
people. If he refused to do so Lone Wolf had the right to banish
him from the lodge. That would break Quiet Woman's heart.
The eyes of the three trappers steadily watched him, waiting for
him to speak. Vision Seeker glanced away. He felt like a rabbit
cornered by a pack of hungry wolves.

"I went to find beaver grounds," Vision Seeker finally
answered his father. "It is beaver skins these hairy faces seek and
that is what I went to find, beaver streams to give them the skins
they desire. I try to tell them. They believe I lie. They take my
weapons. They bring me to our lodge like a captive woman."

"Hmm!" Lone Wolf grunted. He felt relieved. There had
been no mischief. He had no reason to doubt Vision Seeker's
words. His son was a trial but he did not lie. "Did you find good
beaver streams?"

"Many beaver. They go slap, pop, slap everywhere along
the Bitterroot." Vision Seeker demonstrated with slaps of his

hands to make the sound of beaver tails striking the water.

"Ah!" A gleam of comprehension lit up Yellow Hair's eyes. "Do you mean you went in search of beaver for us, that we have accused you falsely?" Buck rubbed his fresh shaven chin and frowned. "Hmm!" he grunted. Something told him the lad spoke the truth. He would not lie to his father. Buck felt ashamed. He prided himself on his understanding and tolerance of native cultures. Yet here he had jumped to a hasty, erroneous conclusion like so many people of his kind did when judging the Indian. He got up and took Vision Seeker by the hand and pulled him into the circle. "We are ashamed. You were trying to do good and we believed you were up to mischief. We must make this up to you. You will be our partner. For every beaver pelt we take, one out of four will be yours."

The sudden change in the temper of the meeting brought shouts and smiles. Lone Wolf called the women in to prepare food. The trappers dug into their pouches for more tobacco. They filled short blackened pipes, lit them with embers from the fire and passed them to their hosts. Vision Seeker found himself smoking and making talk with the hairy faces like they were old friends. Yellow Hair said his name was not just Buck but Buck Stone. He held up a small rock and pointed to himself.

Running Turtle, who returned from staking out the trappers' horses and mules, watched the goings-on with an open mouth. These huge people fascinated him. He followed their every movement, trying to make out the sign language which he did not know well. When Yellow Hair held up the rock and pointed to himself. He laughed. "He calls himself Buck Rock," he reported to Raven Wing.

Buck Stone who understood enough Sahaptin to interpret the words, shook his head. He dug into his pocket and brought out a small whet stone and began to sharpen his knife. "Stone like this," he said with signs.

"Ah, yes! Buck Rock That Sharpens," Running Turtle exclaimed.

Raven Wing, who remained in the background with Quiet Woman and Grandmother, kept her eyes fixed on Black Hair. He was telling his name. He closed his hand with thumb touching the first knuckle of the first finger, the sign for small. The next sign he made she could not comprehend. She put a hand to her mouth to smother a giggle. He had to be making fun. No one so large could ever be called Small. Black Hair was almost half again as large as her slim brother, Vision Seeker. She longed to ask about the dress beaded with elk teeth but she could not do that. A Nimpau woman did not speak to strangers, especially men. Black Hair turned to glance her way. Their eyes met. Her heart beat quickened. She immediately looked down. Grandmother whispered, "The big man favors you." Raven Wing silenced her with a frown.

The trappers were anxious to get on the trail, but at Lone Wolf's insistence stayed the night. People gathered around hoping they would open their packs of trade goods but the trappers refused, shaking their heads; they did not wish to trade. The next morning Vision Seeker proudly led the three trappers away from Sun River camp on the trail south. Everyone gathered to see them off. For a while a group of youthful horsemen rode with them, among them Weasel Face's son, Toohool. "I wish I could go with you," Toohool said wistfully when they parted.

"Ride along," Vision Seeker invited. "The hairy faces are friends. They will welcome you."

"Good!" Toohool's face lit up, then darkened. "No, I must stay. Father would miss me too much." Toohool reined away. He held up his hand in farewell. Vision Seeker answered with a salute. He suddenly felt sad for Weasel Face's son. He could not make a move without his father's approval.

Vision Seeker found the company of the now friendly hairy faces so exciting and enjoyable he forgot about the signs which foretold they were forerunners of misfortune. Around the evening campfire Buck Stone made him understand in remarkably good Sahaptin he wanted to learn the myths and legends of the Nimpau.

When Buck did not know a word he asked its meaning by sign language. The quick way the man with yellow hair learned astonished Vision Seeker. At each campsite they talked late into the night. No one, not even Rabbit Skin Leggings, spoke of such interesting things as Buck Stone.

They pushed on through Hellgate Pass and into the Bitterroot Valley. Vision Seeker guided the trappers to one beaver stream after another. The beaver bounty astonished them. It took days for them to decide where to set their first trap lines. Beaver sign was everywhere they looked.

"By gum!" No Hair On Head exclaimed. "The varmints're thick as skeeters in a swamp."

The trappers chose a protected canyon for the permanent campsite. They erected a lean-to shelter and began to prepare their deadly steel traps. Vision Seeker, who had fulfilled his mission by guiding the hairy faces to the beaver grounds, announced it was time for him to leave. He had remained with them longer than he intended. He felt it impolite to ride away before the trappers had time to set up camp and settle in. He did not like this business of trapping beaver. There was the belief among his people beaver had spirits the same as two-leggeds. Beaver families lived together, worked together and protected the lodges they built much as did people. When he got astride his spotted pony ready to ride away, the trappers pleaded with him to stay.

"Remember, we are partners," the man called Buck said, making the sign of four, pointing to Vision Seeker as the fourth finger. "Stay with us. We share beaver pelts."

Buck's invitation delighted Vision Seeker but he had to return. He did not wish to displease his father again. "Lone Wolf needs me. Buffaloes come soon. I help hunt." He was surprised how easily the hairy faced ones' words came to his tongue.

Buck nodded. He understood. "Lone Wolf needs hunters. We must not keep his son. We can't let him travel home with no gifts. Tomorrow we hunt. We'll send a mule with you to carry fresh meat for your people."

Vision Seeker hesitated. It would be impolite to refuse. Now that he and the hairy faces were friends he must not offend. He agreed to wait until morning. The next day he wondered if he had done right. During the night a heavy snow began to fall. A bitter wind howled in from the north. Throughout the following day it continued to storm. High drifts piled up to block the trails. Vision Seeker knew he would never make it through Hellgate Pass. He had no choice but to remain. It would be foolish to battle against the wind and snow.

In a way the situation pleased him. He wanted to learn more about the ways of the hairy faces, especially the words they spoke so easily to each other. Perhaps if he knew their language he would understand why the signs told him they brought trouble.

The canyon where the trappers camped was well protected from the howling wind that rose up to pile high drifts of snow in the open where the valley widened. The horses and mules were shielded by a thicket of cottonwoods. In spite of the comfort and protection the camp provided, Vision Seeker began to feel un-easy. Confined with the trappers in the small lean-to he felt smoth-ered and caged. The strange smell of the hairy faced ones that filled the enclosure reminded him of the caves of hibernating bears.

The chores the trappers did to while away the time con-fused him. These men did women's work. They scraped and stretched beaver skins. They made bone beads and cut quill to decorate hat bands, rawhide shirts and leggings. Little Ned spent his spare time cutting, polishing and sewing quills onto the dress Raven Wing coveted. The sliver of iron called a needle looked so small in the big fist it made Vision Seeker smile. Why did he spend so much time on this elk skin garment? He was worse than Grandmother who spent days weaving, dyeing and shaping a buf-falo hair pouch. Black Hair painstakingly made tiny holes in the buckskin with an awl, then thrust the needle through, pulling the thread tight. When he finished a seam, he knotted the thread several times to make certain it would never pull loose. Perhaps he had a mate in his home village who was very particular. Black Hair said few words but when he did speak, Vision Seeker noted, his partners listened. He felt honored when the big man told him his people lived in a big village called Boston.

"This will please Boston woman," Vision Seeker said one evening, admiring the addition of square cut beads that encircled the neck of the elk skin dress. He struggled to form the words in English. He did not want to make a mistake and offend the big man, so repeated with sign language.

Little Ned shook his head. "No Boston woman. Gone to Great Spirit Land."

Vision Seeker glanced away. Now he understood this silent man. He had lost a loved one. Out of respect for her memory he kept his peace. Words were not needed. The spirit of the one who had passed to the other side was always present. That was the way with his people. Names of those who left this world were never spoken. But if his woman was gone why did he work so over the elk skin dress? Vision Seeker stared into the fire. He was baffled. The hairy faces worked on meaningless things as hard as they did their trap lines. If Raven Wing could see the dress now she would be wild. "Oh-ha!" The startling thought struck him. Was he doing this for Raven Wing? Black Hair knew Raven Wing coveted the dress but had nothing to trade for it. Did that mean this man called Little Ned had his eye on her? He would use the dress to bargain for his sister?

Vision Seeker sat stunned. Thoughts flashed through his mind like streaks of lightening. Would he take her for his play thing or as his mate? A hairy face in the Lone Wolf clan. It never could happen ... Never! Vision Seeker pushed the thought from his mind. He could not imagine this big man living in the long lodge. He would break his head every time he went in and out the door. Yet, perhaps it could happen. Hairy faces of the Redcoat trading places took native women for mates. It was said their children did not look or act much different than any others. Would Black Hair take his sister away, perhaps to the land beyond the

River of Many Canoes. That would not be good. To have his family scattered from one end of the country to the other was too terrible to contemplate. Whatever happened, the family must remain together.

Vision Seeker got to his feet and stepped outside. He had to clear his head, get some place where he could think straight. It was crisp and cold. The snow covered ground crackled beneath his feet. He glanced up at his friends, the stars. Running fox, flying horse, the dove, fish and hawk signaled their welcome. He was cold yet felt comforted. He was at home under Father Sky. The fresh air, the whisper of the trees, the quiet rustle of the creek, the far off cry of coyotes -- these were the things he understood. There was something about the talk and ways of the hairy faces that disturbed him. He had heard Rabbit Skin Leggings say the coming of these people from beyond the River of Many Canoes would change the way the Nimpau looked at life. Now he knew what the White Bird meant. He had no desire to abandon the way his people lived. It was a hard life but one he loved.

Vision Seeker walked a bit farther. He heard the horses and mules stamp their feet and snuffle. All of a sudden he had a terrible urge to jump on his spotted pony and ride away, leave this evil smelling lodge of the hairy faces behind. He longed to be among his own people. He entered the pole corral that held the horses and mules. He patted one animal and rubbed the muzzle of another. He hesitated by his spotted pony, rubbing his hand through the furry coat.

"Would you like to go home?" he asked. The horse lifted its head. In the distance came the plaintive cry of a wolf. A sharp, damp breeze ruffled the horse's mane. The tree branches overhead began to sway and moan. Clouds scuttled to blot out the light of the stars. The signs were very clear. More snow was on the way.

Vision Seeker shivered, his thoughts bleak. Like the beaver caught in the hairy faces' steel jaws, he was trapped. Not until the Season of Melting Snow would he be able to escape.

XIII

The wolves are in great number . . . at the distance of two or
three hundred yards I counted 27 about
the carcass of a buffalo . . .

Meriwether Lewis

Vision Seeker's gloomy prediction was correct. The occupants of the lean-to shelter awakened to find a new foot of
snow blocking the path to the cottonwood grove where the stock
was kept. It took all day to make the round of the traps. Some
the trappers could not get to and had to leave untended. Vision
Seeker stoically accepted his fate. He had no alternative but to
remain with the trio of hairy faces. He cheerfully pitched in doing his share of chores, mainly tending to the needs of the horses
and mules.

Gradually, Vision Seeker became accustomed to living
cheek to jowl with the trappers. He even began to look forward
to the long evenings watching and listening to the three hairy
faces. They reminded him of three bears growling, scratching
and bumping into each other in the small living quarters.

As the trappers and Vision Seeker learned each other's
words, they engaged in lengthy conversations, sometimes lasting
late into the night. Black Hair said little. No Hair On Head made
up for the big man's silence. He chattered and scolded like a
chipmunk, talking so fast and strangely Vision Seeker seldom
could understand what he said. No Hair On Head often quoted
from the Great Spirit Book called Bible, explaining what people
must do to make the journey to a place called heaven. It was
Buck Stone's conversations Vision Seeker enjoyed most. He had
a breadth of knowledge that seemed to cover everything. He said
he learned much of what he knew from study at Harvard College,
a Boston school. Buck had a little pack stuffed with black bound
books. From time to time he would open one and read aloud.

When this happened Vision Seeker sat fascinated, barely breathing, intent on every word. Some of the sayings were so full of meaning Vision Seeker often asked to have them repeated. Like a village crier, he wanted to have them committed to memory so as not to make the slightest mistake in their retelling.

One night the stars were unusually bright. After seeing to the livestock Buck and Vision Seeker stopped to admire the brilliant canopy overhead. Vision Seeker pointed out running fox, dove and hawk. He asked Buck if the wise men of his people studied the stars.

"Ah, yes," Buck replied. "Stars have intrigued our people since ancient times. They search the sky with special instruments called telescopes. There were people called Babylonians who believed stars were gods. They believed these god stars were so powerful they influenced everything that happened on Mother Earth. Then there were learned people called Greeks who named stars after monsters, animals and battlefield heroes.

"People in those olden days told time by the stars and sailed over the great uncharted waters guided by the stars. The Bible tells of a star that guided wise men to the place where the son of God, Jesus Christ, was born. Every year during the Season of Deep Snow, Christian people remember this event with a feast called Christmas."

Vision Seeker fell silent, thinking over what Buck had said. Not only was he a person of book learning but he was a man of infinite wisdom. He spoke of things in this world and of things in the next world. Suddenly, he felt close to this man who was so different than any human he ever had known. He was comfortable with him for he made him feel worth while. His obsession with Father Sky was not as odd as some of his people believed.

On the feast day, Christmas, the hairy faces did unusual things. Short, round Deacon whitened his beard with flour and put a funny cap on his bald head. He beat on a kettle and shouted, "Wake up! 'Tis Santa wishin' yuh a Merry Christmas!" From a pouch on his back he handed out gifts. Each of the trappers gave

Vision Seeker a present. From Little Ned he received a buckskin pouch decorated with quills. Deacon gave him an Appaloosa pony carved from wood and spotted with daubs of clay to resemble his own Appaloosa. Buck gave him a knife that opened and closed, hiding the blade inside the handle.

After the gift giving they sang songs of the holy night when Christ Jesus was born. Deacon read from the Great Spirit Book. Then he produced from his pack a small jug which he held aloft. "Christmas comes but once a year, when it comes it brings good cheer," he proclaimed, putting the jug to his lips. He passed it on to Little Ned who drank and passed it on to Buck. Not wishing to give offense as he did at their first ceremonial smoke, when it came his turn Vision Seeker took a big swallow. He almost choked. The liquid burned his mouth and throat and lay on his stomach like a slow burning fire.

"Good, ain't it?" Deacon asked. He took the jug and tipped it up for another swallow.

"Yes, but I must tend to the horses and mules," Vision Seeker quickly replied. He did not want another drink and did not want to give offense. He also was distressed. The hairy faced ones were so generous and he had no gifts to give to them in return.

Only twice did Vision Seeker work the traps lines. On the first day after making camp Little Ned invited him to help set traps. Vision Seeker did not care to take part in the beaver killing but felt it impolite to turn the big man down. Besides, he felt honored the usually silent Little Ned would ask for his company. Instead of setting the steel jaws around the beaver dams as Vision Seeker expected, Little Ned walked upstream. He studied the beaver tracks, the depth of their trails and the beaver runs and slides. He pointed toward a stand of aspens, some of which had been recently cut down by the beavers' sharp teeth. Abruptly, Little Ned stepped into the cold water to wade against the current and motioned for Vision Seeker to do the same.

"Never leave your scent," Little Ned instructed. "The

smell of man scares these critters away quicker'n anything. Don't think these beaver are dumb. They have more sense than many who attempt to trap them."

At the foot of a well-used beaver slide, Little Ned stopped. He pried open a set of jaws and set the trigger. Carefully, he placed the trap in the water at the foot of the slide. With a piece of wire, he fastened the five foot trap chain to the submerged root of a tree. To mark the location, he tied a thong to the chain. On the opposite end of the thong he fastened a marker stick that bobbed up and down in the slow moving stream.

After making certain the trap was satisfactorily set and marked, Little Ned waded ahead to another beaver run and placed two more traps. Over these he placed floating markers which he dipped into a bottle of liquid. "This draws them like ants to honey," he explained.

When Vision Seeker asked what the bottle contained, Little Ned shook his head. "It's a secret formula. Beaver can't resist it. They sniff it from a distance. They come and bang go the jaws of the trap. It gives me the power to catch more beaver than most anyone alive. It's best you don't know any more than that. People have tried to kill for the secret."

The next morning Vision Seeker walked with Little Ned to check the traps. The jaws of the first five traps each held a beaver. The sixth trap was missing. Little Ned found it in a tangle of brush. When he reached out to retrieve it, a beaver, caught in the jaws, began to thrash about. Vision Seeker grabbed for the struggling animal, attempting to seize it by the back of the head. He was not quick enough. The long, sharp teeth snapped on to a finger bringing a spurt of blood. With the butt of his hand ax Little Ned gave the trapped animal's head a brutal whack. The teeth released their hold. The little eyes dimmed, but not before they gave Vision Seeker an accusing look.

Little Ned quickly took his hand to examine the wound. He clucked sympathetically. "It's a bad one. Looks to be cut to the bone. I should have warned you. You have to approach these critters with care. They put up a mean fight. Those teeth can nip off a finger quicker than you can say scat." From a bag he took a clean piece of buckskin and expertly wrapped it around the wound. Vision Seeker marveled at the big man's tender touch and sympathetic manner.

Back at camp Deacon took charge. He unwound the rawhide wrapping that protected the cut; the blood resumed its flow. "My, my," Deacon muttered. He took the little Christmas jug from the pack and doused the wounded digit. Vision Seeker sucked in his breath. The liquid made the wound burn like fire.

"Where's yer needle?" Deacon asked Little Ned. "I'd say a bit of sewin' needs done." He offered Vision Seeker the jug. "Yuh'd better take a few pulls; this's goin' ta sting."

Vision Seeker pushed the jug away. The pain, sight of the exposed bone and raw whiskey fumes, already made him feel ill. A swallow of the burning water would only make him feel worse.

Vision Seeker did not go out on the trap line again, partly because the trappers warned him to keep the wounded hand out of water; but mostly it was because the eyes of the beaver Little Ned clubbed to death haunted him. The message the dying animal delivered kept going through his mind. "I'm only a creature like you. I want to stay alive and do the things the Great Creator put me on Mother Earth to do."

Just when the trapping was at its best, a storm worse than the first two howled down from the north. The tall trees writhed and moaned under the impact. The creek froze over until it was a single block of ice. When the wind ceased to blow the snow piled up in a thick blanket so heavy the shelter where the trappers worked and stored their pelts collapsed. The roof of the living quarters had to be swept every few hours or it, too, would have been demolished. As it was, the shelter became more snug than ever. Banks of snow on every side insulated it against the worst of the cold.

"Now we know how the Eskimos live so well in their igloos of ice," Buck observed. Since Vision Seeker had never heard of either Eskimos or igloos Buck went on to tell about these people far to the north who lived in near darkness half the year and then had days when the sun barely set. Although Buck illustrated with a ball of snow how the earth tilted to make the sun disappear that brought the long nights and then tilted back again to make the long days, it was still beyond Vision Seeker's imagination. How could they live on a spinning ball that circled around the sun, tipping this way and that? He glanced at Deacon. No Hair On Head grunted.

"I don't understand it either," he said. "God jest made it thet way. Jest proves He kin do anythin' He puts His mind to."

The snow was waist deep and continued to fall. The men dug a trail to where the horses and mules were sheltered. The animals had nibbled at tree trunks until they were bare of bark. For water they lapped the snow like thirsty dogs. The hair on their hides increased in thickness. They stomped and whinnied when the men came near. It was all Vision Seeker and the three trappers could do to cut and drag in sufficient tree branches to keep them satisfied.

"I don't know how long we can keep this stock alive," Buck said one afternoon. "The poor critters get thinner each day. Then there are the wolves. Unless I miss my guess, they must be near starvation. They'll be nosing around before you know it. So what can we do to keep these animals safe? The ground is too frozen to set poles and build a secure shelter."

Silent Black Hair, who often put on snow shoes to scout the land, had the answer. "There's a canyon up here with a deep cavern in one wall, provides protection on three sides. If we could drive them there -- hold them in the cavern and keep a fire going at the entrance. That would keep the stock safe."

It took a struggle that lasted much of the day but the horses and mules were moved to the cavern. Every night someone stood guard. It was miserable duty. When the snow quit falling the weather turned bitterly cold. The air was so clear at night and the stars so bright and near, they appeared to hang in the tree tops.

The cold crisp air magnified every sound. A limb heavy with ice snapping off could be heard a half mile away. The hoot of a distant owl sounded like the bird was perched next to one's ear. Then came the dreaded baying of wolves. Their threatening cries drifted over the hills, carried into the canyon by breezes that cut like a knife. Each night sounds of the howling wolf pack came nearer and nearer.

"We'd better git prepared; they're slobberin' an' slaverin', jest thinkin' of the meal they'll be makin' of our tender back-sides," Deacon said one evening as the trappers sat smoking in the lean-to quarters. "They sound 'specially snappy an' ravenous tanight."

"Yep," Buck agreed. "Wouldn't surprise me none if they show up on our doorstep before morning. Then the fun will be-gin. Vision Seeker, it's your turn to stand guard. You'd best make a bonfire in front of the cavern and keep your weapons handy. Who knows what these starving creatures might do. Fire may not be enough to keep them at bay."

Vision Seeker hurriedly fastened snow shoes over his moccasins and leggings. He had heard wolf packs many times in the past but never did they sound like this one. These howls were savage, cruel, and bloodthirsty. He almost could see the flaming eyes and the rows of glistening carnivorous teeth. Never before had he covered the path between camp and the canyon cavern so quickly. He built a big fire and hunkered down behind it. His main fear now was running out of firewood. He got up and fran-tically dug through the snow. Load after load he stacked in the cave. The wood was wet but hopefully would burn.

The trappers also looked to their wood pile and went in search of more. In their absence, a wolverine clawed a hole through the wall of their living quarters. Before the trappers dis-covered its presence, the animal had gnawed a hole through the sack containing their supply of dried meat. What the wolverine did not devour, it soiled so thoroughly it was uneatable. Deacon stomped around the shelter in a wild fury.

"What's goin' ta happen next?" he raged. "Every livin' thing in these mountains is about ta starve, includin' us. All thet's left're a couple of bags of meal. Who kin keep up strength on pots of gruel? When that meal runs out, then what're we goin' ta do, start boilin' our buckskins?"

They next morning the trappers awakened to thrashing sounds that seemed to surround the shelter. They seized their rifles. Cautiously, they pushed the door open.

"Oh! My God!" Deacon said irreverently. Not more than fifty yards away a small band of elk kicked and bucked their way through the snow. A short distance behind them a pack of snarling wolves skittered back and forth, intent on the elk.

"Careful," Buck cautioned. "Here's meat on the hoof delivered right to our door, but we're going to have to fight to keep it. First we knock down the elk and then go for the wolves. Every shot counts."

They carefully aimed and fired, reloaded and fired again. Then, before they could reload a second time, the pack of wolves bounded over the snow and onto the carcasses. Snapping and snarling, they went straight for the downed elks' still throbbing throats. The trappers shot into the pack. Before the wolves retreated, five of their number lay dead beside the carcasses of the elk. They went no farther than the first row of trees where they sat on their haunches and howled.

"I hope thet Injun kid's all right. These damned wolves ain't gonna go away. After finish caterwaulin' they may go on a beeline fer the horses," Deacon said.

#

Vision Seeker had encountered the band of elk and trailing wolves before the trappers. He armed his bow, pulled the bowstring taut, took aim and let the arrow go. One elk fell, then a second. The wolves swarmed in to attack the carcasses. Vision Seeker alertly seized a blazing limb from the fire and hurled it into their midst. Yipping and snarling, the wolves took flight. For a while they stood at a distance, whining and licking their chops, longing to return and finish their meal. Then a big gray wolf, larger than the rest, took after the remaining elk which were disappearing over the hill. The restless pack soon followed its leader. Vision Seeker quickly pulled an elk carcass next to the fire and began to butcher.

#

When the wolves retreated the trio of trappers also began to butcher the elk they had killed. To keep from freezing their fingers they had to wear mittens but before they could open the carcasses and clean out the innards, the offal had frozen. It was like working with ice. The wolves watched from the timber line, whining and fighting among themselves. Now and then the big gray wolf darted from the pack toward the trappers. He came at them so fiercely the trappers reached for their guns. Gradually more and more wolves followed the big gray. They came so near the trappers could see their lips curl up, exposing glistening white fangs. Buck shot one, Little Ned downed another. Deacon sent a big gray and white one limping away.

"Shucks!" Me bloomin' eyes must be goin' bad. I thought I had him dead to rights,"the former preacher groused.

The pack withdrew but the wolf threat had continued long enough to freeze the elk carcasses, making them impossible to butcher. Even the sharpest of knife blades could not slice the frozen layers of flesh. Disgusted, Deacon finally took a hand ax and chopped off a haunch, carrying it into the shelter where he skinned it by the fire. Buck and Little Ned also gave up and came inside. After Deacon pulled the hide away from the haunch, he swore and tossed it away. It was all skin, sinew, gristle and bone, no meat at all. When the trappers withdrew the starving wolves returned to attack the carcasses. The bodies of the elk were frozen so hard they received little satisfaction. Soon they, too, gave up and left. The trappers morosely watched them go.

"There's enuff meat out thar ta feed an army. Fer all the good it does us it might as well be on the moon. Me poor stomach's growlin' fit ta be tied," Deacon complained.

"Hey! Hey!" A shout echoed down the canyon. It was Vision Seeker. He waved from the top of a hill. "Feast! Feast! Roasted meat! Almost ready to eat."

XIV

Look upon the snow today —
tomorrow it is water.

Spotted Tail, Brule Sioux

The departure of Vision Seeker with the hairy faces disturbed Lone Wolf more than he would admit even to himself. He had sent his son away with strangers, people he knew little about. Would he be safe? He was defenseless against these heavily armed men, two of them giants. What if the men from beyond the River of Many Canoes did not find the beaver streams to their liking? In their anger they might believe Vision Seeker had played a trick on them. If they found the streams rich with beaver there was also danger. They could go back on their word, not wish to share their good fortune with an outsider. To keep all for themselves they could slay his son, pitch his body in the Bitterroot River.

He was the one who had placed Second Son in this terrible predicament. He should have used his head and sent a party of men along to keep his son safe. Of course that was out of the question; any day the buffalo herds might arrive. Every man who could ride and handle a weapon was needed for the hunt.

Quiet Woman and Grandmother did nothing to lessen Lone Wolf's worries. "The man with no hair on his head does not like our son. He could do him much harm -- did you think of that when you sent him away?" Quiet Woman questioned.

"My daughter, your words are wisely spoken," Grandmother said from her corner. "They say hairy faces keep slaves, never allow them freedom. This black man called York who came with the exploring hairy faces was a slave. He came from a far-away country where all people have black skin. The hairy faces made him travel with them, never did he see his home again. Poor Vision Seeker, if that should happen to him . . ."

"Quit sniveling, woman," For the first time in memory

Lone Wolf was short with his mother. It was not like her to look on the dark side. He left the lodge only to run into Two Kill who gave him cause for more worry.

"The buffalo herds do not come," Two Kill said. "The season is late. A new moon has come and gone. The full moon is here and will soon lose its shape. How many moons will we wait?"

Lone Wolf looked away. The great hunter was politely telling him the buffalo hunt was in jeopardy. The people were desperate. He knew what they were saying -- something had gone wrong. Did the hairy faces leave a scent that kept the buffaloes away? All other animals had fled before their approach. Did the hairy faces defile the grasslands on which the buffaloes grazed? These were some of the terrible thoughts that passed through Lone Wolf's mind.

"Let us speak to the *tewat*. Perhaps we have not properly prepared for the buffaloes arrival."

"Your thoughts are good," Two Kill agreed. "Our people forget buffaloes are sacred creatures. They must be paid homage, greeted with honor."

Lone Wolf and elders met with the *tewat* to plan a proper welcome for the buffalo. A ceremony was held. The *tewat* led the people in songs and prayers. The *tewat* dusted off his buffalo headdress and raised it above his head to face the direction from whence the buffalo would come. He placed the headdress over his head and did a dance and said more prayers. Hunters rode as far as a range of distant purple hills to greet the buffalo. The people watched them leave with hopeful hearts. Not a buffalo did the searchers see. There was nothing on the horizon but row after row of distant clouds.

The day after the sacred ceremonies were performed the storm struck -- the same one that collapsed the trappers' work shelter and blocked the trap line trails. The Sun River camp was taken completely off guard. The herd, including the hunting mounts, were in the pasture fields. That morning Lame Horse had taken his men down river in search of small game. A screeching wind filled with stinging snow descended with a fury, making children run screaming inside. Camp dogs, tails between the legs, scurried for cover. Smoke hole flaps were hurriedly secured and entrances sealed to keep the wind from gusting in to sail flimsy tipi coverings away. Seeing his tipi creak and strain, Lone Wolf was thankful he had ordered Running Turtle to double the stakes that held the buffalo hide covering secure to the ground. He learned from his father, Great Wolf, to take great pains in setting the tipi. "Always face it east and tilt it slightly forward and the winds will never blow it away," his father had instructed.

#

As usual, Many Horses' first thought was of the herd. He started toward the pasture grounds, bent almost double to make headway against the wind. When he came to the open space beyond the cottonwood groves, a fierce gust knocked him off his feet. The blow was so sudden he was unprepared. For a moment he lay on the frozen ground, stunned. He could not believe the power that pushed him around as if he were a pinch of goose down. The wind buffeted his body and pulled at his clothes until he thought they would be torn away. Every inch of skin stung and burned from the whipping, battering beating.

During a brief lull Many Horses got to his knees and pulled himself forward by clutching tufts of buffalo grass. At the top of a crest that bordered the pasture field, the stinging wind hit him full force again, sucking away his breath. Like a fish out of water he lay gasping. The driving wind whipped the snow into his eyes, blinding him. With his eyes closed and breathless, he struggled forward. How strange he felt, as though he was about to fly into space. He finally caught his breath to have the air sear his lungs as if he inhaled hot coals. He coughed; tears rolled down to freeze on his cheeks. For a short while the wind let up. He opened his eyes. The herd was nearly hidden by a curtain of white. He half crawled and half clawed his way across the snow swept ground to where the horses stood. Another herder crawled alongside. In the lee of the horses they managed to stand. Together they drove the horses into the thickets of willows bordering the river. The miserable animals huddled next to one another, their rumps pressed together bearing the brunt of the storm.

Behind the willow trees the force of the wind lessened. Using the willow trees as a wind break, the two herders started for camp. Many Horses' companion stumbled and fell to his knees. He struggled to his feet. A sudden blast of wind twisted him around. He stumbled and slipped on an icy patch of grass. Before he could right himself, another gust of wind sent him off balance. He fell down the slick river bank slope. Many Horses watched in horror as momentum carried his fellow herder onto the river's frozen surface. The ice cracked, then broke. Freezing water closed over the herder. His frantic shouts were carried away by the wind. Before Many Horses could reach him, his companion was a corpse, stiff and cold as the ice that enclosed him.

Many Horses crawled into the tipi more dead than alive. The skin on his face had turned pale, nearly white. Quiet Woman took one look at her son and pulled him into her arms. She seized a rawhide cloth, immersed it in warm water and began to pat the tender, discolored flesh and softly moaned, "My poor son! My poor son!" She ordered Raven Wing to take off Many Horses' leggings and moccasins. The stricken man lay still until feeling began to return to his nearly frozen limbs.

Running Turtle, who watched with wide eyes, piled wood on the fire. It warmed the lodge but only increased the torture. Many Horses could not keep from uttering painful moans as blood began to circulate in the frostbitten flesh.

Lone Wolf sat silently in the shadows. Many Horses' every moan and cry pierced his heart. Weasel Face had been right, he should have stayed the winter in the snug long lodge. Why was he not content to lead a normal life? It was his pride that was to blame. Ever since he could remember he had to prove himself, do things that others would not attempt. What evil power drove him to do these things? Why did he place his family, his friends and those who depended upon him in danger? He stared into the fire, tormenting himself sick with self-accusing thoughts.

Many Horses finally became quiet but continued to shake and shiver. His teeth chattered so, it was impossible for him to drink the warm herbal water Quiet Woman put to his lips. No amount of covers kept him warm. Finally, he drifted into troubled sleep only to jerk awake with a shriek. He stared down at his hands and feet, uttering incoherent words. Under Quiet Woman's crooning, he closed his eyes and drifted off only to jerk awake and scream again and stare at his hands and feet and mumble to himself. Over and over the same sequence of events occurred.

The horrified watchers finally understood. Each time he drifted off a dream came to Many Horses. A head with vacant eyes and icicles for hair appeared to rise out of the ice covered river. In the terrible reoccurring dream, instead of his herder companion, it was he, Many Horses, who had fallen into the river. Each awakening he looked down at his hands and feet to make certain they were still there; they had not turned to ice.

It was a miserable night for everyone in the lodge. The flimsy tipi covering whipped back and forth like bulrushes in a fierce whirlwind. Unlike the trappers' shelter, the snow did not drift up to help insulate the inhabitants against the penetrating cold. No matter how near one pushed up against the fire, the chill remained, one side of a person was hot, the other side freezing cold. The wind shifted to the east, gusting down the smoke hole to make the flames dance. It came so swiftly and with such force Running Turtle's hair was scorched. Cinders, ash and smoke swirled around the tipi interior. The sulfuric, acrid air made the occupants cough and sneeze. Running Turtle tore open the tipi flaps, thrust his head out and quickly jumped back. The escaping light from the lodge fire outlined furry shapes. A dozen eyes glowed like red hot embers.

"Wolves -- wolves!" Running Turtle stuttered. "They wait to eat us alive!"

"Foolish boy, stay in the lodge. It is no time to go gandering like a goose," Grandmother chided.

Late into the night Quiet Woman watched over her first-born, rocking him back and forth, sometimes keening, sometimes muttering prayers. She looked at her mate with tears dripping down her face. She, uttering a mournful moan, "I felt it in my bones. We never should have left the home lodge. We will meet our deaths before the Season of Melting Snow. Our son, Vision Seeker, is out in the cold. We should never have let him go."

"Stop it, woman!" Lone Wolf commanded. "There is no need to snivel. The storm cannot last forever. Everything will be all right once the wind ceases to blow."

Lone Wolf looked away from his mate. He did not want her to see he, too, was almost in tears. His precious horses were freezing. His second son and the White Bird hunters, who were down river searching for game, may have frozen to death. The whole camp was in dire need of food. He foolishly had depended upon the early arrival of the buffalo herds. The onslaught of the storm could prevent the shaggy animals from coming at all. If they did not arrive the whole camp would surely starve. For the first time in years, Lone Wolf put his arm around Quiet Woman, pulled her to him and held her so tightly she barely could breathe.

Early the next morning Running Turtle awakened before the others. Hurriedly, he slipped out of the sleeping robes and, shivering uncontrollably, unfastened the straps that held the tipi flaps. He desperately had to relieve himself. He threw open the tipi flap and plunged into the snow. He ran head-on into a dark furry hide. It startled him so his bladder let go.

"Buffalo! Buffalo!" he cried and ran back inside to seize his brother's lance. He dashed out again. The big animal turned to face him, its nostrils snorting puffs of steam. The shaggy beast lowered its head and glowered, its eyes as round and large as full moons. One sharp hoof pawed, scraping a slit in the snow. Grasping the lance in both hands, Running Turtle stood his ground. Here was his chance to slay a buffalo but how? Two Kill said a thrust in the heart was the sure way to bring a buffalo down. When a hunter faced one head-on how did he manage that? The shaggy beast did not wait for Running Turtle to make up his mind. Uttering a steamy snort, it charged. Scrambling to get out of the way, Running Turtle tripped and fell in the deep snow. Desperately, he thrust the lance; the sharp point caught the buffalo in the chest. The impact of the big beast's momentum sent the flint lance head deep into the flesh. Mad with pain, the buffalo plunged headlong into the tipi, trampling the occupants inside.

Quiet Woman, smothered under sleeping robes, tried to get up. She was pinned to the ground. Lone Wolf, who lay beside her, also was trapped. The sharp hooves of the buffalo did a crushing dance on his shins. Many Horses awakened in a daze. All he could feel was the agonizing pain of frostbite. He had no idea what was happening. He suddenly found himself out in the cold. The tipi covering had ripped from its moorings. Wearing the tipi covering like a hooded cape, the buffalo charged back and forth trying to free itself from the tenacious, blinding thing that covered its head.

Many Horses reached for his weapons. He could find nothing until his frostbitten hand fell on Lone Wolf's heavy-bladed hunting knife. His fingers pained him so greatly he hardly could grasp the polished bone handle. Gritting his teeth, he plunged the knife blade into the buffalo's side time after time. Warm blood flowed down his hand and arm. The frostbitten areas burned like they had been set afire. His thrusts only seemed to make the animal more frenzied. Finally, a deep thrust brought the shaggy beast to a standstill. Breathing a heavy sigh, it rolled over on its side, gave a last few futile kicks and died. The knife dropped from Many Horses' hand, he fell back to lay senseless beside the great animal's body.

The other tipi occupants cut and clawed their way out of the shambles. Lone Wolf could barely get to his feet and hobble. The buffalo had stomped him so badly he was amazed his feet and legs had not been crushed. Freed from the smothering sleeping robes, Quiet Woman and Grandmother emerged, blinking like

moles seeing sunlight after a long spell in the dark. They spied
Many Horses' body and quickly rushed to his side. So much
blood covered him for a moment they thought he had been killed
along with the buffalo. Only temporarily dazed, Many Horses
stirred and sat up. He reached over and ran his frostbitten fingers
through the heavy fur that covered the neck and shoulders of the
dead buffalo and frowned. "Are we mad? Do we not hunt the
buffalo in the open where they can face death with honor?"

Other hunters crawled outside to find buffaloes virtually
blocking their tipi entrances. They quickly discovered a band of
buffaloes huddled in the willow trees alongside the surviving
hunting mounts. There the shaggy creatures had taken shelter,
their backsides turned to bear the brunt of the wind-driven snow.
Uttering yelps of astonishment and joy, men, women and children descended on the nearly defenseless bison. Within yards of
camp more than a dozen of the great beasts fell to the thrust of
the lance and knife.

The fear of starvation was a thing of the past. Dry wood
was brought out of lodges to start bonfires to keep the carcasses
and butchers warm. Fire pits were chopped out of the frozen
earth. Cooking fires were built. Spits were made. Large slabs of
meat were put on to roast over open coals. That night a great
feast was held. The next day the White Bird hunters struggled
into camp. They had taken refuge in a ravine until the storm
passed. Their safe return was the cause of more rejoicing.

During the festivities, Lone Wolf painfully hobbled around
camp greeting everyone. No gift among Mother Earth's basket
of wonders gave his people more pleasure than that of the buffalo. As Lone Wolf limped by Weasel Face's lodge his face broke
into a smile. Weasel Face would have to find something else to
grumble about now. No one but a fool could say the hunting trip
had failed. Now, if Vision Seeker would return, everything would
be just fine.

XV

Knowledge was inherent in all things. The world was a library and its books were the stones, leaves, grass, brooks . . .

Luther Standing Bear, Oglala Sioux

The ordeal with the wolves brought the four men on the Bitterroot trap lines closer together. No Hair On Head claimed Vision Seeker had saved their lives with his elk kills which he had turned so quickly and efficiently into succulent roasts. After the feast Deacon, whose paunch had nearly disappeared during the starvation period, patted his midriff and appreciatively belched.

"Them was mighty good vittles. I couldn't hev asked fer better. I'm much obliged. From now on I'll never say another word again the Injun. Bless 'em, when the chips're down they come through. 'Course, this had ta be God's work. He tested us good an' proper. When we was down ta eatin' our bootstraps He said we had enuff -- sent the herd of elk an' Vision Seeker ta save our miserable hides. Yes sir, does wonders fer a man's soul. Makes a body 'preciate bein' alive."

Buck Stone, puffing on his short black pipe, nodded. "Yep, as they say, afflictions are sent to us by God for our good."

Life at the trappers' camp soon fell back into its regular routine with each man taking care of specific chores. No Hair On Head cooked the meals. Little Ned helped clean up afterward, maintained a supply of firewood and kept the shelter neat. Buck saw to the drying, storing and counting of the beaver skins. Vision Seeker tended to the livestock, which was no simple job. Chopping and dragging distant branches to the animal shelter was hard work. His voracious charges tore into the offerings, chomping the forage down as soon as it was laid before them. Often times it took him all day to collect sufficient feed to satisfy but he did the work gladly. It kept him in the fresh air surrounded by Mother Earth's beauty. This country which the trappers called wild was to him home, the place he belonged.

As the days passed Vision Seeker took more interest in the tasks the hairy faces did when away from the trap lines: the bead and quill work that occupied Little Ned; the wood carvings and woven items Deacon made; and the writings on talking paper that kept Buck Stone busy. Not only did the man with yellow hair write things down, he made drawings of birds, fish, trees, rocks and once a particularly spectacular sunset that he did in color with paint kept in a small metal case. The drawings were much like ones the Nimpau did on cured elk skin. The native work did not have the intricate detail of Buck's drawings. He made it look so easy, his pen going back and forth putting feathers on birds, manes on horses, quills on porcupines, stripes on a skunk or chipmunk until each feather, quill and hair took shape. It was magical, delightful to watch.

Buck took a special interest in Vision Seeker's Appaloosa. He spent half a day measuring, inspecting and sketching the horse, then made a perfect drawing of the animal. It was so lifelike Vision Seeker stared in astonishment. The pony looked as though it would utter a whinny and nibble at the fringes of his hunting shirt, begging for a handout. Buck noticed the wondrous expression on Vision Seeker's face

"You have a beautiful animal with a tremendous history. This breed of horses had its origin years before the time of Christ. These spectacular marked creatures were the favorites of kings and emperors. A king named Xerxes rode an Appaloosa when he led an army that invaded ancient Greece. The emperor of China, Wu Ti, possessed a herd of Appaloosas he called "Heavenly Horses." He coveted them so greatly he sent his army to raid a country called Turkestan for breeding stock. The army was successful but at a cost of 40,000 soldiers' lives and a loss of 100,000 horses. Yes, this animal has a great history. By breeding such fine stock your people are making it even greater."

Vision Seeker looked at his mount with new eyes. He had a possession even more precious than he ever had dreamed.

His admiration of Buck Stone also increased tenfold. Here was a man who possessed unbelievable knowledge. He could speak with authority on almost any topic that came to mind. He was generous with his knowledge, often offering it without being asked.

"I know a story you should like," Buck said one evening after the chores were finished. "It's about a man who tamed a winged horse."

Vision Seeker was immediately all ears. "A horse that flew in the sky like a bird?"

"Yep. It happened long before your people knew horses existed. Many strange things took place in those ancient times. Not only was there this winged horse named Pegasus, but a terrible beast that terrorized people and carried off animals and children and devoured them. The frightful creature had the head of a lion, the body of a goat and the tail of a snake. It breathed fire and smoke, burning forests, crops and villages.

"A brave man named Bellerophon decided to put an end to this monster. He caught the winged horse. The horse was like one of your wild Appaloosas. He did not want to be ridden. Pegasus tried to shake off his rider. His bucking and whipping back and forth, took Bellerophon high into the sky. When they were high above Mother Earth they saw the monster. They were of the same mind -- the monster had to die. The monster saw them coming and tried to hide. Bellerophon rained arrows at the beast but the monster breathed such fire flying horse and rider were driven away.

"Undaunted, they made a second attack. This time Bellerophon hurled a lance that pierced the side of the beast. In a flame of fire, the monster died. To reward the flying horse for its great service, Bellerophon gave Pegasus his freedom. Instead of flying away, the winged horse remained with Bellerophon to be his special mount. For years afterward horse and rider could be seen riding high in the sky guarding the countryside."

"Hmm!" Vision Seeker grunted in awe. How wonderful it would be to ride above the clouds close to the stars.

"Yuh shouldn't tell the lad such silly things," Deacon scolded. "Yuh'll get him all muddled up. Flyin' horses, fire belchin' dragons, goblins an' sech. It's all a bunch of hogwash - - fairy tales. He's liable ta go back an' tell these things ta his folks. They'll think he's lost his wits. Yuh should be tellin' about the Good Book, do missionary work. Prepare him fer what's ta come. Before yuh kin say Jack Sprat the Bible thumpers'll be hightailin' it across the plains, jest achin' ta save the pagan Injuns."

For the first time that winter the trappers quarreled. "So these legends are hogwash, are they? What's the matter with your brain? You are talking like an uncivilized ignoramus. These tales are classics; they have come down to us from the great civilizations," Buck retorted. "If you're so all-fired anxious to get him squared away on religious matters, explain to him Jonah and the whale, Daniel in the lion's den, Moses and the burning bush, the parting of the Red Sea, the plagues of Egypt or Samson pulling the roof down on top of himself."

"Yeah, I guess they's some bits of the Old Testament thet're hard fer an unbeliever ta swaller."

"Old Testament! What about the New Testament?" Little Ned who had remained silent all evening, suddenly spoke. "The Immaculate Conception, The Holy Trinity, Christ walking on water, feeding a multitude with five loaves of bread and two fishes, Christ rising from the dead and ascending into heaven to sit at the right hand of God. I'll warrant your pagan Indians will find them hard to swallow, too. I am sure it will be much easier for them to understand a horse with wings."

"Yeh! Yeh!" Deacon muttered. "No use talkin' ta people who ain't had no Christian upbringin'. I ain't sure but what yer more heathen than the Injun."

That night Vision Seeker wrapped himself in his sleeping robe and lay awake too confused to sleep. There was so much he did not understand. Was he pagan? Was he a heathen? He had wanted to ask the meaning of the words but the argument among the trappers had gone on all evening. So many new words were tossed around he could not follow what was said. Old Testament, New Testament, Holy Trinity, Immaculate Conception . . .? They must be words of a special Christian language the trappers did not think he would understand. "Ah!" He was so ignorant. There was so much to learn, so much he would like to know. In frustration, he turned over and pounded the sleeping robe.

The quarrel did not keep Buck from telling the long ago tales. In the nights to come he told other stories, many of them taken from his supply of books. Like a squirrel collecting food for a long winter, Vision Seeker stored them in his memory. To repay Buck, he told legends of his people, of the mythical days when animals lived and acted like humans. Instead of storing the words in his memory, Buck carefully put everything on talking paper. The story Buck liked best was of the cunning coyote. Like the legend of the flying horse, Vision Seeker's story also contained a monster. Buck wrote every word down and then, much to Deacon's disgust, read what he had written to Vision Seeker.

"In olden days before the Nimpau existed there lived a monster so terrible he devoured all living things. The coyote, the cunning trickster of the animal world, thought to himself, if we ever are to live in peace we must remove this monster from Mother Earth. He placed himself in the monster's path and allowed himself to be swallowed alive. In the monster's stomach coyote started a fire. By the light of the fire, with stone knives, he cut out the monster's heart. In the monster's death throes all the animals he swallowed were set free. To make certain the monster never again would come alive, coyote cut him into little pieces. He flung each piece across the face of Mother Earth. Each place a piece of the monster landed became the home of an Indian people. When he finished, the only place left was where the monster had lived. Coyote sprinkled it with the monster's blood. It became the home of the Nimpau, the land where these people live today."

Vision Seeker listened with awe. How well the story was told. He never had heard it told better, even by Grandmother who was a legendary teller of Nimpau tales. How he wished he could make paper speak like Buck. To achieve that ability would give him much greater satisfaction than a battlefield coup.

Buck was not happy with the talking paper. The story was not finished. He chewed on the pen quill and reread what he had written. "Hmm!" he grunted. "You call your people the Nimpau, The People. Is that not so?"

Vision Seeker nodded. "Some people call us Chup-nit-pa-lu, people of the cut noses. This is false. We never cut our noses."

Buck Stone nodded. "French trappers, I understand were the first to call your people Nez Perce. Then came the explorers, Lewis and Clark. They called you Chopunnish. That's the trouble with people of European stock. We don't take time to find the truth. We give a name to someone or something with little thought. How did your people live before the coming of the horse? From my calculations you cannot have had the horse for more than four or five generations, maybe one-hundred years."

Vision Seeker pondered. What did he know about his ancestors? Only what he had heard around lodge fires. Grandmother was the keeper of such knowledge. Now he wished he had listened to her more carefully. She remembered stories her grandfather told her of when he was a boy. In those days, Grandmother said, the Nimpau lived in small villages along the River Kimooenim. They were fishermen and half their diet came from salmon and other fish. In the summer and fall all families went to dig for kouse root and camas bulbs. As First Son, Grandfather Dark Wolf was given the responsibility for seeing to the dogs. They were the beasts of burden. With small packs on their backs or dragging travois, the dogs carried supplies to and from the digging grounds. The dogs were troublesome, they did not like to work. They quarreled and fought. Dark Wolf had his hands full in keeping them ready for travel.

One day, while Dark Wolf prepared the dogs for a trip to dig for camas bulbs, a party of Cayuse came to visit. They were leading two huge four-leggeds carrying packs on their backs. The villagers could not believe what they saw. The huge beasts had great long heads with pointed ears, large round eyes and nostrils as large as prairie dog holes. They stood taller than a man, with broad backs, long tails and hooves that were solid and round. As the astonished villagers stared, the long head of the lead animal lowered, black puffy lips opened to expose broad teeth unlike they ever had seen before. The teeth clamped on a tuft of grass, tearing it in half. The head came up, the long jaws began to grind, the large eyes watched the onlookers as if to ask, "Why are you two-leggeds gawking?"

"What is it?" an incredulous villager asked. "What is the name of this large beast?"

"It is called horse," a visitor answered.

"Oh-hah!" Dark Wolf's father exclaimed. "Where are these creatures found?"

"They come from a place called Mexico. We took these from the Shoshoni."

Dark Wolf's father fell silent. He had friends among the Shoshoni. That was where he must go. He would not rest until he possessed this animal called horse.

The wealth of the Shoshonis astonished Dark Wolf's father. In their pasture fields grazed horses of many colors: black, brown, gray, red, yellow and white. How did these people get so many of these animals and the Nimpau had none? Now, more than ever, Dark Wolf's father was determined to possess these handsome animals. After much hard bargaining he returned to the home village with a stallion and mare with colt.

Soon Dark Wolf was given the responsibility of caring for the horses, instead of dogs. He was proud of these animals. They were so much easier to keep than dogs. They did not quarrel and fight. Instead of meat they ate grass and could live off the land. The horse carried four times the load of a dog and traveled twice as far.

Over many moons the Nimpau built up the herd. At first

they used the horses as pack animals, then one day Dark Wolf leapt on the back of a mare. The mare danced around and threw him off. His companions hooted and laughed. This angered Dark Wolf so he had friends hold the mare and again jumped on her back. Using two long sticks, one on either side of the horse, he balanced himself as his friends led the horse forward. He quickly gained confidence and did not need the sticks. He could remain upright by clenching his legs around the horse's ribs. His friends were envious. They began to mount up and ride. Soon men were riding everywhere. With this new found mobility Dark Wolf's family left their Kimooenim River bank home. They traveled from one place to another, carrying with them everything they possessed. Meat replaced fish as their main food. Life for Dark Wolf's family was never the same after the coming of the horse.

Everything Vision Seeker said Buck put on talking paper. "Why do you put these things on talking paper?" Vision Seeker asked one day.

"My memory is not as well trained as yours," Buck replied. "For that reason I write down everything I wish to remember. Someday I will put these things you tell in a proper book so all men can see the words you speak, a book like this." He pointed to the book that contained the tale of Pegasus, the flying horse.

Vision Seeker stirred uneasily. His words in a book all people could see was not good. They would learn of the Nimpau and their homeland. They would desire to see this beautiful country. A tremor of fear struck at his heart. He once had a vision of hordes of strangers overwhelming Nimpau lands, taking over the pasture fields and driving villagers from their lodges. Vision Seeker clamped his lips tightly together. His words written on talking paper could make these signs come true. He vowed not to say more.

THE LONE WOLF CLAN

XVI

*Christians see themselves as set apart from the rest of the
animal and plant world by superiority,
even as a special creation.*

Tatanga Mani, Stoney

The Sun River camp continued to prosper. Another herd
of buffaloes descended and then another. The supply of meat,
hides, bones, horns and hooves mounted until every lodge had
more than the occupants could manage. Two Kill said it was the
greatest hunting season since he was a youth.

Lone Wolf suddenly found himself in high favor. Although
his bruised and battered shins kept him from riding in the hunt,
he was praised for making the harvest of buffaloes possible. The
trials and tribulations of the journey up the Kooskooskie were
forgotten. The people put the terrible storm and its losses behind
them. Now they looked forward to returning home. Bearing all
their new riches, the people could journey to Lapwai Valley in
triumph.

However, not all was well. Many Horses' frostbitten hands
continued to pain him. The medicine man had to trim away flesh
that did not respond to Quiet Woman's treatments. Every twitch
of pain reminded Many Horses of the terrible night when his companion rolled into the river and fell through the ice. Visiting his
four-legged friends in the pasture continued to bring him sadness. So many of his trusted friends were gone, frozen to death in
the storm.

Lone Wolf and Quiet Woman also had many bad moments.
Not a word did they hear from Second Son who left with the
hairy faces. Search parties went out but the trail had been long
obliterated. There was nothing anyone could do but wait and
hope Vision Seeker had not met his death at the hands of the
hairy faces or lay buried beneath the deep winter snows. Raven
Wing remained lazy and rebellious. Along with her constant com-

panion, Small Goat, she spent most of every day away from camp, avoiding the work of scraping hides, preparation of meat and fashioning useful articles garnered from the bountiful buffalo harvest. Scoldings and warnings fell on deaf ears.

"Do not worry," Grandmother said. "When weather warms daughter will settle down and Second Son will return."

Yet, when soft breezes came to sweep away the snow, Raven Wing did not change her ways and there was no sign of Vision Seeker. In spite of his injuries, every morning Lone Wolf mounted his horse and rode to a far range of hills to stare at the distant horizon. The only signs of life he saw were flocks of blackbirds, magpies, a few spring robins and circling hawks. He would return to report to Quiet Woman whose eyes would take on the tragic look she had the day Baby Young Wolf slipped into the Kimooenim and drowned. Then one day Lone Wolf's heart leaped for joy. Riding across the grasslands were three horsemen. He spurred his mount down the slope and loped toward them. He waved and shouted. The horsemen took no notice. They were busy talking among themselves. Something was familiar about all three . . . . Suddenly, he recognized them.

Fury blinded Lone Wolf. He viciously struck his mount with the quirt. He pulled up in front of the now halted riders. He was too enraged to speak. He jabbed his quirt in Toohool's face. "Go!" he ordered.

"Are you unhappy, Father?" Raven Wing innocently asked.

"Unhappy! Our son and brother is lost. Daughter does no work, all the time she rides with Weasel Faces. If you like them so, why do you not move to their lodge?"

"That is what Toolhool asks."

Lone Wolf brought his quirt down on the rump of Raven Wing's mount and chased her all the way back to the Sun River camp.

That evening, just as the white-breasted killdeers came out to sound their strident cries, Many Horses, standing guard over the herd, saw a lone rider coming up Sun River. He knew the newcomer instantly. "Hi-yeh! Hi-yeh! Vision Seeker!" he shouted, galloping wildly toward his brother. The brothers were in such a hurry their horses nearly collided. Vision Seeker took his brother by the hand and shook it in the manner of the hairy faces. His heart throbbed with love and pride. The smile on his brother's face beamed a light brighter than sunlight on snow. There was no greater gift Earth Mother could give after a long absence than the greetings of a brother.

As they rode toward camp Many Horses told Vision Seeker of the events that had happened in his absence: the deadly freeze; the bountiful bison kills; how the herder lost his life in the storm; the injuries the buffalo inflicted on his father's shins; the sadness Vision Seeker's absence had caused Lone Wolf and Quiet Woman and other news that affected family and friends.

"Where are the beaver furs the hairy faced ones promised?" Many Horses finally asked. "Father believes the words of these people are not good."

"The words of the hairy faces are good. We have many pelts, too many to bring. The hairy faces will keep them until the Season of Tall Grass. They invite Lone Wolf and our people to a place called rendezvous. Trappers from all over the mountains come to trade. Pack trains that carry goods from the banks of the River of Many Canoes come there. Buck, the yellow-haired one, says besides beaver skins, hairy faces trade for horses, buffalo robes, pemmican and other things."

"Hmm!" Many Horses grunted thoughtfully. "Your news is good. Lone Wolf will be cheered. Our people have much meat, many hides and other things made from the buffalo kills."

The appearance of Vision Seeker brought the villagers running. Children shrieked, dogs barked, the elders cried greetings, Quiet Woman and Grandmother shed tears. Lone Wolf said a prayer of thanksgiving. Afterward, he grasped Vision Seeker by the arm, pulled him out of the crowd and led him to the edge of camp. He wanted to have a few minutes alone with Second Son who had miraculously returned from the dead. Lone Wolf was moved by paternal emotion but also wanted to know how many beaver skins awaited Vision Seeker at the camp of the hairy faces.

That evening Lone Wolf called Left Hand, Red Bull, the White Bird leader, Lame Horse, and other family heads together for a smoke of celebration. He ordered the women to prepare a feast. His son had safely returned from the hairy faced ones' camp with good tidings. During the Season of Tall Grass, Lone Wolf announced, the hunting party was off to trade at the place the hairy faces called rendezvous. There the people would see many good things. He sat Vision Seeker in the place of honor and had the women serve him first after himself and the White Bird leader.

Not since he went on his first vision quest had Vision Seeker received such attention. He thought of the story No Hair On Head read from the Great Spirit Book. "After a long absence a sinful son fearfully returned home. Instead of turning him away, the father gave him his best robe and ordered a fatted animal killed. . . ."

A few days after Vision Seeker returned, a party of Flatheads rode into the Sun River camp. Their homeland lay to the west in a beautiful rich grassy valley bordered on the east by mountains that never lost their caps of snow. Lone Wolf greeted them warmly. In his youth he had ridden with Flathead warriors to raid the Snake and Shoshonis. Many of the animals in his herd were descendants of horses taken on those raids.

The Flatheads came to trade for horses. The hard winter had decimated their herds. They also had traded away some of their stock to a brigade of Hudson's Bay people who, to keep from starving, had killed the animals for food. After they smoked and chatted about old times, the Flatheads spoke of the Great Spirit Book. Vision Seeker, who nearly had been lulled to sleep by the droning conversation, perked up to listen. Did Flatheads know the secrets of the hairy faces' religion?

"Yes, you see, we have four Iroquois men in our midst.

They grew up in the east and have much knowledge of the Great Spirit Book," an elderly Flathead reported. "They tell of the many good things it says. If we follow the path of the white man's Great Spirit it will lead us to a place called heaven where game is always plentiful, the air is clean, warm and healthful and pastures are thick and green all seasons of the year. Lodges are built of stone and lined with glittery things called gold. No one dies. No one mourns. There is no pain. Forever, life goes on and on. Our people would like these good things. They want to find this path. We send people to villages along the River of Many Canoes to search for teachers of this Great Spirit Book."

The Flathead paused to puff on his pipe. "There is much we do not understand. The people we send never return. On the banks of the River of Many Canoes there is a sickness that makes them weak. They try to mount their horses but cannot ride. In one, maybe two days, they pass to the other side. Do these hairy faces guard this book called Bible with a sickness that kills?"

The Flathead knocked out his pipe and put it away in its pouch. "We are troubled," he continued. "Other people learn the hairy faces' religion, why not us? The Black Robes of Hudson's Bay have invited sons of Spokan and Kutenai leaders to their post on Red River. For many seasons they remain with the Black Robes to learn the ways of the hairy faced ones' Great Spirit Book. We do not feel it wise to send our young men away. It is better these teachers come to our village. Then we all learn the ways of the Great Spirit Book."

Vision Seeker was impressed. The Flathead spoke wisely. To bring teachers to teach everyone was good. That is what the Nimpau should do. The news did not please Lone Wolf. "Why is it the Black Robes chose to take Spokan and Kutenai to learn of the hairy faces' great medicine? Are we not more respected than the Spokan and Kutenai?" He looked at his sons reproachfully as though in some way they were to blame.

Many Horses got up and walked away. The fingers and toes which had been frostbitten still troubled him. They burned and itched, making it hard for him to remain still. Besides, talk with the Flatheads brought back memories he would just as soon forget. In former days the Lone Wolf clan made regular visits to Flathead country. On one trip a slim maiden with a bright smile and laughing voice caught his eye. He looked upon her with favor. She did not discourage him.

They sat by the beautiful blue lake that bordered Flathead country on the north. They clasped hands and agreed they should marry. Her father frowned on the match and told them to wait. The Lone Wolf family returned the next summer. Lone Wolf was prepared to bargain for the maiden; if need be he would offer a dozen horses, including his prized stallion. Many Horses was pleased. He would return home to Lapwai with a beautiful Flathead mate. Instead, when they arrived in Flathead country, they were told the maiden was promised to an Iroquois man who knew much about the Long Robes' religion that the Flatheads desired to learn.

The painful memory made Many Horses groan. He wished the Flatheads had stayed away. They were here for horses. He counted and recounted the herd. There were only a few good mounts left. He did not want to part with a single one. He did not like people who traded stock to Hudson's Bay. Even a starving man should not kill a horse for food.

Moodily, Many Horses went to where the herd nuzzled in the water sodden pasture for tufts of dry grass and nibbled at tender bark of willow trees. He studied each one of the animals. He did not like what he saw. The horses were thin, their hair long and shaggy. He hated for the Flatheads to see them this way. To protect his favorites from getting traded, he drove them farther into the willow brush. He barely was in time. Before he finished, Lone Wolf and the band of Flatheads arrived to inspect the herd. Trailing behind came Raven Wing and Small Goat. Because he did not want to take part in the trade and witness Many Horses' distress, Vision Seeker remained in camp.

Lone Wolf ordered Many Horses to chivvy the stock around. Raven Wing and Small Goat ran to help. Before he could stop them, the young women stumbled into the patch of willows and flushed Many Horses' hidden favorites into the open. Their actions infuriated him.

"Women! Why do you make this your business? It is none of your concern. Go to camp and do your work," Many Horses shouted.

"Family matters are my business," Raven Wing retorted. "It is important we make good trade."

"Good trade! These Flatheads have no trade goods." Many Horses watched in dismay as the Flathead leader pointed to one of the spotted ponies he had hidden in the brush.

"They may not have trade goods but they have beaver skins, good beaver skins that they received in trade with the Redcoats of Hudson's Bay," Raven Wing curtly informed her brother.

"Beaver skins! We have no need for beaver skins. It is the hairy faces who need beaver skins."

"Do you have anything but emptiness in your head?" Raven Wing gave Many Horses a contemptuous glare. "The Flatheads need horses. We give them horses. They give us beaver skins. When the Season of Tall Grass comes we do as Lone Wolf says, we take our beaver skins to the hairy faced ones' rendezvous and make trade."

Many Horses' anger grew. He understood his foolish sister perfectly. She wanted to possess the froofraw of the hairy faces. She intended to trade his friends for these useless things. "What do you need from the hairy faces that is more important than our horses?" he demanded.

"Black Hair has an elk tooth dress worth any horse, maybe two or more. When we see the hairy faces again Father will make trade. If I do not ride with Toohool again he promised to do so."

Many Horses clenched his jaws until his teeth ached. It was clear the hairy faces had a power too great for the likes of his father and sister to resist. It was a power one did not see or feel. This silent power came like a thief into the lodge to make people angry with each other and make them desire things they did not need. It was a power even greater than that which came from the hairy faced ones' Great Spirit Book called Bible.

XVII

Behold my friends, the spring comes; the earth has gladly received the embrace of the sun . . .

Sitting Bull, Hunkpapa Lakota

Like a giant hand, warm winds brushed away the last of the snow. Flocks of magpies and blue jays flew in to scold and flit about camp. Prairie dogs emerged from their holes to bark; field mice appeared to scamper in search of food. High overhead formations of geese honked their way northward. Dogs lazed all day in the sun. Children raced each other as they did the chores. Adults discovered a new spring in their step. The willows and cottonwoods began to green. Waves of crystal clear water descended from the snow covered heights to make the river overflow its banks. Clouds of mosquitoes descended to hover over the campers' heads whenever they left the protection of the lodge. The Season of New Grass had arrived.

Many Horses went daily to inspect the herd. He kept driving the animals farther from camp to new pasture fields where each of his four-footed charges could eat its fill to become sleek and full of life. How he wished Lone Wolf would decide against the trip to the hairy faced ones' rendezvous. He wanted to take his horses home to the grazing lands of the foothills and plateaus where most of them were foaled. If Lone Wolf got carried away in trade Many Horses feared they would arrive back at their tribal lands with only the mounts they rode.

For Vision Seeker it was also a time of unease. His father kept after him with pestering questions. When would the hairy faces arrive and deliver his share of pelts? How many pelts would he receive? Were they good pelts which would bring much in trade? Every morning after getting up and every evening before retiring, Lone Wolf walked back and forth along the river bank looking anxiously down the trail toward the pass that led to Bitterroot Valley. "Do the hairy faces speak with straight tongues?" invariably he asked. "Will they keep their promise about the beaver skins?"

"Yes, the hairy faces speak true," Vision Seeker assured his father. "It is early. They will take more beaver. This is good. Every fourth one belongs to us."

Lone Wolf was not reassured. "We know nothing of these hairy faces. They leave us blind as moles that never catch sight of the sun." He was all for sending Vision Seeker to the Bitterroot to collect his share of beaver skins.

"There is no need to worry. The man with yellow hair or Black Hair will come or send word. They have many beaver skins, more than their animals can carry. They must come to us for pack animals."

Raven Wing wearied Vision Seeker as much as did his father. To ingratiate herself with Lone Wolf, she avoided Toohool and Small Goat. Whenever Vision Seeker left the lodge, she trailed along. Toohool watched her come and go from a distance, his head and shoulders bowed with disappointment. He tried every way he could to restore his place in her affections. She brushed him off as she would a pesky mosquito. He came up to her one day in the pasture.

"My father will give many horses if we mate," he whispered.

"How many is many?" Raven Wing callously asked. "The storm made your herd small."

Toohool opened and shut his two hands five times. "That many. We have fine herd in Lapwai. Our relatives who live in Weippe Prairie have many more."

"What a small man your father is," Raven Wing scoffed. "I have Cayuse suitors whose fathers will give many, many, maybe as many as leaves on that tree, all Appaloosas."

"That cannot be so, too much stock for any man to manage."

"I do not lie." Raven Wing's dark eyes flashed. "Tell

him, Vision Seeker, a Cayuse man who possesses only fifty horses is a poor man, is that not so?"

Vision Seeker nodded. Her felt sorry for Toohool but he had to tell the truth. "Cayuse men with much wealth have more horses than one can count. They cover the hills and plains like buffaloes on the prairie."

"You people are liars and thieves." Toohool strode away in a huff. Raven Wing's derisive laugh made him quicken his pace. With his long neck thrust out, Toohool had the appearance of an ungainly horse about to break into a trot.

"Why do you treat him badly? He is only trying to do the things Mother Earth put him here to do," Vision Seeker scolded. Sometimes he did not understand his sister. She could be so kind and turn about and be so cruel. She should never have encouraged Toohool. She knew mating with Toohool was not possible. Lone Wolf would die before he would welcome Toohool as a son.

"Well, he can do those things with someone else," Raven Wing retorted. "I will not share my blanket with him, not if he was the last man on Mother Earth."

This was another side of Raven Wing that made Vision Seeker uncomfortable. She spoke more like a ruffian than a virgin maiden. At times she was almost unlikable. Perhaps Lone Wolf should think again about banishing Toohool, Vision Seeker thought. It would serve Weasel Face right if Raven Wing became a member of his family. She and her constant companion, Small Goat, would keep him in such a turmoil of frustration he would not have time to annoy Lone Wolf.

Raven Wing also kept asking about the beaver skins. "How many will we have for trade?" was a question she repeated over and over. Vision Seeker's evasive answers never satisfied her. To have time to himself, every morning Vision Seeker got up early to ride beyond the pasture grounds into the rocky highlands.

One day on his return he encountered No Hair On Head sitting beside the campfire warming himself. The old trapper, the hair on his face as tangled and matted as a horse tail full of burrs, stood up and doffed his cap when Raven Wing passed. A black cloud of mosquitoes descended to land on the inviting pink skin.

"Consarn it! There's enuff of these buzzin' critters 'round here ta carry a body away," he complained, clapping his cap back on again.

Lone Wolf, his face all smiles, did everything he could to make Deacon welcome. He waved Vision Seeker in to act as interpreter. "Tell our friend we are glad he is here."

It was easy to read Lone Wolf's mind. He believed the hairless headed one was the key to a successful summer's trade. Lone Wolf would not let No Hair On Head out of sight until a deal was struck on Vision Seeker's share of beaver skins. To ingratiate himself, Lone Wolf told Vision Seeker to ask the trapper to teach him the ways of the Great Spirit Book.

Pleased by the request, Deacon took The Book from a saddlebag and let Lone Wolf hold it. "The book yuh hold in yer paw tells how the Great Spirit made the sun, moon, the stars an' Mother Earth," he said. "It tells how the Great Spirit made man an' then made woman. It tells of the time when rains came ta cover the earth with water. Ta save themselves, all earth's livin' creatures boarded a big canoe. Forty days and forty nights rain fell." Deacon opened and closed his fists four times. He waited for Vision Seeker to translate.

Lone Wolf thoughtfully puffed on his pipe. "Big storm! Much water! Bad trouble!"

Running Turtle, who listened with an open mouth, held his hand out to signal question. "All fishes, horses, deer, buffalo, skunks, squirrels and people in one canoe?" He stared at Deacon, waiting for Vision Seeker to translate, his eyes round with wonderment.

Deacon nodded. "Thet's what The Good Book say." He took the Bible from Lone Wolf and opened it to read: "They, an' every beast after his kind, an' all the cattle after their kind, an' every creepin' thing thet creepeth upon the earth after his kind, and every fowl after his kind, every bird of every sort . . ." Deacon closed The Book and waved the mosquitoes away. "Yuh see, every livin' thing we know today came from the creatures thet were in thet big canoe called Noah's ark. Thet includes us'ens an' these dad-ratted, blood-suckin' skeeters," he said, swatting at the whining swarm that circled above his head.

Running Turtle, unable to comprehend, looked to his father for an explanation. Lone Wolf stared into the fire and pretended not to see. Legends of the hairy faces humbled him. Compared to this Bible story the Nimpau monster who coyote cut into bits, was nothing. The Flatheads were right. Unless his people acquired the Great Spirit Book and learned its secrets they could well lose their leadership among the peoples of the high country.

The next morning the hunting party broke camp. Deacon informed Lone Wolf through Vision Seeker he would guide them south to where Buck Stone and Little Ned waited with the winter's beaver harvest. From Bitterroot Valley the party would travel over the heights of the Bitterroot Range, drop into the headwaters of the Salmon and from there set a course for the rendezvous place on the shores of Bear Lake.

When told of the destination Weasel Face looked grim. "Old bear, your brain is addled. This trail takes us near the land of Blackfeet and Gros Ventre. These people are enemies. Is it wise to make this journey for a bit of trade?"

Lone Wolf grunted scornfully. Was Squint-Eyes going to give him trouble all the way to Bear Lake? If he was, he should put a stop to it now. "My honored neighbor, if the thought of this journey is too much for you, why do you not take the trail home?"

Lone Wolf turned and walked away leaving Weasel Face sputtering to himself. Later, as Lone Wolf thought the matter over, he had to admit, Weasel Face was right. The Blackfeet and Gros Ventre were enemies of the Nimpau. The route went through territory where they frequently traveled. If raiders attacked in force his party did not stand a chance. He voiced his fears to No

Hair On Head. "Pshaw!" Deacon uttered. "Those blisterin' Blackfeet! They'd better keep thar distance. We've got a score ta settle with 'em. Don't yuh worry. This time we'll bloody thar noses good an' proper."

Lone Wolf grunted doubtfully, but the thought of trade and gambling overpowered his anxieties.

Breaking camp created the usual confusion. Children, dogs, horses, and men, milled about while the women cooked the morning meal and dismantled the tipis. Many Horses and the herders went to the pasture fields to round up the horses. The pack animals were caught and brought in. The winter months of inactivity made them frisky and skittish. They pulled at tethers and shied from packs. When loaded, they bucked and crow hopped in circles hoping to shake off the annoying loads. This excited the dogs. They raced back and forth, frantically barking, snapping at the horses' heads and heels. Finally, everything was calm. Women and children leading pack horses, some with awkward travois dragging behind, filed away one by one from the winter camping grounds. The stay in buffalo country was at an end.

Deacon, who spent the night rolled up in a buffalo robe by a smoky fire in the attempt to keep mosquitoes away, was up early. He sat sleepily on his horse watching the column form and prepare to file away. Beside him, mounted on his special hunter, Lone Wolf also waited, impatient to lead his band down the Bitterroot Trail. He was pleased to see Weasel Face and his family packed, mounted and ready to ride. The silly man would go along for fear if he did not people would think him a coward.

Normally, Lone Wolf set an easy pace. On this trek he went up and down the column urging everyone on. Vision Seeker's share of beaver skins, which he was told would burden two of his best pack mares, excited him. For the first time in his life he would possess trade goods unlike he ever had dreamed. Until they were in his care the least delay irked him.

The column pressed on until late evening. It was dark before the women unpacked and had shelters in place. The long day left man and animal exhausted. In the Lone Wolf camp the evening meal was prepared and eaten in silence. While the women were still eating the White Bird leader, Lame Horse, appeared. He spoke in low tones to Lone Wolf. His favorite son, Spotted Elk, had taken ill. The White Bird families would not strike camp until he was better.

Lone Wolf gave his White Bird relative a terse glance. He might have known these White Birds would not have the stomach for a trip that took them near enemy lands but he kept his thoughts to himself. "I understand," he said. "Travel with sickness is bad. We cannot wait. Perhaps it is best you take the trail over the mountains, back to your home lodges. The rest will push on to this place called rendezvous. We have much trading to do."

Vision Seeker, who overheard, also saw through Lame Horse's weak excuse. Spotted Elk was not ill. That very morning the boy and Rabbit Skin Leggings had helped separate the pack mares from the herd. The White Bird leader told the untruth to keep from offending Lone Wolf. The White Bird families were lonesome for their home grounds. Besides, they did not possess much they could trade. The trip to the rendezvous would do them little good.

Vision Seeker did not blame them for leaving. At this time of year the camas meadows in White Bird country were lakes of blue flowers. The sky was clear and the air fresh. The stars were so near and bright they glowed like giant fireflies. The colorful fields attracted a myriad of Mother Earth's flying creatures. Families were awakened in the morning by the happy song of meadowlarks. Blackbirds and robins swarmed over the land to search for grasshoppers, worms and bugs. Through the midday hours bees buzzed around flowers busily sucking pollen. Butterflies, with black and gold wings, flitted hither and yon. Early evenings, when it was warm and quiet, swallows came to dip and dive after gnats, mosquitoes and fireflies.

Vision Seeker sighed. In a few months bands from all

over the Nimpau homeland would gather for the annual harvest of camas bulbs. For most of the people it was the high point of the year. While women and children dug camas bulbs, the men hunted, raced horses, played games and gambled to their hearts content. Perhaps that dark-eyed beauty from Wallowa would be there.

Vision Seeker groaned. It was not too late. They could join the White Birds and return home, but Lone Wolf would never consider it. His heart was set on trade. "It is all my fault," Vision Seeker thought. If he hadn't found beaver grounds for the hairy faces Lone Wolf also would be taking the trail over Lolo Pass and down the Kooskooskie. Besides longing to see the familiar landscapes of his homeland, the vision of a member of Lone Wolf's hunting party stretched out on a smoke-filled battlefield gnawed at Vision Seeker's mind like an incessant worm. The Season of Tall Grass was here. If the signs were true, any day the terrible event could occur, probably when the Lone Wolf party passed through the lands of the Blackfeet and Gros Ventre. Like the White Bird leader, Vision Seeker had no desire to follow the trail to the hairy faced ones' rendezvous.

The next morning Lone Wolf's band broke camp. Without the White Bird families, the smaller column made travel easier and faster. Near midday they were beyond where the river cut through Hellgate Pass. The grass was green and lush. A flock of geese rose up to continue wending their way north. A brown bear clumped along the river bank, its sharp eyes searching for fish in the swift running stream. When the sun began to slip behind the jagged Bitterroot mountains, the travelers came upon the Flatheads with whom they had traded horses.

Reluctantly, Lone Wolf called a halt. He and the Flathead leader hunkered down to talk and smoke. Upon learning Lone Wolf's band was heading for the trappers' rendezvous, the leader of the Flatheads asked if his people might travel along. Lone Wolf readily agreed. The Flatheads were friends and allies who fought with the Nimpau against the dreaded Gros Ventre and

Blackfeet. The trail ahead was dangerous. It was good to have the added strength the Flatheads provided.

In the upper reaches of Bitterroot Valley, where the timber thinned and the river widened, Buck Stone and Little Ned waited. The carcasses of three freshly slaughtered deer hung from the limbs of a dead snag. The trappers had dug a huge pit and erected a hefty spit. A fire was going.

When Lone Wolf's party from Sun River came into view Buck Stone and Little Ned rode up to greet them. Buck Stone was the first to speak. He waved a hand at the deer carcasses and fire pit. "Welcome! Welcome! You are just in time to join us in the evening meal."

A delighted murmur ran down the column. After the long day's travel the unexpected invitation to partake of a feast was most gratifying. Lone Wolf proudly presented the big trappers to the Flathead leader. The reception greatly pleased him. This was the kind of hospitality good friends extended to good friends but his thoughts were also on Vision Seeker's share of the beaver harvest. Where were his pelts? He wanted to know of their existence, to count them, to plan how much they would bring in trade.

Lone Wolf did not have long to wait. Stacked under the trees, a short distance from the fire pit, were bundles of beaver skins. The trappers had compressed the cured pelts into neat packs, securely tying them with rawhide thongs. Six bundles were set to one side, Vision Seeker's share. The sight so delighted Lone Wolf, he smiled. In the background Raven Wing clapped her hands.

"Hoh-hah!" Lone Wolf uttered. "We shall smoke and feast. First we must thank The Creator for all the good things He has provided."

As the pipe made its rounds Vision Seeker thought back to the day when Lone Wolf first met and smoked with the hairy faces. The vision he had seen came vividly to mind. He took a puff and watched the smoke waft up to fade away in the twilight. It told him nothing. He took a second puff and passed the pipe to his left. Perhaps the signs had been false. He fervently hoped so. It would be a calamity to have death destroy the peace and tranquillity that finally had descended upon the Lone Wolf lodge.

XVIII

*Everything as it moves, now and then, here and there,
makes stops. The bird as it flies stops in one place
to make its nest, and in another to rest . . .*

Ohiyesa, Santee Sioux

The column moved southward. Over Lost Trail the travelers struggled, the going so rocky and steep the horses and mules were in danger of slipping into the cascading creek that dashed and bounced around and over boulders in the canyon below. On either side of the trail deep snow still lay in shady hollows. Through rugged rocky outcroppings of the upper Salmon River the column descended to encounter swarms of mosquitoes that attacked man and animal. The insects especially liked to feast on the sweet blood of the hairy faces. Deacon was in a constant battle with them. His high-pitched voice could be heard from one end of the column to the other as he vainly attempted to fight them off, often blaspheming, taking the Lord's name in vain.

"Listen to that man! It is a wonder the god he calls Jesus does not strike him dead," Running Turtle exclaimed. "He carries on like a spoiled child. How shameful, making a fuss over Mother Earth's smallest of creatures."

The travelers came to a spring that fed into the turbulent Salmon River. A perfect campsite surrounded by trees and plentiful pasture greeted them. A band of campers already occupied one edge of the inviting meadow. They popped out of makeshift shelters to watch them file in. They were members of the people called Snakes. For many years the Nimpau and Snakes had been deadly enemies. Only in recent years did they get together to smoke the pipe. They were still wary of each other. Old enmities were hard to forget. Lone Wolf and his men rode up with hands on their weapons. The new arrivals had nothing to fear. The leader of the Snake camp walked toward Lone Wolf, his hand held up in the gesture of peace.

"Ah-hoh! The people they call cut noses and those with flat heads. Welcome! Welcome! You honor us by your presence." The Snake leader, a spare man, wore an elaborate bone neckpiece and beaded bands around the biceps of each arm. He was all smiles. He waved his hand toward a shady knoll, inviting the men to sit with him and join in the smoke of friendship.

Women came to help the travelers unload the pack mares and set up camp. A bevy of barefooted, sparsely clothed youngsters, at first shy, began to run back and forth trying to lure the newcomers to join them in play. The dogs mingled, walking stiff-legged to sniff and growl, then retreated to hide behind their masters' legs.

The Snake campers had fished the river. Much of their catch had been sliced into strips and lay in racks to dry in the sun. The smell of offal was overpowering. Sticky flies drawn by blood and guts, were everywhere. They clung to the people's skin like leeches. They were in eyes, noses, mouths and hair. Deacon violently waved his hands and swore. He did not want to stop and smoke. He wanted to continue down the trail, away from the flies and smothering stink of fish. Buck and Little Ned would not hear of it. They might not find another place to camp for miles.

"Light up that black odoriferous pipe of yours," Buck Stone suggested. "The fumes it puts out would drive away a pack of skunks."

"These pesky ding-danged flies don't know the difference 'tween smoke an' fresh air. Nuthin' short of a bee keeper's rig'll keep the buggers away. Dad blast it. I wish yuh fellas had my tender skin. Yuh'd be leavin' here quicker'n lice hoppin' off a scalded dog," Deacon grumbled.

That night there was a fish feed that went on until dawn. There was little attempt to sleep. It was a festive occasion with much joviality, yet in the back of the minds of both the Nimpau and Snake people there was the niggling thought they camped with former enemies. They did not completely trust one another and were afraid to lower their guard. The people visited, ate, visited and ate some more. In spite of all Lone Wolf's efforts to get an early start, it was midday before the column left the Salmon River camp. As they prepared to mount to ride away, the leader of the Snake took Lone Wolf and the Flathead leader aside.

"Take care. Blackfeet are nearby," he warned. "They say they will kill every stranger who enters their land. Guard your four-leggeds well. These people are born thieves. They like to sneak up and steal a horse or two before anyone suspects they are around."

After the column wended its way down the trail, the Flathead leader, who had more men than Lone Wolf, ordered riders ahead to scout for hostiles. Lone Wolf instructed Many Horses to take charge of the rear guard. The trappers, trailed by the long-eared pack mules, rode on either side of the column with their long-barreled rifles ready to fire.

In spite of Lone Wolf's scowls and Quiet Woman's scolding, Raven Wing rode with the outriders, usually by the side of Little Ned. For some reason she was drawn to this man who appeared so fierce with his black beard. They would ride for miles beside each other. Only occasionally did they pass a word. Yet she knew he enjoyed her presence. He seemed to accept her as a companion. One evening near dusk he motioned toward a flowering bush that the sun's late rays had turned to gold. The next morning they passed a spectacular formation of rocks. He waved a big hand toward it and shook his head in wonder. His special appreciation of Mother Earth's beauty surprised her and pleased her that he should want to share these joys.

Once after such a moment she turned back to catch him watching her. He quickly glanced away. He remained silent, as taciturn as before but there had been a deeper tint to those blue eyes than ever before. Was he thinking of her or did she remind him of someone else, perhaps a woman he had left behind who he sorely missed. She reined her horse away to gallop back to join her mother who trudged beside a pack mare.

Sometimes, to tease her father, she chose Toohool as a

riding companion. Lone Wolf had yet to bargain with Black Hair for the elk tooth dress. She did not want him to forget his promise. Toohool always received her attentions with such devotion, she was ashamed. She was reminded of a friendless dog wriggling all over upon receiving a kindly pat on the head.

Raven Wing was not at all discreet. Her boldness had tongues wagging up and down the column. Quiet Woman who overheard the whisperings, was furious. "Why do you keep doing these things? People are talking. They say the Lone Wolf maiden is no better than a camp woman who flits from one lodge to another.

"First it is Toohool, now it is Black Hair. Yesterday you were back with Toohool. What is the matter with you, foolish child? You know you cannot mate with either one. Your behavior spoils your chances with all men. No man wants a bold woman in his lodge. If you want a mate, act like a Nimpau woman should. Walk alongside the pack animals with the children and women."

"Daughter has a mind of her own," Grandmother said. "She will do what she wants to do until she mates. Then her man will teach her to behave."

"Wagh!" Raven Wing exclaimed. Why did no one try to understand how it felt to be an only daughter? Her father wanted her gone from the lodge. Her mother found fault with everything she did and Grandmother offered her useless sayings. "Black Hair does not mind when I ride with him," Raven Wing retorted. "He takes pleasure when I am with him. If I wanted, he would take me for a mate. Perhaps that is what I should do. Father would be happy and you would not have to scold."

Grandmother uttered a disapproving cluck. Quiet Woman vehemently turned on her daughter. "Foolish girl, you have not the sense of a goose. To want a hairy face for a mate is not good, not good at all. Hairy faces do not make good mates. They quickly tire of their women. They make them big with child, then leave the lodge. The women are left to look out for themselves. Is that what you want?"

Raven Wing tightened the last strap of the pack which contained her meager possessions and strode off without looking back. She made straight for her pony, mounted and rode to where the big man, Little Ned, was saddling his mount. He finished tightening the cinch without looking up. Raven Wing turned away in search of Toohool. Quiet Woman was right. She could not imagine living in the same lodge with this man who looked like an overgrown bear.

"Ah me! Ah me! Daughter is like the yearling colt," Grandmother murmured as she watched her granddaughter go from one man to the other. "She has not yet had the feel of bit and saddle."

\#

The Salmon, because of its turbulence, was known as the River of No Return. It plunged and raced through country more rugged than Vision Seeker had ever seen. It was not an inviting land. It was an ominous country. The terrain did everything possible to make the passage difficult. Rocky cliffs, dark evergreen forests, spectacular gorges, narrow canyons and a trail barely wide enough at times to accommodate a single horse, slowed the column and kept the travelers on edge. The crest of each hill and every turn in the trail were ideal for ambush. In advance of the column scouts rode with rifles cocked and hearts in their mouths. A scurrying marmot or fleeing fox could set off wild fusillades of bullets and arrows.

Many Horses, who brought up the rear, equally was nervous. He remembered well the Snake leader's warning words. Blackfeet would consider it a great coup to sneak up, put an arrow in the back of a rider and run off an animal or two. Along with Running Turtle, Toohool and two Flathead herders, Many Horses kept the loose stock close to the column. Each night he circled the herd making certain the animals were tightly corralled and carefully guarded. Only when Buck Stone led the party out of the rugged defiles of the upper Salmon and onto the sagebrush flatlands, did Many Horses begin to breathe easy. The danger of raiders lessened.

The march now took them across terrain where opportunities for ambush were limited. In this stretch of trail the greatest enemies were heat, dust and scarcity of water. For the first time in many days, Many Horses slept through the night. Early in the morning, while he was still befogged with sleep, the frantic shout of a herder jerked him awake.

"Raiders! The herd has been raided!" Toohool galloped into camp wildly waving his arms. "Get up! Mount up! Blackfeet are after the herd."

Still pulling on his leggings, Weasel Face stumbled out of his shelter, his close-spaced eyes darting back and forth like trapped mice. "Son! Calm yourself! Talk sense! Tell us exactly what happened."

Toohool jerked on the bridle reins making his excited mount froth at the mouth. "There is no time for talk. Get the fire stick. The raiders are getting away with the herd. We must head them off."

Little Ned and Buck Stone ran up fully dressed, armed and leading their mounts. "What's this all about?" Buck asked. "Blackfeet, how many? Which way did they go? We don't want to ride into an ambush."

Toohool put out one hand, opened and closed it twice. "They come from the east, maybe north." He motioned the directions with his lips and chin.

"Ten or so, you say?" Buck queried. "That isn't so bad. We'd best get after them. We're already short of stock. We can't afford to lose a single horse or mule."

After several sleepless nights followed by tiring days on the trail, Lone Wolf had pulled his sleeping robe over his head and slept the sleep of the dead. Quiet Woman had to shake him to get him to come alive. He groped his way out of the sleeping robe to see the riders gallop away from camp. "What has happened? Tell me, woman, where are these people going? Is there trouble?" he frantically asked his mate.

Armed, but most of them still half dressed, the horsemen swept out of sight over the nearest hill and into the pasture grounds, the Nimpau and Flatheads waving their weapons, shouting war whoops and shrieking threats. The dreaded Blackfeet had to be taught a lesson. On the far side of the hill Buck Stone held up his hand. The riders stopped and fell silent. The scene was peaceful. A lone herder astride a roan, watched a pocket of horses graze in an open space. When he spotted the riders he came toward them at a lope. He shouted and waved a hand in the direction the raiders had taken.

Many Horses quickly studied the grazing animals. His heart sank. A fourth of the herd was missing. He glanced up at the sun. It was already three fingers high. If they were to recapture the horses they had to act quickly. He motioned to Vision Seeker, the most sure tracker in the hunting party. "Scout for signs." He did not trust Toohool's report. The young man was a scatterbrain, always jumping to hasty conclusions. He was just as likely to report three enemy where there was only one or none.

A group of youths whipped their mounts into a gallop. They raced over the nearby hill and into the next hollow, raising great clouds of dust. Vision Seeker shouted in a futile attempt to stop them. Any tracks the raiders left would be lost. The young riders returned to report there was no sign of the raiders or missing horses. It was as if they had melted into the sagebrush covered terrain.

Weasel Face rode close to his son. "What happened? What did you see? From where did the raiders come? How many animals did they take? Speak! How can we catch them if you do not tell us what you know?"

Toohool pulled on his whiskerless chin and glanced uneasily around the circle of riders. "I do not know exactly what happened. I did not see the raiders. I did not see the horses go. Before we knew it the horses were missing, disappeared right before our eyes." The second herder, a Flathead man, agreed.

"That was the way it was. The horses were here and then,

whoosh! They were gone."

Weasel Face ignored the Flathead and turned on his son. "Do not tell lies. Speak with a straight tongue. You fell asleep." Weasel Face pulled Toohool from the saddle. Many Horses stepped forward. He feared the angry father would strike his son in front of everyone. It was an act that neither he nor his son would ever live down. He knew what had happened. The raiders had slipped in and led one horse away at a time. Under the cover of darkness they could do this almost in front of the herders' eyes. When the raiders had a dozen or two, they drove the stolen animals away before the sleepy guards discovered anything was wrong.

Weasel Face lowered the threatening arm. "Did you track them? Did you find which way they went? Perhaps there were no raiders. Perhaps the horses wandered off by themselves. To keep from getting into trouble you blame the Blackfeet."

"They did not wander off. The raiders left their mark." Toohool pulled himself free of his father's grasp. From inside his shirt he took a piece of bark. On it was drawn the outline of a tomahawk.

The sight of it fueled Weasel Face's anger. "Stupid one! You were fast asleep! These people could have cut your throat. Instead, they left their mark to tell you how near you came to death. This is the Blackfeet way of counting coups. They sneak up and touch the enemy with a coup stick, then leave their mark to let you know how near you came to losing your scalp. This Blackfeet man has challenged you to come after him. Are you brave enough to answer the challenge?"

Toohool turned away from Weasel Face and swung up on his mount. "Give me the fire stick. I will face these raiders and bring the stolen animals back."

"Foolish lad!" Weasel Face said scornfully. "These people will swallow one rider like a fly trapped in a spider web. We all will go after these horse thieves." He glanced around the circle of men for support.

"Hold on a minute!" Buck Stone held up his hand. "Let's not go off half-cocked. This is just the type of thing the Blackfeet want. These people are not stupid. Yes, one of them may be having his little fun by trying to draw this young man into a fight. There also is the chance this is a ruse to steal our gear and pelts. While we are chasing after the people who stole our horses a war party may slip around and take everything we have: women, children, goods -- everything we possess." A murmur ran through the crowd. Buck glanced at Vision Seeker. "Do these people understand what I say?"

"Your Sahaptin is good. The people are astonished you speak so well."

Belatedly, Lone Wolf rode up, sliding to a stop in a cloud of dust. He was furious with himself. He, the leader of the band, had been caught fast asleep. Enemy raiders had taken him completely off guard. The hated Weasel Face made the embarrassment worse by taking charge. Lone Wolf started to speak but the Flathead leader held up his hand for quiet. Yellow Hair was addressing the crowd. He caught the last words of Buck Stone's warning. "These raiders may circle back and take everything we have, women, children, goods . . ."

The thought of losing the recently acquired beaver pelts spurred Lone Wolf into action. Horses he could afford to lose. To lose the wealth of precious trading goods was another matter.

"Our friend with yellow hair speaks straight," Lone Wolf said. He stepped into the center of the group. "We have lost horses. That is bad. To lose everything in camp is worse. Some of our men must stay. The rest will ride after the raiders and bring back the horses."

"Time is wasting," Weasel Face loudly reminded the group. The carelessness of his son's behavior brought him great shame, a shame that could not be removed until the enemy was faced and the stolen horses recaptured. "While we talk these thieving Blackfeet are getting away."

The Flathead leader also insisted the rescue party should

leave at once. He could not afford to lose a single horse. Lone Wolf hesitated. He looked to Buck Stone and Little Ned for support. Buck raised his hand for silence.

"Lone Wolf is right and so is Weasel Face and so is our Flathead friend," Buck said diplomatically. "We must guard the camp and we must rescue the horses. Let us organize ourselves so we can do both."

XIX

Even if the heavens were to fall on me,
I want to do what is right . . .

Geronimo, Chiricahua Apache

Everyone wanted to take revenge on the crafty Blackfeet. The boldness of the raid on the herd was an insult that could not be ignored. In spite of Buck Stone's warning of Blackfeet trickery hardly a single Flathead or Nimpau wanted to stay behind. The clamor to be chosen to go after the raiders was so great Lone Wolf could not make himself heard. Suddenly a rifle shot rang out. The stunned crowd turned on the shooter, only to face the stern, rugged features of Two Kill.

"Are you warriors or cackling geese?" Two Kill demanded in the same tone of voice he would reprimand an errant hunter. "The hot blood that pounds through your hearts makes for bad thinking. Stop and ask yourselves, why do these Blackfeet people send a small band to raid for horses? Is it because these are young bucks out to make fun? If that is so why send the whole camp after them? It will make us look foolish; many after few. If these raiders come from a large camp why do not more riders come and take all our horses?

"Remember, these people are cunning like Brother Coyote. They make a small kill which they use to lure large prey into their trap. Perhaps the Blackfeet want us to believe this band of raiders are hot-headed youth making coups on their own. When we go chasing after them the main body of warriors will attack our camp. If we fall for this trick we are worse than the greedy blue jay that darts after every crumb, paying no attention to the danger that lurks in the shadows. We are not only acting silly, we are acting stupid. I do not wish to be stupid. I will remain and guard my family and possessions. If enough of us stay the Blackfeet will see we are strong; that we are not fooled. They will not attack."

The men glanced at each other sheepishly. Two Kill's scolding made them feel like unruly children. He was right and they knew it. These Blackfeet were known for their tricks. They would do anything to make coups. Yellow Hair had tried to tell them it could be a trap but it took the great hunter Two Kill to get their attention. What silly fools they were, thinking of making coups instead of protecting their families and possessions -- everything most dear to them.

The brief period of self-analysis was all the opportunity Lone Wolf needed. "We move quickly," he said. "A small war party of fast riders is best. It is only right Toohool should go. He must have the chance to redeem himself. Who else? A tracker. There is no better tracker than my son, Vision Seeker. He can pick up the trail of an ant on bare rock. Many Horses! He knows stock so well they come when he calls. Our Flathead friends cannot be left out. Some of these young riders anxious to count coups should go. Since the hairy faced ones did not lose any animals and have many beaver pelts at risk, it only is right they stay to guard the camp."

Weasel Face was appeased. His son would have the opportunity to uphold the honor of his lodge. He did not even argue when Many Horses was chosen to lead the warriors. Besides Toohool, Many Horses and Vision Seeker, Left Hand, Red Bull and a half dozen Flatheads made up the party. After properly equipping themselves and saying hurried good-byes to loved ones, the riders galloped away from camp. Toohool, carrying his father's heavy fire stick, rode in front alongside Many Horses.

Raven Wing, with her friend Small Goat, watched the warriors leave. Raven Wing had said good-bye to Vision Seeker and Many Horses at the lodge after Lone Wolf had tapped each son with his coup stick and said a brief prayer for their success and safe return. Raven Wing also had wanted to seek out Toohool to wish him well. The slender youth, carrying the long fire stick that was almost as tall as himself, looked so vulnerable. She had the greatest urge to call to him and tell him not to go. He was not a warrior, just an overgrown boy who yet had to gain the experience needed to go into battle.

At the pasture grounds the horsemen stopped briefly to count what was left of the herd. The losses were not great but the sight still made Many Horses sick -- three of his favorites were missing. The herd that left Lapwai the previous fall had faded away like the winter snow. Coming up the Kooskooskie trail three animals went to their deaths. The snow storm took a far greater toll. Now Blackfeet raiders had picked the best of the animals that had survived the winter. It would take years of breeding and training to bring the herd back to the state it was before leaving Lapwai. How he wished he had added his voice to that of Vision Seeker and resisted Lone Wolf's decision to make the disastrous trip to buffalo country.

Vision Seeker did not bother to count the horses. He would know by their tracks how many had been lured away. The trail the raiders left was not hard to find. He counted the tracks of a dozen loose horses and about ten sets of deeper hoof prints made by horses that carried riders. The tracks led east toward a range of low lying hills almost hidden in the morning haze. If the raiders made a stand it would be there, Vision Seeker decided. The trail was so easy to follow the horsemen rode at a gallop. Then, in the rocky outcroppings at the base of the hills, the tracks faded away. Vision Seeker dismounted. His searching eyes picked up clues here and there -- a broken branch, a bent tuft of grass, a disturbed anthill . . . He stopped. There was something wrong. Someone had brushed the ground clean. He held up his hand. "Two or three of us should scout ahead, the rest remain behind. The enemy may be hiding behind this ridge."

Many Horses handed the reins of his mount to Red Bull. "From here we walk."

Toohool came forward, struggling with his father's heavy rifle. "I am at fault. It is right I face the enemy first."

Many Horses studied the determined youth and agreed.

He did not have much faith in the young man but he had the right to be out front. Perhaps this son of Weasel Face would surprise him.

In single file the three scouts crawled up the long slope, using low growing brush as cover. They stopped frequently to rest and listen. Any moment the enemy could shower them with arrows or send down an avalanche of rocks and dirt. Step by step, they labored to the crest. At the summit Many Horses, who was in the lead, held up his hand. A single horse grazed in an open space; otherwise there was no sign of life.

Vision Seeker and Toohool crawled alongside Many Horses. Vision Seeker shaded his eyes against the brilliant rays of the sun. In the draw below the pony lifted its head. It had a strange white mark on its muzzle. It looked their way and nickered.

"That's my pony!" Toohool exclaimed. "I named him Badger because of the mark on his nose." He started to crawl forward but Many Horses pulled him back.

"We cannot leave him there. It is hot in the sun. I must go after him," Toohool protested.

"Use your head, man. That is exactly what the Blackfeet want you to do. This is another one of their clever tricks. The pony is hobbled. The Blackfeet left it there as bait. The enemy is waiting in that thicket. Go for the horse and they will shoot. In that open space you do not stand a chance."

The pony pointed its ears toward the crest and nickered again, as if pleading for help. Toohool groaned. "Badger knows I am here. He wants me to come. I have cared for him since he was foaled. I will run to him as fast as I can. It is not far. I can be back before the enemy knows we are here."

"No! You will get yourself and your pony killed," Many Horses said harshly. He knew exactly how Toohool felt. He probably loved the pony better than he did any member of his family. He would not rest easy until he had it back. "Patience! Patience!" Many Horses said more kindly. "It will not hurt your pony to stand in the sun. Wait until dark. We will go for your pony then."

"What about the other horses? Perhaps the raiders left Badger there to hold us up while they drive the rest of them away; that is the trick they play."

"You speak wisely." The same thought had occurred to Many Horses. Was he over cautious? Should he order the men to charge across the open space and into the stand of trees? He would look very foolish if he waited all day on the hot hillside only to find the ambush he envisioned was a fake.

Yet, he could not take the chance. If the enemy was present as he thought, a charge across the open space was certain to cost the lives of several men. The last thing he wanted was to return home with dead bodies. Perhaps they could circle around and come up behind the enemy. He studied the lay of the land. The terrain was hills and valleys. The unseen Blackfeet held the only defensible location. After dark was the time to attack. Under the cover of darkness they could storm through the Blackfeet camp and run off the horses without danger to a single man. That was the best strategy. Many Horses settled back to wait.

Toohool fidgeted. He laid his father's fire stick to one side. He took out his knife and whetted the blade. He removed his powder horn and bullet pouch. He sat and stared at the hobbled pony. Rivulets of perspiration streamed down his face. "I can run across that open space before anyone can get off a shot," Toohool pleaded again. "In a flash of an eyelash, I can cut the hobbles and ride back. If I lose Badger for not trying, Weasel Face will never let me live it down."

"Your father will never forget it if you get killed either. Ah! What's that, brother?" Many Horses motioned toward the far side of the draw. "Did you see movement in the trees?"

Vision Seeker carefully studied the stand of trees. The ambush site was perfect. Not a spear of grass or tree limb appeared to be disturbed. Yet, the enemy's hiding place was some distance away. Would their fire be accurate? He almost agreed with Toohool, a fast runner could cut the pony's hobbles and ride out of danger before the ambushers would be able to shoot him down. He was tempted to try it himself.

They sat for another hour, rivulets of perspiration pouring off their bodies. Sand flies and gnats tormented them. Toohool continued to fidget, scratch and squirm. Suddenly he jumped to his feet. Before the brothers could stop him, Toohool made a long leap down the slope. "Stop! Stop!" Many Horses cried out. "Are you trying to get yourself killed?"

Toohool did not hesitate. He slid the last few yards down the hill and ran across the grassy open space as fast as his feet would carry him. For a moment it appeared Toohool would make it to his pony. The brothers silently cheered. Then, when Toohool was within a few feet of the pony, a barrage of arrows whistled out of the thicket. For a step or two Toohool staggered like a drunken man, then fell face forward. From the trees came an earsplitting war whoop. A painted warrior brandishing a toma- hawk, ran toward the fallen man intent on completing his coup.

"Quick! Toohool's fire stick! Shoot! Shoot! Do not let him reach Toohool," Many Horses cried.

Vision Seeker grabbed the heavy iron stick. In one quick motion, he cocked it, took aim and fired. The recoil jolted him. The explosion made his ears ring. The warrior tumbled over and over and finally came to rest, partially hidden in the grass. Vi- sion Seeker stared numbly at the brown mound that minutes be- fore had been a living, breathing creature like himself. With one tug of the finger he had taken his life.

"Good!" Many Horses exclaimed. "Another great coup, a mountain cat, now a Blackfeet warrior."

Vision Seeker did not answer. He was afraid he would be sick. How easy it was to kill. Point the iron stick and pull the trigger and one of Mother Earth's creatures was gone forever. He tossed the weapon aside and would have walked down the slope in view of the enemy if Many Horses had not pulled him back.

"What is it brother? You act like you did a terrible thing. Be proud. The Blackfeet raider is done for. He will never steal again." The rifle shot brought the men who waited at the base of the hill scrambling forward. When they arrived at the crest Many Horses signaled caution. He pointed to the clump of trees.

"The enemy is there. Hard to say how many. Toohool went after his pony. We tried to stop him. His body lies in the grass alongside a Blackfeet warrior Vision Seeker shot. We cannot do anything until dark. Then we will go after Toohool's horse and bring his body back."

"Perhaps Toohool lives," exclaimed a youthful Flathead. "I will get him, carry him to the hill."

"No! You will get killed. Toohool is dead. The enemy shot many arrows. Toohool could not escape. He fell. . . ." Many Horses glanced at the sun. It was still two hands above the horizon. It was going to be a long, long wait.

The party of scouts watched the sun inch across the sky. A flock of buzzards began to silently and ghoulishly circle over the meadow where the bodies lay. Lower and lower they swooped until one dipped its wings and skidded to a stop in the tall grass. Wings half raised, it gave a couple of hops in the direction of the bodies. Many Horses armed his bow and loosed an arrow. The arrow dropped harmlessly beyond the curved beaked carrion eater.

Before he could rearm the bow, a second arrow came out of nowhere. The buzzard's wings flapped. The bird squawked and attempted to take off. Instead, it tumbled over dead. The watchers murmured. Where did that arrow come from? They studied the thicket of trees. Not a leaf or stem of grass stirred. An uneasy feeling fell over the watchers. One of the hidden enemy was a deadly marksman.

The afternoon dragged on slowly. The sun beamed down mercilessly, baking the watchers. Nerves grew taut. Eyes burned from staring at the woods where the enemy lay hidden. The watchers' heads ached. Their tongues grew thick for the want of water. How many enemy warriors did they face -- three or thirty? They discussed the numbers among themselves. They did not think it too many but even a handful made a daylight attack impossible.

Many Horses suffered more than physical torture. He was

the leader. He was responsible for a dozen lives. He already had
lost one. Weasel Face would be grief-stricken. Every member of
a family was precious, but none as precious as a first son.

Many Horses berated himself. He should have stopped
Toohool, kept him out of harms way. He groaned. What more
could he have done? The boy was uncontrollable. He would not
listen to reason. He could not wait to rescue his pony. Now
Toohool would never see his precious pony, Badger, again, not
until they met in the next world.

Many Horses tried to shake the torturous thought from
his mind. Suddenly his ears picked up a sound. It came from the
grassy hollow. Vision Seeker heard it too. Was it an enemy trick?
Were the Blackfeet trying to get them to expose themselves? The
circle of buzzards flew lower. Another moan and a pitiful cry.
Toohool's pony lifted its ears and uttered a plaintiff whinny. Many
Horses' blood ran cold.

"It is Toohool! He is alive!" the leader of the Flatheads
exclaimed.

"It could be the Blackfeet," Many Horses said. He tried
to close his ears to the heart-wrenching cries.

"It is not the Blackfeet. It is Toohool," the Flathead insisted.

The sounds of pain were more than the watchers could
stand. No one should suffer like that. One after another the men
beseeched Many Horses to let them go to the rescue of their
wounded companion. Many Horses remained steadfast. It was
hard enough to report one death without adding more.

Vision Seeker agreed with Many Horses' decision but the
awful cries seared his brain. If it was Toohool, he felt beholden
to rescue him. He was a neighbor, a fellow villager. If it was the
enemy, he felt responsible for wounding him. As the afternoon
slowly passed the pitiful cries became weaker and weaker until
they finally died away and stopped altogether.

When dusk began to fall, Vision Seeker could wait no
longer. "Keep watch on the enemy," he instructed the men. "I

will go for Toohool." He slid down the hillside and crawled through the grass. If the enemy saw him they remained quiet. He came to Toohool's body. In the fading light he could see two arrows sticking out of the stricken man's back. He crawled up to feel for a heart beat. He was alive! It was Toohool they heard crying. How could he get him to safety? He could not do it by himself. He started to crawl back for help only to find Many Horses coming toward him.

"Toohool is alive."

"Sh-sh!" Many Horses cautioned. The brothers fell silent. From the direction of the grove came rustling sounds. Many Horses and Vision Seeker froze. The enemy was crawling toward them! Vision Seeker reached for his skinning knife. Many Horses pulled out his hatchet. Their hearts pounded so loudly they were certain the crawlers could hear them. The noises stopped and then resumed. The brothers could hear a mumble of voices. The sounds came nearer and nearer. Gripping his knife, Vision Seeker rose to his knees. He would take the first warrior, Many Horses the second. If there were more . . .! Suddenly the sounds began to recede, finally they faded until there was silence.

Many Horses put his hatchet away. "They came and took the body of their fallen brother. Let us do the same."

They crawled to where Toohool's still form lay. The two arrows sticking out of his back made them shudder. Should they remove them or leave them? It was a ghastly business, but Many Horses decided to remove them. He seized the slender shaft and gave it a tug. As he feared, the shaft broke. Toohool uttered a piercing moan that struck at the two men's hearts. Many Horses made no attempt to extract the second arrow. It could wait until they had better light.

"It is best to get him back where we can see what we are doing," Vision Seeker said. "Fetch the horse. The darkness will protect us."

Many Horses cut the rawhide hobbles that held Badger's legs and led the animal forward. The brothers lifted the inert body of Toohool. Although not heavy, the unconscious form was difficult to handle. The brothers carefully folded Toohool's long form face down over the pony's back. At the top of the hill Toohool moaned again. Vision Seeker, who was astride the horse holding the body in place, leaned forward to hear if Toohool would speak. The wounded youth remained still. Vision Seeker felt for his heart beat. There was none. Toohool's spirit had passed to the next world.

THE LONE WOLF CLAN

XX

There is no death, only a change of worlds.

Seattle, Duwamish

The death of Toohool left the party of horsemen stunned. Except for the Flathead leader, they were men with little exposure to battlefield tragedy. They had looked on the effort to recover the stolen livestock as a lark, an exciting adventure that would bring coups they could brag about for years to come. Toohool's agonizing moans and cries seared their minds.

They had not thought once of getting wounded, and to have wounds cause so much suffering was beyond their ken. Death on the battlefield was supposed to be glorious, quick and decisive, not end in slow excruciating torture. The men avoided each other's eyes. Their thoughts were not ones of courage and valor, but thoughts they could not share with anyone, not even their best friends. The glorious adventure they envisioned had turned into a frightening nightmare. They had stood by and listened to their companion's cries for help and did nothing. If they had shown Toohool's courage they would have stormed through the wooded thicket, slain the enemy and recovered the stolen horses and saved their companion from death.

That is what they should have done. Instead, like frightened children, they cowered behind the hill safely hidden from the enemy. The shame of it was almost more than they could bear. Their leader was to blame. He had held them back. They had pleaded to rescue Toohool but Many Horses would not let them. They began to grumble and talk angrily among themselves. Sensing the dangerous mood, Vision Seeker came near to his brother.

"Things are not well with the men. They believe we are to blame for Toohool's death. We must do something quickly. These people will soon be more dangerous than the enemy."

Many Horses felt as distressed as anyone. Had he been

too cautious? Should he have ordered an attack on the woods? His head told him he did right; his heart said he did wrong. "Ah!" he agonized. There was no glory in being a leader when things went amiss. But right or wrong, he had to face the consequences. Somehow he had to calm the men. He raised his hand for silence.

"Hear my words." His voice was clear and steady. "What has happened cannot be undone. The Great Mystery has taken our companion. We cannot bring him back to this world, nor should we if we could. Instead, we should sing his praises. He showed a courage few warriors possess. He went to save a four-legged and fell to his death. Not many love our four-legged companions as he did. Now it is time to take him home. Two of his friends should do the task carrying him on Badger, Toohool's own pony. The rest will stay. At first light we attack the Blackfeet. Refresh the animals and prepare yourselves. We ride at dawn."

Many Horses paused. What else could he say? The men had fallen quiet but it was too dark to see their expressions. He searched for the Flathead leader. He stood to one side, surrounded by his men. "Is the plan wise?" Many Horses asked. The Flathead did not answer but moved deeper into the shadows. Many Horses inwardly groaned. This was the worst thing that could happen to a leader. The men had lost their trust in him. A Flathead rider, embarrassed by his leader's silence, finally spoke in his place.

"The plan is good. The Blackfeet will sleep. We will surprise them -- make many coups -- take back the four-leggeds. Our herd will be whole again."

Many Horses breathed a sigh of relief. The men might not like what he did but would still follow his lead. Even so, the night was an uneasy one. The two riders who left with the body of Toohool, did so in an atmosphere charged with emotion. In the distant hills a band of coyotes began their mournful chorus. A night bird uttered a sharp cry. The regular thump of the departing horses' hooves made the eerie sound of death drums. Only when the sight and sound of the departing funeral party disappeared did the men who remained prepare themselves for the conflict on the morrow. They did not roll up in their robes and rest. They were too perturbed to sleep. Instead, they worked on their weapons and talked among themselves.

At the first light of dawn they mounted up. They spaced themselves a lance length apart and then, in a line abreast of each other, advanced across the meadow. In spite of their attempts to be quiet, a horse snuffled, another stumbled. The creak of leather and plop of horses' hooves was thunderous. For certain the enemy was awake and waiting for them. When they were within arrow range of the trees, they charged. Caution was thrown to the winds. Whooping and shouting threats, the horsemen galloped into the thicket and out the other side. No enemy rose to challenge them. They turned and raced back. Again there was no resistance. The riders pulled up and stared about them. They were dumbfounded. Where were the Blackfeet? Where were the stolen horses?

Vision Seeker dismounted to better inspect the abandoned campsite. It was clear the Blackfeet raiders had fled taking everything with them but the willow bough pallets they slept on. The horsemen milled about in disgust. They had ridden across the open space with their hearts in their mouths, believing any moment an arrow shaft would strike them down. To find their fears had been for naught made them feel foolish. None felt worse than Many Horses. He had been too cautious. He should have mounted a night attack. He had let the dreaded Blackfeet escape.

"This is no good," he uttered in disgust. He turned on Vision Seeker. "Look for the trail. Which way did they go? What are their numbers? Hurry! We already have wasted too much time."

Vision Seeker's keen eyes examined the land around the tree grove. It was not difficult to locate the tracks. The enemy had made no attempt to cover them. "The trail leads east." Vision Seeker motioned toward the rising sun. "Small party, probably youths on their first raid." He counted the willow pallets and flattened spots in the grass where the enemy had rested. "Not more than fingers on two hands."

"Oh-hah! About the same as we. We ride on, should catch them before midday. We must not let them get away."

"Hey! Hey!" a youthful Flathead shouted. "We find them -- kill them -- teach them lesson."

Vision Seeker dismounted to examine the tracks. He held up his hand in the sign of caution. "They have a good start, left last night, probably right after they carried away the dead one. They are now deep in enemy country. They could be waiting in ambush."

"The stolen herd will give them trouble and slow them down. When Father Sun is full height we will catch them. They will wish they never raided our camp," Many Horses said with an assurance he did not feel.

Vision Seeker turned to mount up. He put a hand on the horse's mane and stopped to steady himself. He suddenly felt dizzy. Early in the night he had a dream that had shattered him. It was so real and intense he could not go back to sleep; over and over he relived it. He could not brush it from his mind. It clung to him, wrapped around him like the snake in the sky world, squeezing his strength away. The scene almost was identical to the one that appeared when Lone Wolf and the hairy faces had their first smoke. This time, lying near the dead warrior, was a bloody scalp. From the black hair protruded two feathers. The dead man could not have been Toohool. He had worn a single feather and his scalp was intact. It meant another member of Lone Wolf's band was doomed to die.

"It is not good. Do not go," Vision Seeker urged. "The signs are bad."

"I do not care about your signs," Many Horses angrily interrupted. "What do you take us for, cowards? The Blackfeet are getting away with a fourth of our herd. We cannot return until we get these animals back." Many Horses waved his band of riders forward. The two feathers in his hair, one pure white and the other white tipped with red, did a little dance, glistening in the brilliant morning sun.

Vision Seeker stared. "Come back!" he shouted. His words were lost in a cloud of dust. Vision Seeker turned to catch his mount. The horse, excited by the departure of the riders, followed the party, its head held high and reins at trail. The riderless animal topped the ridge and disappeared. Vision Seeker stopped, too weak and shaky to make the effort to go on.

Vision Seeker sat down in the shade. There was little he could do on foot but wait. In spite of his worries, he fell into a deep sleep. Near midday he was awakened by the thundering return of Many Horses and his warriors. Without their best tracker they had lost the trail. He was so happy to see Brother alive and well Vision Seeker jumped up and ran to meet him -- only to be rebuffed.

"What is the matter with you?" Many Horses asked angrily. "You are worse than an old woman. When we need you most you are not there. You stay behind and sleep under a tree like a lazy camp dog. Bagh! What kind of warrior is that?"

Many Horses dismounted. He walked back and forth snapping a quirt against the leg of his pantaloon. He acted and looked so much like Lone Wolf when irritated, Vision Seeker smiled. It was a mistake. His brother thought he was making fun. "This is serious business and you make light of it," Many Horses accused. "Nothing has gone right. We wait all night to attack the Blackfeet. When we ride into their camp we find them gone. We travel all morning to bring back our stolen herd and lose our way because our tracker is not there. Toohool is killed. We rescue no horses. We return to camp like a pack of whipped dogs. Weasel Face and Lone Wolf will run us out of camp and well they should! We are a disgrace to our people and all you can do is smile."

\#

When the party led by Many Horses returned empty-handed, Lone Wolf met them at the edge of camp, his face a mask of disgust. "A dead man, no horses, no plunder, no enemy scalps, no prisoners . . ." The harsh voice lashed at the riders like blows from his rawhide quirt.

Shamefaced, the Flatheads drifted away leaving Many Horses and Vision Seeker to bear the wrath of the Lapwai leader. As Many Horses expected, after enduring Lone Wolf's rage, the brothers were pounced on by Toohool's grieving family. Weasel Face stormed out of his shelter followed by his remaining sons. In the lodge behind the angry man, Weasel Face's two wives were keening, ripping at their clothes and tearing their hair. Their wild eyes and tortured screams sent shivers up Vision Seeker's spine. The more subdued, but penetrating cries of Small Goat and The Weaver added to the unearthly din.

"What kind of a leader are you, sitting safe on a hilltop watching my son attack the enemy by himself?" Weasel Face shouted at Many Horses. He turned to Vision Seeker, his narrow set eyes vicious. "And you . . . Where were you? Why did you not do something? You and Toohool were friends. Shame! Shame! Shame! What kind of people are you, leaving my son all day crying in pain? No hearts! No feelings! No courage! What have you to say? Nothing! Cowards! Leaders! Wagh! You should not be allowed to lead a horse to water." He raised his long arms as if to pull the brothers from the saddles.

"Stop this mad talk!" Lone Wolf jumped in to stand between his sons and Weasel Face. "We are sorry about Toohool but calling names and rebuking my sons will not bring him back," he said not unkindly. For the first time ever Lone Wolf had empathy for his tormentor. Weasel Face was just another human being. He loved his sons like any father. "Should I lose a son would I act differently?" Lone Wolf asked himself. The thought was too terrifying to consider.

Buck Stone also had sympathy for the grieving Weasel Face clan. He met with family members and suggested they stay camped a day longer to allow time for Toohool to be laid to rest. A cloud of gloom hung over the camp. The shrieks and cries of mourning penetrated every lodge and carried to the pasture, making the horses snort and pitch their heads. Camp dogs whimpered and howled. Coyotes in the hills added their voices to the mournful dirge. During the night it began to rain and continued into the morning. Low clouds hung above the campsite like a gray shroud. A bitter wind blew down from the north, so cutting and cold people wrapped themselves in blankets and robes and still could not get warm. Hardly a soul got any sleep that night.

The column departed the ill-fated camp, but grief and bitterness were not left behind. The Weasel Face clan formed a little party by itself. They made separate camp and rode as a group. They did not let their horses mingle with the communal herd and stood their own watch. Their actions made everyone uncomfortable.

"This is no way to grieve," Lone Wolf remarked to Quiet Woman. "I don't like it. The Weasel Faces should stay with the column. The Blackfeet may be following. They could pick off the Weasel Faces as easy as plucking ripe berries from a bush."

The mood in Lone Wolf's camp was little different than that of Weasel Face's. Deep in his heart Lone Wolf blamed his sons for Toohool's death. They knew what a scatterbrain the youth was. They should have watched over him. When he leaped up to run down the hill, they should have jumped on Toohool, if need be, hobbled him like an unruly pack mare. Anything was better than having Weasel Face's son killed. As long as Weasel Face lived he would hold Toohool's death against the Lone Wolf clan.

Lone Wolf also brooded over the lost horses. Here again, his sons let him down. Many Horses had grown careless. And Vision Seeker, for all his signs, did not warn of the impending danger.

After his first outburst, Lone Wolf did not censure his sons. He spoke no words to them. He gave no orders; he did not even glance their way. Quiet Woman, who watched and listened, began to fret. What was happening to her family? They were like a bunch of strangers. She, too, fell into a sour mood: packing, unpacking and tramping all day without noticing what she did or where she was going.

Raven Wing also was subdued. She had liked Toohool. He was so good to tease. He was foolish but his heart good. She had to admit his attentions were flattering. Yet she had treated him badly, scorned him, made him feel inept and foolish. How she wished she could call back those cruel words. For the first time ever, she willingly helped with camp chores. No longer did she ride with Little Ned or in front with the scouts. "If I had treated Toohool more kindly he would not have been so reckless and gotten himself killed," she confessed sadly to Vision Seeker.

The tragic events struck Many Horses equally hard. Only at meal time did he venture into camp. He wanted to avoid Lone Wolf, but also his fear of losing more animals kept him close to the herd. He watched over the horses, counting and recounting those that remained. He lay awake at night thinking of ways to recoup the losses. Only one thought gave him comfort. Perhaps at the rendezvous he could persuade Lone Wolf to use Vision Seeker's stock of beaver pelts to trade for horses and rebuild the herd, but deep inside he knew the thought was in vain.

The raid on the herd and the failed rescue attempt affected Vision Seeker most of all. For days the calls of the wounded man haunted him. He could not sleep. As soon as he closed his eyes the face of Toohool appeared. He heard the wounded man call for help. The pitiful cries started loudly then gradually faded into moans. They stopped only when Vision Seeker jerked awake. Was it Toohool who called out or the enemy warrior? It nearly drove him mad trying to decide.

Almost worse, was the reoccurring vision he saw on the night after Toohool was slain: a dead warrior abandoned on a field of battle. The gory scalp with two feathers made his blood run cold. He groaned so loudly he awakened Grandmother.

"What is it, Second Son?" she called out.

"Nothing, Grandmother. Bad sleep," Vision Seeker replied.

XXI

*Miles were to us as they were to birds. The land was ours
to roam in as the sky above was for them to fly in.*

Luther Standing Bear, Oglala Sioux

The threat of an attack by the Blackfeet did not go away.
From time to time distant riders could be seen keeping pace with
the Lone Wolf column. The shadowing horsemen remained out
of rifle shot range. Some days there were three or four mounted
riders on small but fast steeds. For a couple of days only two
riders appeared. Then the four riders were back again.

"The miserable critters're as annoyin' as a swarm of
skeeters," Deacon complained. "They're jest waitin' ta nip in
an' take all we hev."

Deeper into sagebrush country the column penetrated.
Each day brought new vistas. A stretch of trail crossed a barren
waste where nothing grew, the soil dry as powder. Clouds of
choking dust rose up to blind eyes and clog nostrils, causing a
hacking cough that lasted for days afterward. They passed into a
rocky land filled with weird formations and twisted, struggling
clumps of evergreens.

For a while they rode along a huge swamp area covered
with bulrushes. Flocks of water birds darkened the sky. They
flew a short distance only to descend again, filling the air with
flapping wings and squawking cries. A group of hunters went to
shoot game birds for the evening meal. Few had luck. Many of
the birds that fell came down far from shore. The swamp was too
dangerous to enter. One rider urged his horse in to have the poor
animal sink to the withers. It took hours to pull the animal free.

The column passed immense stretches of black lava. Buck
Stone said hundreds of years ago the surface of Mother Earth had
burst open, spilling great rivers of molten rock and soil that flooded
the plain. When the river cooled it turned black, leaving a wil-

derness of jumbled jagged rocks and deep crevices avoided by man and beast.

"Must've been like a taste of hell," Deacon commented. "'Magine a bloody river of fire rollin' across the prairie settin' everythin' in its path ablaze -- trees, sagebrush an' every livin' creature thet couldn't skitter outta the way. Makes a body wonder what's deep beneath our feet, maybeso thet's where the devil lives."

One night the travelers made camp near the edge of the black desolate field of lava. Near dark Vision Seeker and Running Turtle rode over to view the awesome phenomenon. A keening wind whistled across the barren area. Geckos darted out of their path. A scorpion flicked its deadly tail and disappeared under a rock. A long tailed kangaroo rat gave three great hops and dropped into a hole. A prairie falcon swooped down, its sharp talons thrust out. The rat was too quick. It was safely out of sight before the cruel, curved talons could snatch it up.

Running Turtle shivered. "Let us go back to camp. I do not like this place. It makes me think of death."

On the ride back the brothers passed near the Weasel Face camp. Small Goat and The Weaver were staking out the horses, a task Toohool formerly had done. When they saw the brothers approach they turned their backs. From the hastily erected shelter came Weasel Face's strident voice, scolding his sons and berating his mates. The sight and sounds of the unhappy family left Vision Seeker feeling terribly sad. Would the tragedy of Toohool's death ever pass?

Gradually, the scenery became more inviting and travel easier. Each new day brought more water and more abundant pasture. One afternoon the travelers topped a ridge to see the glittering surface of a lake ahead. Like a shiny jewel, it nestled in a cul-de-sac of mountains. East of the lake, bare reddish-brown hills rose abruptly from the water's edge. To the west, an inviting strip of quaking aspen beckoned. Above the greenery rose wispy tendrils of smoke that evaporated into the haze of a sky so blue and bright it hurt the eyes.

"There you are," Buck Stone announced. "That's Bear Lake."

"Yep! Now bargainin' an' funnin'll begin," Deacon said to Vision Seeker. "Yuh hev ta look sharp. Yuh'll be meetin' galoots with tongues as slick as silk. An' maybeso varmint's as obnoxious an' uncivilized as wild hogs. Me advice is ta stay clear of 'em both. Oft'times yuh cain't tell which is which but I guess yer paw'll do most of the tradin'. He's keepin' a eye on those pelts of yers like a hen on its chicks. I spect he's larned a few tradin' tricks in his day, too. He may be a match fer these slickers from the east. Main thing is ta watch out fer firewater. It don't take much ta make a Injun act as silly as a loony goose."

A short distance from the rendezvous place Lone Wolf and his party stopped to camp. The trappers urged them to press on but Lone Wolf and the Flathead leader were adamant. It was important to make preparations before entering the camp of strangers, Lone Wolf explained.

While the women set up camp, Lone Wolf took charge of the men. He sent Many Horses to bring in fresh mounts from the herd. He ordered Running Turtle to fetch colored clay from a special pack. Working alongside his sons, Lone Wolf began to paint the animals. The ceremony of painting was a tradition tied to the coming of the horse. In an important meeting like this, one must show the people's great pride and respect for the horse and to thank The Creator for this great gift. The paintings depicted the rider's exploits and accomplishments that the horse had enabled him to achieve. The colorful drawings covered heads, sides, necks and rumps. To the bridles the riders tied beaded rawhide fringes and colorful ribbons. Eagle feathers interwoven in the manes and tails, gently fluttered in the breezes that swept off the blue-green waters of Bear Lake. It was late evening before Lone Wolf was satisfied and ordered a halt.

Next morning the men painted and decorated themselves. Lone Wolf put on the Dakota headdress acquired in trade from

Buck Stone. Around his neck hung his prized bear claw neck-lace. A thong around each upper arm held trinkets of tinkling seashells.

"My, my! Doesn't Father look fine," Grandmother's qua-vering voice came from the shadows. "His presence will give honor to this place called rendezvous."

Lone Wolf puffed out his chest at the praise. Yes, he looked the part of a leader of the Nimpau. He waited for Quiet Woman and Raven Wing to comment but they said nothing.

Many Horses, Vision Seeker and the Flathead youth did not possess Lone Wolf's finery. Still, they painted their bodies, put plumes in their hair and otherwise adorned themselves. Many Horses did the task reluctantly. He had no desire to enter the hairy faces' trading place. For some reason he sensed it was not a good place for his people. The hairy faces played games, drank firewater, gambled, laid with women, often times in front of oth-ers who watched, joking and shouting, awaiting an opportunity to join in the orgy. These things were not for the Indian. They made him lose his dignity, made him look silly. Many Horses wanted to express these thoughts to his father. He knew it would do little good. Lone Wolf was still irked with his two older sons. The part they played in Toohool's death had brought dishonor to his lodge.

Near mid-morning the men, carrying drums and shields, mounted up. They were ready to make their entrance into the hairy faces' trading grounds called rendezvous. Led by Lone Wolf, they galloped out of camp in single file. The women and chil-dren shouted and waved in delight. They were proud to see their men so stalwart and handsome. They looked forward to seeing the wonders of the rendezvous. In a short while they would break camp and follow.

At Lone Wolf's request, Vision Seeker fell into line close behind his father and the Flathead leader. His heart told him it was not right. The wealth of beaver skins put him in the ceremo-nial place which rightly belonged to Many Horses, the first son.

He glanced back at his elder brother. The paint on Many Horses' face obscured his expression. Before Vision Seeker could catch his brother's eye, the column came to a halt.

Many Horses rode up to stop at Vision Seeker's side. The two feathers fastened in his hair, one pure white, the other tipped with red, hung above his right shoulder. The terrible dream flashed through Vision Seeker's mind. He put out his hand to hold his brother back. He should warn him while he had the chance. Many Horses frowned and shook the hand away. He did not like to be touched. This was not the time or place to show brotherly affection. He sniffed the air and scowled.

"This place is not good," he said. "There is the smell of evil." His dark eyes searched the sides of the trail. His fingers tensely clasped the shield he carried. "As soon as we dare, we should leave."

Although it was warm and the sun shone brightly, Vision Seeker shivered. The shimmering surface of the lake, the bright white bark of aspens and brilliant blue sky dotted with fleecy white clouds, presented Mother Earth at her best. They were surrounded by friends. There was no reason for him to shiver or for Many Horses to sense evil. However, appearances often were deceiving. Sometimes trouble came when one least expected. Many Horses had to be warned. He urged his mount forward. Before he could get his brother's attention, Lone Wolf waved his hand for the column to move ahead.

The colorfully ornamented riders and their mounts marched on the rendezvous encampment singing, drumming and beating on shields. A welcoming party of trappers and traders were grouped together watching the column approach. The horsemen formed a single file circle around the spectators. The riders urged their mounts into a canter and then into a gallop. Whooping and shouting, they rode faster and faster, around and around the spectators. Abruptly, they pulled the horses to a halt. The riders leapt from their mounts to land on their feet facing the crowd. "Ya-hee!" they shouted.

The watchers laughed and clapped their hands. A red faced fellow with an enormous paunch and wearing a shiny top hat, gave a speech. Few, if any, Indians understood a word he said. After finishing his speech the red faced man bowed as though he had performed a feat of skill. Buck Stone then came forward and welcomed them in their own language. He gathered them around and led the way to the trading grounds where he proudly introduced his guests to the wonders of the encampment. Lone Wolf walked by his side, his eyes popped out like those of a hunting possum. On blankets and robes were displayed a variety and quantity of wares unlike he had ever seen. He did not know where to look first. Not even sullen faced Indians, numb from firewater and who stolidly watched, kept him from fingering the goods and smiling his appreciation.

The noise, confusion, dust, smells and jostling crowd made Many Horses retreat to a vacant plot of ground. Why did his father take such pleasure in places like this? There were so many clean, unspoiled meadows where they could have camped. Besides, there were things that needed done. Two stallion colts should be gelded. A mare was about to foal . . .

As Many Horses thought of these things Lone Wolf, his eyes bright with the thought of impending trade, rode up and ordered his oldest son to ride back along the trail to hurry the pack train. He was anxious to unpack the beaver pelts and pit his skills against the hairy faced ones called merchants. Many Horses lifted his shield in salute and galloped away. Vision Seeker started to follow but his father held him back.

"Stay. You should be here. Someone may wish to talk trade."

While Lone Wolf and Vision Seeker waited for the column with the camping equipment and trading goods to appear, they watched the trappers and traders enjoy themselves. Four bearded men seated on bundles of furs, gambled with little squares of talking paper that had strange drawings and squiggles on them called playing cards. To Vision Seeker's surprise, another group squatted in a circle engaged in the Indian game of hand. It always amazed him that people could get so excited over the simple guessing game. The hairy faces made heavy wagers on which closed fist held the hidden pebble. Gleeful shouts and angry curses burst from the group. Still wearing the shiny top hat, the man who made the welcoming speech, picked up his winnings, a dozen beaver pelts. Immediately, he threw them into the cluster of gamblers to wager on another chance.

In a nearby glen, shooting competitions were underway. At one target the hairy faces demonstrated their marksmanship with long-barreled fire sticks. At another target they vied in shooting the bow and arrow. An expert bowman, Vision Seeker itched to test his skill.

A bearded bowman missed the target by the length of a bow. The shot was so wild Vision Seeker grinned. "Damn it all to hell!" the shooter complained. "No one in his right mind would use such a weapon." He noticed Vision Seeker's smile. "I guess yuh think yer pretty good at these things. Well, show us greenhorns how it's done!" He thrust the bow and an arrow at Vision Seeker.

The shooting stopped as everyone expectantly eyed the slim, dark-faced youth. "Thank you," Vision Seeker said in Boston accented English learned from Buck Stone. "If you don't mind, I will shoot with my own bow."

The trapper doffed his cap and made a mocking bow. "Well, la-te-da, if we ain't got a edjucated one. Maybeso, yuh don't know the mechanics of firin' thet bow any better'n the rest of us, bein' schooled an' all." He glanced at his companions, winked and guffawed.

Vision Seeker took an arrow and armed his bow. He drew the string taut. He deliberately aimed the arrow at the trapper's big paunch. "I make certain my arrows fly straight and true," he said, watching the trapper's eyes grow large with alarm.

"Hey! Quit foolin' around. Them arras ain't playthings." The trapper skittered backward, nearly stumbling over his feet.

A thunder of hooves put a stop to the drama. Three Flatheads who had remained behind to guard the women and children, galloped wildly into the encampment.

"Raiders! Blackfeet!" the lead rider shouted. Waving war lances toward the north, the horsemen whipped their mounts about and galloped away.

"What the hell's that all about?" someone shouted.

"Maybeso it's that camp of damned Injuns we saw comin' in. They looked mean enuff ta bite theirselves. I said ta meself, these people're jest thirstin' fer blood," a voice answered.

"What the hell are we doin' sittin' an' jawin'. Let's git after 'em."

Trappers and traders ran for their weapons and mounts. In a flurry of dust and confusion they mounted up and rode after the Flatheads. Lone Wolf and his riders quickly followed. A single bearded horseman galloping down the trail from the north, attracted everybody's attention. He rode a painted Indian pony and waved a dripping scalp. "The enemy's thataway," he shouted.

Lone Wolf wheeled his mount about and seized the rein of the bearded man's horse. He swung his gun barrel up to point it at the man's chest.

Vision Seeker, who had been left behind, pulled up alongside his father. His heart skipped a beat. The bearded horseman, his shifty eyes going from Lone Wolf to his son, attempted to pull away. Vision Seeker seized the other rein. The hairy face was astride Many Horses' gelding, still colorfully marked with clay. Clutched in his hand was a shock of long black hair. From it a pure white feather and another tipped in red danced ever so gently in the Bear Lake breeze.

THE LONE WOLF CLAN

XXII

*If a prophet had come to our village in those days and told us
that the things were to take place which have come to pass,
none of our people would have believed him.*

Black Hawk, Sauk/Fox

The tragic turn of events was almost more than Lone
Wolf's mind could grasp. Moments before he had spoken to Eldest Son, told him to ride back and hurry the column. Now he
was no more. In less time than it took to blink an eyelash, Lone
Wolf's mood turned from supreme jubilation to the depths of
despair. The death of a first son was a loss almost too grievous to
bear. There was no doubt that he was dead. There was his horse.
There was his scalp. He would recognize the two feathers any-
where. He had given them to Many Horses himself. One came
from a northern goose he had shot on a hunt along the Umatilla
with his Cayuse friend, Stickus. The other was an eagle feather.
He had bargained for it at the Chinook trading center on the Great
River. It came from the far north where in summer months the
sun barely set.

Lone Wolf turned on his son's killer. The hairy face with
the tobacco stained beard, shifty eyes and grease fouled garments,
filled him with revulsion. Why were vermin like this allowed to
soil Mother Earth? This creature had less worth than the snake
that crawled from its hole to search for prey in the darkest hours
of night. The arrogant way the man sat Many Horses' mount
made him blind with fury. He raised the rifle barrel until it was
even with the shifty eyes and pulled the trigger. He was too late.
Vision Seeker had thrown up his hand to knock the barrel aside.

Before Lone Wolf could go for the knife at his belt, Buck
Stone, Little Ned and Deacon rode up. "What goes on here?"
Buck demanded, taking in the painted horse, the dripping scalp,
Lone Wolf's fury and the bearded rider in one quick glance. He,

too, swung his rifle barrel up and thrust it into the man's face. "You ignoramus! You killed one of our friends."

"But-but, the fella was in war paint," the bearded man stuttered. "Fer all I knowed he was hellbent afta me scalp. Yuh cain't condemn a man fer defending hisself."

"Idiot! Your life wasn't in danger. He was wearing ceremonial paint, not war paint and the lad was unarmed. These men have every right to make you answer for your crime." Buck gave the rider a vicious swipe with the heavy rifle barrel, knocking him off the horse and onto the ground. Freed from its rider, the horse jerked its head up and bolted, galloping away.

Stunned with grief, almost too horrified to comprehend what had happened, Vision Seeker swung down from his mount. He plucked his brother's scalp from the man's hand and carefully placed it in the rawhide pouch Little Ned had presented him on Christmas day. He had lost a kin, the brother he loved most. He was so sick at heart he could not think. The world that went on around him was unreal. There was rifle fire and shouting. It seemed to come from faraway.

Two bloodied, nearly naked hairy faced ones ran down the trail, gasping like wind-broken horses. In breathless snatches they reported the grim news. "Blackfeet! Maybeso a hundred on the trail ta the north. Shot partner. Ran off animals. Got pelts. Got packs! Got everthin' we possess. Damned stinkin' thieves. Entire winter's work gone ta hell."

A band of horsemen from the rendezvous site rode past at a dead gallop. "After 'em, lads," the leader shouted. "We'll larn 'em ta interfere with our fun."

War cries, wild curses and scattered reports of rifle fire drifted down from the north. "We'll deal with this idiot later," Buck said, glaring down at the bearded man on the ground. "We have to settle the hash of these Blackfeet first." The three trappers spurred their mounts toward the sounds of battle.

Lone Wolf reloaded his rifle and spat on the hairy face who groveled in the dust. Revenge could wait. Buck, the man with yellow hair, was right. First the pesky Blackfeet had to be crushed.

Vision Seeker suddenly came to his senses. A great anger seized him. He vaulted on his mount and galloped into the heart of the battlefield. He charged through a line of trees. An unhorsed rider rose up with bow and arrow. The arrow shaft whistled toward him. He ducked. The deadly missile passed so near the feathered tip grazed his cheek. Before the enemy could rearm his bow, Vision Seeker was on him. Rage gave him superhuman strength. He jerked the horse around and made straight for the Blackfeet. He swung his tomahawk. Iron met flesh. The enemy went sprawling on the ground. Vision Seeker urged his mount forward. It would take more than one slain Blackfeet to avenge the death of his brother.

A wave of rendezvous horsemen following close behind Vision Seeker, also hurled into the enemy ranks, shooting, stabbing, swinging hand axes, clubs -- any weapon that would maim or kill. No quarter was expected or given. Stunned by the ferocity of the attack, the enemy wheeled their horses about to scatter like dry weeds before a storm. Vision Seeker remained in the chase until his arms were weary and his horse had run itself out. He pulled his spent mount to a halt and slowly, retraced his steps.

The rage that had consumed Vision Seeker was replaced by a feeling of shame. He had acted worse than a wild beast, killing for killing's sake. No number of dead Blackfeet would bring back his brother from the other side. He would have to spend the rest of his life without this man who had shared everything with him since childhood. There was not another person in the Lapwai band as wise and kind. Many Horses treated every living creature as though it were special. He said they all were the creation of the Great Mysterious and had souls like people. If one did harm to them, one did harm to the Great Mysterious.

#

The battle was won. The attackers had been routed. Loot and scalps were taken. The pelts and pack animals lost to the enemy were recovered. The herd the Blackfeet had stolen from the Nimpau and Flatheads was back in the hands of the rightful owners and many captured horses were divided among the victors. The triumphant defenders of the rendezvous encampment came together to brag, lie about their exploits and consume great quantities of firewater. The Flatheads and horsemen of other tribes who had joined in the fray launched a victory dance. The beat of drums, shouts and happy laughter; the excited barking of dogs and the sharp yelping cries of the dancers, rose up to echo against the hillsides and resound back across the placid lake.

In the camp of the Nimpau there were no sounds of celebration. The death of a second member of their band at the hands of the Blackfeet was a tragedy that had to be avenged. The elders gathered to council. Should a war party be formed to trail the hated enemy to its lair or should they accept their losses and wait until a more favorable time? The young men did not bother with talk. They wiped away the ceremonial paint and colored themselves with stripes of war paint, black for death, red for blood, and white for victory. It was explained to them that Many Horses did not die at the hands of the Blackfeet but was killed by a hairy faced one. At first they refused to believe the report. When it was confirmed, their wrath turned on the rendezvous encampment. They mounted up and would have stormed the makeshift village of tents, lean-tos and lodges of the trappers and traders but it was the great buffalo hunter, Two Kill, who put a stop to it. Although his bones were stiff from age, he walked with quick determined steps into the horsemen's midst. In a commanding voice he ordered the young men to dismount. He snatched up their weapons and threw them into a heap.

"Stop this foolishness," he ordered. "Ride into the hairy faces' camp and you ride to your death. Every one of them is armed with guns and they know how to use them. Right now they are crazy with firewater. They will tear you apart like a pack of wild wolves. Put your horses away. Go to your lodges. Say a prayer to the Great Mysterious. Give thanks for delivering you from death on the battlefield."

There was much grumbling but the young men obeyed. Except for the keening sounds that came from Lone Wolf's lodge, the camp fell silent. But the feeling of injustice did not die away. The hairy faces had brought them to this place then killed one of their kind. This was unforgivable. Someone had to pay. All through the midday hours thoughts of revenge smoldered until by late afternoon feelings ran so high it took all of Two Kill's skill to keep the young men under control.

Lone Wolf was too busy searching for the body of his first son to take part in plotting revenge. Immediately after the battle he met up with Vision Seeker. Together, they set out to follow Many Horses' tracks. It was an impossible task. Every foot of ground was crossed and recrossed by hundreds of hooves. To make matters worse, the Blackfeet had fired the brush and weeds leaving behind ashes, cinders and scorched debris.

Lone Wolf was not deterred. "First Son must be found. He still may live. Losing a scalp does not mean death. What's a scalp anyway? It's only a mass of hair." Lone Wolf plunged on, barely able to see the ground through tears. He only talked to keep from breaking down. He knew full well that a man who lost his scalp only did so after death. But still they searched, hoping against hope they had missed a clue that would lead them to the body of son and brother.

As the long afternoon waned and the sun became a ball of red fire in the western sky, Lone Wolf finally stopped to lean against his horse and mop his face. He was so tired he hardly could stand. Worried over his father's health, Vision Seeker suggested Lone Wolf go to camp and rest while he remained to continue the search.

"Rest! I'll not rest until our son and brother is found and his killer is dead. Why did you keep me from shooting that worthless hairy faced one? He deserved to die!"

"Yes, he deserved to die. But is it wise to kill a hairy face at their rendezvous? It could make big trouble for our people. Is it not best the hairy faces punish this man themselves?"

Lone Wolf grunted sourly. "Let us see to it they do." He wearily threw a leg over his horse's back and pulled himself upright. Together they reined their mounts toward the rendezvous site. The place was a kaleidoscope of confusion. The streets of the encampment were like rabbit runs. For short distances they ran straight, then zigzagged to the right or to the left for no reason. Barrels of whiskey had been opened and blocked the way. The acrid smell polluted the pine scented air. Boisterous men with tin cups in hand and bloody scalps hanging from belts at their waists gathered in motley groups, everyone talking at once.

In one alleyway two buckskin clad, bearded trappers with big noses and big bellies wrestled, rolling in the dust, snapping and snarling like two dogs. Another trapper was busy undressing an Indian female, who feebly attempted to ward him off but was too filled with firewater to avoid his clutching hands. The trapper's companion, with jug in one hand and black cheroot in the other, avidly looked on. Lone Wolf's lips curled in distaste. He glared at Vision Seeker as if he were to blame for the hairy faces' disgusting behavior.

They threaded their way through stacks of bundles, barrels, boxes and a hodgepodge of lean-to and tent shelters until they came to where Buck Stone and his partners camped. The three trappers saw the riders coming and rose to meet them.

"We are sorry about the death of your son and brother," Buck said, sadly shaking his head. "He was a good man. But at a time like this what good are words?" He spoke in English, forgetting Lone Wolf did not understand.

While Vision Seeker translated, Lone Wolf looked on grimly. "We came for my son's killer," he said tersely. "It is time he paid for this terrible crime. Where is he to be found?"

"The man is gone. He took to the forest. Who knows where he is," Deacon answered in sign language.

Lone Wolf stared, wondering if he understood No Hair On Head. "What is it you say? The man who killed my son has run away and you do not know where?"

Deacon nodded. "Yep, he vamoosed."

Lone Wolf turned on Vision Seeker. "Do my eyes and ears betray me? Did these people let the man who killed my son go unpunished? What kind of friends are they? This evil man killed and scalped Eldest Son. They saw these things. Why did they not hold him here? Do they not know spilled blood must be answered with spilled blood? Are not these the words of the Great Spirit Book?"

Buck Stone understood Lone Wolf's flow of angry words. "Yes, the Bible does have words like that."

Lone Wolf turned again to his son. "Ask them why they treat us like this? Did we not smoke the pipe with these people? Did they not call us friends? Did you not find beaver streams for them so they take many skins? Did they not lead us here to this place called rendezvous? Did we not travel with them -- place our trust in them? Why is it they do not help us when our son and brother is killed?"

Buck Stone nodded and answered in Sahaptin. "What Lone Wolf says is straight and true. We are indebted to you for many things. We are your friends. We grieve with you for the death of your son and brother. The man ran while we were doing battle. Who knows where he went. By now he is far away. That does not mean he won't be punished. If he remains in the mountains someday we will find him, judge him and see justice is done. That is the way of our people."

The words were spoken clearly but Lone Wolf did not believe them. These people did not speak with straight tongues. They said they were friends but no friend would let an enemy get away. Lone Wolf turned on No Hair On Head with such vehemence the rotund trapper flinched. "Why is it you did not follow the teachings of your Great Spirit Book and kill this man? If your stomach was too weak, we would have taken this burden from you. Tell us where to find this man. All we wish is to see that our son and brother's death is avenged. Is that too much to ask of friends?"

"It was a terrible mistake," No Hair On Head said in sign language. "The man thought your son an enemy warrior."

Lone Wolf took a step forward. "What kind of talk is that? What is the matter with you people? Someone that stupid should not be allowed to live. How many innocents will he kill like he did my son?" Lone Wolf reached for his knife. He brandished the cold steel blade in Deacon's colorless face. "Suppose we had taken you for enemies in buffalo country. You would not be talking today. You would be dead! Dead! Dead!"

Vision Seeker moved in front of Lone Wolf to face the trappers. His heart was torn between his father and his hairy faced friends. He had lived with these people, worked with them, nearly starved with them. They had been good. They had taught him many things. And he had been good to them. He had helped make them rich with beaver skins. He had fought wolves, protected their horses and mules. When he did these things they treated him like a brother, yet now they acted like strangers. Did they not know how painful it was to lose a brother and a first son?

"Why do you treat us this way? Do you not know the terrible burden of grief that has fallen on our lodge? Not to avenge Many Horses' death is a disgrace the Lone Wolf family can never live down."

Vision Seeker glanced from one face to another. Only Little Ned who had remained silent looked him in the eye. "Lone Wolf is right," Vision Seeker continued. "I misjudged you. You are not friends. You say good things but your heart is cold. You tell us things the Great Spirit Book says we must do. In your lodge you read the talking paper that says the Great Spirit demands an eye for an eye, tooth for tooth, hand for hand, foot for foot. I remember these words well. I was happy to hear all the good things the Great Spirit Book said. If people lived by these words everything would be good. Now I see these are worthless words. You people say these things but in your heart you do not believe them and do not live by them." Vision Seeker glared at

Deacon who during the Season of Deep Snow had read to him many times from the book called Bible, warning him if he did not do the things it said he would burn forever in hell.

Deacon glanced nervously at his fellow trappers. "It's a turrible misunderstandin'. Yuh see, the Bible's in two parts. There's a Old Testament an' a New Testament. The old un says a eye fer eye, tooth fer tooth . . . The New Testament says, 'Whosoever shall smite thee on the right cheek, turn unta him also the other.'"

After Vision Seeker translated, Lone Wolf looked at Deacon pityingly. "Your Great Spirit Book is like a summer wind that whirls around to pick up leaves and twigs. It goes hither and yon blinding people with dirt and dust. If I do as your new Great Spirit Book says, I would give this man who killed my first son, my second son. When he kills my second son, I give him my third son. The man does more evil. What do I have left to give? All of my sons are gone. Do I give my daughter? What kind of fools do you hairy faces take us for?"

Lone Wolf spat on the ground. "It was a bad day when you people came to us out of the snow. You bring us big bad trouble. We listened to you, smoked with you and followed you to this place because we believed you honorable people. You are no more honorable than our enemies, the Blackfeet. Keep your beaver skins. They are no good. They are evil. They caused my son's death."

On the way back to camp Lone Wolf encountered Weasel Face. He stiffened and looked the other way. Weasel Face did not take offense. He put out his hand and laid it on Lone Wolf's shoulder. "I am sorry, old bear. I know the sorrow you carry in your heart."

Lone Wolf went into his tipi and closed the flap. He blindly lowered himself onto a sleeping robe and sat staring at the blank tipi walls. Never again would he see First Son's face. Never again at councils would First Son sit by his side. Never again would his precious horses feel First Son's kind touch or his call.

So full of misery was the Indian leader he did not notice Raven Wing and Grandmother who sat grieving in the shadows nor did he hear Quiet Woman's low moans of mourning coming from the pallet she made on which to lay the body of her first-born.

XXIII

What is life? It is the flash of a firefly in the night.
It is the breath of a buffalo in the winter time . . .

Crow Foot, Blackfeet

The encounter with his former trapper companions left Vision Seeker sick at heart. It was the calm manner in which they accepted Many Horses' death that bothered him most. It was as if his brother's life had no more worth than a beaver caught in one of their steel traps. He had overheard one of the drunken trappers say the only good Indian was a dead one. Is that what these three hairy faces believed?

Vision Seeker rode to the highest ridge he could find. Perhaps from that vantage point he could see something that would give a clue to where Many Horses had fallen; circling buzzards, hawks or a flock of magpies might lead him to the body. Carrion seekers who roamed the sky had uncanny knowledge of where to find dead and wounded after a battle. He had to hurry. In the west a high bank of clouds was beginning to form, covering what was left of the setting sun. The glistening waters of Bear Lake had already darkened to take on the look of polished black ice. Cool lake breezes made the boughs of a lone pine tree shiver and sigh. There was no doubt in Vision Seeker's mind that the tree was sending its message of grief. The mournful sound struck the very depths of his being.

Vision Seeker slid from the saddle. He felt like throwing himself down on Mother Earth and crying. He could blame the trappers all he wanted but it was he, himself, who was really at fault. The gods sent him the signs that foretold the tragedy. Not once but many times it came to him, a warrior of the Lone Wolf clan stretched out in death on the field of battle. Why had he not warned Many Horses? He should have stayed with him, ridden by his side wherever he went. To vent his grief and frustration,

Vision Seeker beat his head against the tree trunk. The wind sighing in the boughs brought him to his senses. It was as if Many Horses called his name and spoke to him. "I am not dead. I am the whisper of the grasses. I am the sunlight on the clouds. Come to me. I am as near as the pine needles in this tree."

Vision Seeker stood motionless. Was he losing his mind? Had these words been spoken or were they his imagination? He listened, straining every nerve, but heard nothing. The wind had died away. Not a breath of air moved. Evening swallows dipped and skimmed back and forth across the shiny surface of the lake. Clouds in the west towered like mountains smothered in snow. A shaft of light shone upon white peaks making them come alive. Like flying horses with heads held high and manes swept by the wind, the line of clouds climbed higher and higher. Vision Seeker watched in wonderment. The display was more awesome than the vast sea of stars in Father Sky.

The magical winged horse that carried Bellerophon to do battle with the fire-snorting beast came to Vision Seeker's mind. He could imagine Many Horses riding such a steed. The thought gripped him until the line of chargers became real. Out of the pack a great gray and white stallion reared above the others, the rider expertly holding his mount in check. Two feathers swept back from the rider's head -- one pure white, one tipped with red. In a burst of speed the stallion galloped off to disappear in a fog of white. The rider, his two feathers bobbing in the wind, faded out of sight. The illusion was so real Vision Seeker imagined he could feel a breeze the flying horse created as it swept past.

For a long while Vision Seeker sat musing over the un-canny experience. First he heard Many Horses speaking through the sighing boughs and now he came riding out of the sky. Surely these had been signs but what did they mean? He glanced at the sky again. There were no flying horses. The clouds over Bear Lake formed one solid blanket. Then like a giant hand had parted it, the blanket broke apart. In the opening was a field of flowers. No, they were bulrushes. Lying in the bulrushes was the body of a warrior! Vision Seeker closed his eyes. Why did he see these things? He opened his eyes. It was still there, almost identical to the sign he had seen at the first meeting with the hairy faces. What was it trying to tell him this time? Many Horses was dead. It would take more than signs to bring him back to life. He groaned. This mystical power he possessed was driving him slowly but surely mad.

Vision Seeker arrived back at Lone Wolf's lodge in time to hear his father scolding Raven Wing. "You have no pride. You have no feeling. You trail about camp like a wanton woman. You belittle the memory of your dead brother. You bring dishonor to our lodge."

"Dishonor! Any dishonor in this lodge is yours. You brought us to this place of evil. Many Horses would be alive if we had stayed away," Raven Wing retorted.

"In your grief you forget yourself. Remember your place, daughter," Lone Wolf's voice thundered.

"My place! I know my place. In this lodge it is no better than a camp dog or a piece of trade goods. Do this. Do that. Raven Wing why do you not have a mate? A proper mate, not one like Toohool. The son of Weasel Face is not good enough for the Lone Wolf family!"

"Silence!" shouted Lone Wolf.

"Stop it!" Quiet Woman ordered. "This lodge is in mourning. How can you quarrel when Eldest Son lies out there, his body unprotected from buzzards, coyotes and wolves?"

"Ah-ah-ah. Ah-ah-ah," came the sound of Grandmother moaning. "Death has come to the Lone Wolf lodge."

Vision Seeker could not bear to listen. He had to get away from this tortured, guilt-ridden, place. But he could not leave. Now that Many Horses was gone, he was number one son. He must learn to do all the things Many Horses had done: it was up to him to geld the stallions; it was up to him to see the mares were bred and properly foaled; and it was up to him to make certain the herd was protected and pastured. There were myriad of other things he must do: he had to set an example for Running Turtle; act on his father's behalf when he was not around; and, if something should happen to Lone Wolf, take over, guide and protect the family.

To escape the tension-filled lodge, Vision Seeker mounted up and rode to the pasture. The captured horses swelled the herd until animals overflowed the field. Thoughts of Toohool crossed his mind. How pleased he would be to know the stolen horses had been recovered and the Blackfeet had paid dearly for the tricks they played on him.

#

Raven Wing also could not stand to remain in the oppressive lodge. She slipped away to walk aimlessly about. She wanted to go to Small Goat but that would not do. The Weasel Face family remained in mourning for Toohool. Her wanderings took her in the direction of the rendezvous trading grounds. The Blackfeet who came to raid and plunder had interrupted trade but trappers and traders were quickly back in business.

The packers, who brought trade goods from the east, were anxious to dispose of their wares. Signs scrawled with prices were tacked to posts, tree trunks or haphazardly propped against lean-to shelters. Offers to buy and offers to sell were listed side by side. Beaver skins brought $5.00 per pound, otter hides $3.00 and the lowly muskrat twenty-five cents. The traders' goods were likewise priced: $2.50 a pound for gun powder; $2.00 per pound for sugar; and the same for coffee and tobacco. Three point blankets were $15.00 and scarlet cloth $10.00 a yard.

The exciting sounds that drifted from the trading square were more than Raven Wing could resist. She wandered from one trader's place to the next, eyeing the displays. The traders waved trinkets and gewgaws to attract her attention. Trappers, smoking, visiting and idling in passageways, called out to this shapely Indian beauty with amorous invitations. Raven Wing did not understand the words but knew their meaning. She held herself aloof. Her skin crawled at the thought of the rough hands of these bearded, dirty hairy faces touching her. She had nothing but scorn for the Indian girls who offered themselves to men for a few yards of calico or a trinket or two. Little did she know her aloofness made her all the more alluring.

At the edge of camp, Raven Wing turned back. The sun had disappeared. The long summer twilight had set in. The haunting music of a violin, the twang of a banjo and singing voices, cast a magical spell. In the Indian encampment warriors, heated by the battlefield victory and firewater, started a scalp dance. The wild thump of Indian drums sent Raven Wing's blood racing. A dark-faced man with fresh scalps hanging from his belt, lurched from behind a tent and into Raven Wing's path. Startled by his nearness, she backed away only to find herself blocked by a wall of stacked bundles of beaver pelts. She was trapped. The tall man came so near she could smell the acrid odor of whiskey on his breath.

"Do not be alarmed, little beauty," he said, doffing his wide brimmed hat. "I won't hurt you. Why not stay and visit a while with Francois? You and I could make the big romance."

Raven Wing did not understand the words but the bold, dark eyes seemed to devour her. She shrank back. The stranger fascinated her, at the same time she felt repelled. She wanted to run but her limbs refused to move. The stranger reached out to her. The touch of his hand sent a shiver through her body like none she had ever known, a feeling so powerful it made her want to scream. Out of the gloom loomed another man. In a daze, Raven Wing recognized the big man, Little Ned. He seized the dark-faced stranger and jerked him away. There was a sharp crack like a dry limb had snapped. Raven Wing did not wait to see or hear more. She turned and ran toward Lone Wolf's lodge as fast as her legs would move.

#

In the pasture field Vision Seeker inspected the animals as he had seen Many Horses do. He went from one animal to another to make certain they had not suffered in the battle or been badly treated by the Blackfeet. He came to a gelding still bridled. It raised its head and took a step toward him. Vision Seeker stared. Its head and flanks were colored with clay! From its mane fluttered a red ribbon. It was Many Horses' mount, the one he had raised from a colt and the one that carried him to his death.

Vision Seeker caught the trailing reins and led the horse away from the herd. He hoped somehow it might provide a clue where his brother had fallen. Inspection of the horse did not help. Except for the clay paint, the animal was unmarked. Vision Seeker lifted a hoof. Mud caked the frog. Did the triangular pad inside the horse's hoof provide a clue?

"Oh, ha!" Marshy ground! The sign in the clouds! West of the row of trees where the battle with the Blackfeet took place there was a field of bulrushes. That was one place he and Lone Wolf had not searched. Of course! The sign was telling him Many Horses had fallen in the marsh.

Vision Seeker threw the bridle reins over the horse's neck, swung on the back and galloped for the swampy field. He did not have much time. The long shadows of evening were already forming. Vision Seeker pulled up and glanced hurriedly around, his sharp eyes searching the ground. It was not a large area but thick with growth, tender green sprouts of new bulrushes thrusting up amongst last year's brown stalks. A dark spot where new plants were flattened and the old ones lay crushed, beckoned. Keeping the crushed spot in sight, Vision Seeker rode around, following a solid ridge of ground. He came to the crushed bulrushes and sucked in his breath. Curled up like a sleeping baby lay Many Horses, his denuded head seemed to move; crawling, flying insects had descended to do their ghoulish work .

Vision Seeker quickly jumped down and brushed the vermin away, cradling the body of his brother in his arms. He received the shock of his young life. Many Horses was breathing! His brother was not dead! He was alive!

XXIV

*We see Miracles on every hand . . . . Nothing of the marvelous
can astonish us — a beast could speak or the sun stand still.*

Ohiyesa, Santee Sioux

The return of Many Horses brought great jubilation to the
Nimpau camp. Lone Wolf slowly carried his son into the tipi
lodge and laid him on the buffalo robe covered pallet of boughs
Quiet Woman had carefully prepared. Quiet Woman busied herself cleaning the wound and cooking broth. Grandmother came
off her pallet making soothing clucking sounds like a quail that
has found a brood of lost chicks. All night the two women hov-
ered over the sick man, trying to make him comfortable, watching for any sign he would come out of the deep coma.

"Fetch the medicine man," Grandmother ordered early
the following morning. Qoh-Qouh, a man with a long hooked
nose that was red as a ripe cherry at the tip, arrived carrying the
tools of his trade: ashes, bones, herbs and fetishes of which only
he knew the content. He entered the lodge warily. He knew the
story of this man's near escape from death. He had treated many
wounds but never a patient that had been scalped. His instinct
was to wash his hands of the whole affair. He had a successful
record of healing. He did not want to jeopardize it now. From all
accounts this one already had a foot in the next world.

"Look to this man," Grandmother ordered. She had known
Qoh-Qouh since he was a child. She did not think much of him
then and did not think any better of him now. Yet, unless they
went to the Flatheads, he was the only medicine man they could
call. His record of successes was due to the fact he treated only
those he was certain would get well.

"Do not stand there, tend to him," Grandmother's voice
suddenly took on a commanding tone. "Do what you can. No
one expects miracles."

Qoh-Qouh nodded grimly and bent over the pallet. The wounded man breathed heavily. There was a disturbing dry rattle as he exhaled. He did not like the sound of it. He wished he had never been called but now he was trapped. If he left the man unattended he would be named a coward. No one would want to be treated by him again. If he tended the man and he died the people would lose faith in him. Since the injured man was the leader's son he might even be accused of murder. He and Weasel Face had long been close friends. Everyone knew Weasel Face blamed Lone Wolf's eldest son for Toohool's death. If the man now died under his care . . . He groaned silently. The scandal could cause him to lose everything he had achieved.

Qoh-Qouh called for more light. When the firelight brightened, he got down on his knees. He inspected the wound, and ran his fingers over Many Horses savaged head. He blew out a puff of breath then chanted an incantation in a tongue none of the listeners could understand. He called for a pot of boiling water. He took something from behind Many Horses' ear and plunged it into the pot.

"Get the crier," he ordered. "This man is very, very ill. The spirits of sickness are very strong. If we are to make this man well all the people must help."

Running Turtle scurried away. In a few minutes he was back. A parade of tribesmen followed. In front was the camp crier, Man of Many Words. The crier and the medicine man met outside to confer. Qoh-Quoh took the crier aside and told him of his fears. "The injured man is already well on the path to the other side." The crier's face turned gray. He did not want to have anything to do with announcing death. But he could not shirk his duty. In a sharp piercing cry he started to chant. From every corner of the camp people scurried to gather in front of the lodge where the leader's son lay dying.

A drum began to beat and was joined by another. The gathering picked up the crier's chant. The medicine man came out again. "Louder. Louder! Louder! The bad spirits are starting to leave." He returned to the lodge and came out again, his tightly closed fist held above his head. "I have the sickness in my hand. What shall I do with this bad spirit, send it east or send it west, north or south?"

"Send the bad spirit to the horizon where the sun rises. Let it descend on the Blackfeet warrior who scalped Many Horses," a voice in the crowd shouted.   A flock of blackbirds flew overhead. Qoh-Quoh drew back his fist, threw his arm forward toward the birds and opened his fingers. "Blackbirds!" he called. "Carry this man's sickness away. Take it far from here. Turn this evil spirit onto our enemy."

Qoh-Qouh congratulated himself. He'd made a bad situation better. By asking the crowd to take part, if the patient did not recover the blame would not fall entirely on him; the people also would be at fault. The spiritual power they all possessed had not been sufficiently strong to ward off the messenger of death. He went back to his patient. He placed a hand on the bloodied forehead and chanted more words. He picked up the pot of water and emptied it outside. He chanted and sang with the crowd and went inside to pick up the medicine bag. He slyly looked to Lone Wolf. "I have done all I can."

Lone Wolf stared straight ahead. He knew, indeed, it would be a miracle to have a scalped man live. Quiet Woman sobbed. Grandmother gave her son's woman a comforting pat. "Your son will not die," she said, but then went to her pallet and wept. Even if he lived who would want to look on him? He was disfigured. He never would rise to the heights he should.

Vision Seeker was the one member of the family who did not despair. The Great Mysterious had given him the power to find his brother. He also would provide the power to keep him alive. The wounded man needed the best attention he could get. He thought of No Hair On Head and the way he had ministered to the ills of the trappers and successfully sewn together the finger the beaver nearly had bitten off. He slipped away from the lodge and made straight for the rendezvous grounds.

The three trappers sat in front of their lean-to lodge watching the morning's trade. Vision Seeker slowed to a walk. He did not want to appear anxious. Besides, he didn't know what reception he would get. When they last met many harsh words were spoken. Would they hold them against him? Would they refuse to help? They were not celebrating the victory over the Blackfeet but did have a jug sitting beside them. This was the whiskey that tasted like fire and made people fall down and act crazy but the trappers seemed to have their senses. That was good.

The three men rose to greet him. "We heard the good news. We are pleased your brother has been found," Buck said. "How is he?"

Vision Seeker shook his head. "He is not well. The medicine man does not know if he will live."

Deacon clucked sympathetically. "I'm not surprised. When a man loses his scalp . . . Thet's mighty bad." He reached for the whiskey jug and held it out to Vision Seeker. "Maybeso, a leetle slug'll make yuh feel better."

"No! I do not wish firewater. It is bad medicine."

"Yep. Yer quite right." Deacon put the stopper in the jug and pushed it inside the lean-to.

"I suppose you have come for your share of pelts?" Buck Stone asked.

"No, our brother lies dying. We have no wish to make trade." He glanced at Deacon. "Many Horses must have a healer. You are the one who can make our brother well."

Deacon scratched his unkempt beard. "Ah! I ain't much fer fixin' people who've lost ther scalps. I only seen one man who survived a scalpin'. An ol' Injun woman doctored him. When she got done doctorin' he wasn't lookin' at all hansome, but he lived. Naaw, my healin' ain't good enuff fer healin' a scalpin'. I kin deal with cuts and bellyaches. Thet's 'bout me limit, serious wounds like a scalpin' . . . Yuh need a proper medical ejucated galoot fer somethin' like thet. Besides, yuh know what Injuns do ta medicine men who don't heal ther patients? I hev enuff troubles without havin' a camp of Redskins ready ta skin me alive."

"Many Horses would not be near death if we had not met you," Vision Seeker reminded. "Your Great Spirit Book tells of the wounded man left beside the trail. No one gives him help. A stranger from a place called Samaria stops and tends to him -- gives up his own horse to carry him away. The man lives. If a stranger can do these things for one he does not know, can you not do it for one you call friend?"

"Deacon, you can't refuse. This is something you must do," Buck Stone said firmly. "Get your things together."

"What about Lone Wolf?" Deacon protested. "Last time we seen him he was ready ta cut me throat. He'll never let me in the lodge."

"We'll think of something when we get there," Buck said.

"A'right," Deacon agreed. "Maybeso I kin do some good. If I 'member correctly the ol' woman, Paiute she was, fixed up the feller who lost his scalp with a poultice of bear grease an' skunk cabbage. It'll stink worse than thet fish village we passed.

"Maybeso thet's what brought the feller 'round. 'Twas either git weller or suffercate. Never cared fer the fella much, he never lost the smell of skunk. Let's git a hustle on. Round up a tub of buffalo grease. Buffalo lard'd probably do. Thar's no time ta lose."

While the two big trappers scurried out to find grease and skunk cabbage, Deacon went through his supply of medicines, bandages and medical tools. "I 'spect I'd better take Little Ned's needle. Sewin' might be needed."

Vision Seeker anxiously watched the preparations. Now that No Hair On Head agreed to see Many Horses the next problem was how to get Lone Wolf to allow him into the lodge? If No Hair On Head tended the wounded man and he died! Did he do right by asking the hairy faces for help? Before he could make up his mind, Little Ned was back with a container of buffalo tallow and Buck followed with an armful of skunk cabbage.

Deacon clucked his approval. He picked up his bag and

strode toward the Indian camp, walking so fast Vision Seeker had to stretch his legs to keep up. Buck and Little Ned brought up the rear. As Vision Seeker feared, Lone Wolf would not allow Deacon inside the lodge. Vision Seeker attempted to explain to his father.

"No treacherous hairy face is going to touch my son," Lone Wolf snapped. He glared at the trappers, went back inside and sealed the tipi flaps. The men glanced at each other. What could they do? Buck started forward and then held back. Within the tipi sharp words were exchanged between Quiet Woman and Lone Wolf. Grandmother's quavering high-pitched voice also could be heard.

Vision Seeker's heart sank. By calling in the hairy faces he only had made matters worse. He had started a quarrel that might last half the night. He glanced helplessly at the trappers. Buck Stone shrugged. If the head man of the lodge turned them away there was not much they could do. The tipi flaps opened. Grandmother came out.

"Never mind your father," she said to Vision Seeker. "Tell your friends we welcome any help they can give."

The fetid air hit Deacon like a slap in the face. The skunk cabbage he carried made matters worse. "Open the flaps and roll up the tipi skirts," he ordered in sign language.

Lone Wolf glowered but Quiet Woman, Raven Wing and Grandmother quickly obeyed. Deacon knelt by the pallet and examined the wound. The sight of it almost made him retch. The remaining flesh on the skull had blackened. Dribbles of yellow pus oozed from all parts of the wound.

"Git ta makin' hot water," he ordered. From his bag he took a bottle of whisky and sloshed the contents over the blackened skull. He dipped a cloth in the pot of warm water Grandmother placed at his elbow. Carefully, he moistened the black area, wiping away the pus. He tried to remember exactly how the Paiute woman applied the poultice. The key was to keep the raw flesh moist and yet not interfere with the healing magic of the herbal ingredients.

When he finished, Deacon sat back and wiped the perspiration from his brow with a shirt sleeve. "Thet's the best I kin do. It's up ta the Great Spirit now. Yer lucky the lad's alive. He must have the constitution of a horse. Of course, he has the constitution of Many Horses." The figure of speech made Deacon smile. He turned to find Lone Wolf's fierce eyes upon him, his hand on the handle of the knife he carried in a sheath fastened to his belt.

"Let us pray," Deacon said quickly. He folded his hands and looked up at the tipi smoke hole. "Our Father . . ." From the corner of his eye, Deacon saw the hand on the knife handle gradually relax.

Deacon packed his bag, putting away the whiskey bottle last. "Why not give him a sip?" Deacon said more to himself than anyone present. He pried the slack mouth open and poured a few drops through the parched lips. Many Horses uttered a small gasp. His eyelids fluttered. Quiet Woman, her face bright with hope, dropped to her knees beside the sick man's pallet. Lone Wolf came close to put his hand on Quiet Woman's shoulder.

"So you are going to live, my son," Lone Wolf said, his voice harsh with emotion. Many Horses' eyelids fluttered again as if to answer.

For days Many Horses lingered between life and death. Every morning and afternoon Deacon came to tend to him. Every time Lone Wolf greeted him with a hard look and motioned him inside the lodge with a curt wave of his hand. Deacon paid no attention. He ministered to his patient pretending his life was not at stake. He said a prayer before entering and upon leaving the lodge. He also mumbled a prayer when taking his patient's pulse. Sometimes he felt his prayers were being answered and at other times he was certain they were not. Then one night he took the scalped youth by the hand and was astonished. The patient pressed his hand back. He barely could contain himself. He knew at that moment Many Horses was going to live. He hurriedly packed his medicine kit and left, ignoring Lone Wolf's sour glance. Outside the tipi lodge he kicked up his heels in a little dance.

That night Many Horses awakened and uttered his first words. The next morning Lone Wolf greeted Deacon with a beaming smile. The little bearded medicine man had performed a miracle. No Hair On Head had brought his son back from the dead.

XXV

*Generally speaking, everybody behaves according
to his heart and his understanding,*

Balthasar Gracian

Over night the mood of the Lone Wolf camp turned from gloom to joy. News of Many Horses' awakening swept from lodge to lodge; their leader's son's life was saved! Each member of camp personally felt responsible. Their chants had made the recovery possible. Even Weasel Face turned to his two wives and smiled. No one knew better than he what a blessing it would be to have a son return from the other side. He went as far as to congratulate his medicine man friend, Qoh-Quoh, giving him credit for bringing the dead man back to life.

Qoh-Quoh was not one to hide his talents under a bushel basket. He accepted the praise as duly earned. He strutted from lodge to lodge thanking the people for helping him cure the sick man. The wily medicine man was careful not to overstate the importance of his role in performing this miracle of healing. He merely had been an instrument of the gods, he said. It was those who chanted away the bad spirits who brought the dying man back from the edge of the grave. The part No Hair On Head played was ignored. What did a hairy face know about driving evil spirits away?

The people forgot the faults of their leader. They left the hardships of the trail behind. They rejoiced in the victory over the Blackfeet. Their lost herd was recovered and increased by captured enemy ponies. The Weasel Faces emerged from their deep mourning. Small Goat and The Weaver were allowed to visit the Lone Wolf lodge again. The entire camp celebrated with a feast. Hunters went into the hills and brought back the carcasses of two deer, a bear and a variety of water fowl and other small game. The most tender and most tasty parts were prepared and taken as gifts to the sick man's lodge.

However, joy in the Lone Wolf lodge was brief. Many Horses' recovery was slow. The constant flow of well-wishers, The Weaver, ever present, and the coming and going of Small Goat in the already crowded lodge, got on Lone Wolf's nerves. He was impatient with everyone, mostly himself. He could not shake the nagging thought it was his fault Many Horses had lost his scalp. It was he who had sent Eldest Son into harm's way and then had done the unforgivable. He had allowed the man who mutilated his son to go free without punishment.

Lone Wolf groaned. The great trading he looked forward to with such anticipation had turned to ashes in his mouth. He could not bring himself to accept Vision Seeker's share of the rich beaver harvest. Even though Many Horses was found, and under No Hair On Head's care recovered, he could not forgive the trappers. They had let the man who attacked and scalped his son go free. The memory of this disgrace would hang over his head as long as he lived.

Every time he looked at First Son's hairless head and scared skull it made him ill. They were a constant reminder of the slack jawed, tobacco chewing, unclean hairy face who shot and scalped his son. No, he could not be friends with people who let a creature like that go unpunished. They had no sense of justice. They had no regard for the feelings of their fellow beings. It was best he have nothing to do with them, leave the rendezvous place as soon as possible. With nothing to trade there was no reason to stay. But before they could travel, Many Horses had to get well.

Every morning Lone Wolf sat by the side of Eldest Son. "How are you today, Son? Are you ready to ride?" he invariably asked.

"Of course he is not ready to ride," Grandmother scolded one day. "How can he get well with you pestering him all the time?"

Raven Wing also chided Lone Wolf. "Grandmother is

right. You should leave him be. He needs rest and quiet."

Lone Wolf turned on her. "What do you know about such things?" he demanded. "You never have mated and brought forth children. From the looks of it you never will."

The sharp, angry words of her father were like dagger thrusts to Raven Wing's heart. How could a father speak so disparagingly to his only daughter? All he thought about was getting her mated and bred like one of his mares. "Aagh!" she said so loudly and fiercely Many Horses stirred uneasily and opened his eyes. Lone Wolf answered just as sharply. The two of them snapped at each other like quarrelsome dogs. Quiet Woman and Grandmother attempted to intervene. Their efforts were ignored. The wrangle between daughter and father continued. Only when Many Horses weakly cried out did they stop.

When the quarrel was at its height Vision Seeker returned from the pasture fields. He did not enter the lodge but lingered outside, listening, sick with despair. The bitter words Raven Wing and Lone Wolf spoke were tearing his family apart. He saw no end to the constant quarreling. As long as Raven Wing and Lone Wolf lived in the same lodge there was bound to be trouble but what could he do? One did not dispose of a daughter and sister like a worn out pair of moccasins.

Vision Seeker knew the source of the trouble. Lone Wolf had promised to bargain for Little Ned's elk skin dress. He never did. Now it looked like he never would. Vision Seeker turned away from the lodge with heavy heart. What could be done? Lone Wolf was as unbending as a seasoned lodgepole and Raven Wing as stubborn as a balky colt. Neither one would give in. From now on they would be like two angry mountain cats caught in a trap. Somehow this terrible hostility had to cease. Lone Wolf had to free his mind of guilt. Raven Wing had to accept her lot in life. If he could get his father to accept the beaver pelts and get him involved in the joys of trading . . . Vision Seeker stopped short. A bright thought began to shine through the gloom. Perhaps not all was lost.

He turned to walk toward the rendezvous site. Buck Stone and Little Ned always had treated him well. If he explained the troubles . . . Vision Seeker quickened his pace. Little Ned! The man with the black hair was the solution. Little Ned and his elk tooth decorated dress could bring the Lone Wolf family back together. Vision Seeker's pace slackened. No, it was a foolish thought. How could he ever bring it about? They would laugh in his face. But there was the conversation he and Little Ned had during the Season of Deep Snow. He had no mate in his Boston lodge. Surely he would not want to live alone the rest of his life. There was Raven Wing . . . She did not want a mate but she would do anything for that elk skin dress. Vision Seeker found the three trappers busily packing and cleaning their quarters.

"Glad you came," Buck said. "We are getting ready to leave and need to get your beaver skins off our hands."

Ah, yes, the beaver skins. They had to be dealt with. To refuse them would be an insult and until Lone Wolf got over his irascible mood he could not accept them. To avoid giving an answer he stalled for time. "You are leaving so soon?"

Buck nodded. "If we stick around here, we'll spend all we've made. Now, about these beaver skins, shall we load them on our mules and take them to your lodge?"

Vision Seeker glanced at Little Ned. "Did you finish work on the elk skin garment?" he asked. Little Ned shook his head. Vision Seeker thought he would not speak but finally he did. "I guess I'll never finish fiddling with it. It's become my personal albatross."

Vision Seeker looked away. What was an albatross? He did not dare ask. He had to get Black Hair thinking about Raven Wing.

It was almost as if baldheaded Deacon could read Vision Seeker's thoughts. "Raven Wing takes ta thet elk skin garment like a duck ta water," Deacon exclaimed. "Little Ned, yuh oughta loose up, start thinkin' right smart on takin' a wife. Thet dark-eyed beauty'd be a ketch. Sit here with Vision Seeker an' drive a bargain. No time like the present ta make a deal. Vision Seeker kin speak fer his sister. Yuh better let me speak on yer behalf."

Little Ned stopped packing to give Deacon an angry glare.

"Now lissen ta me, yer lettin' a opportunity of a lifetime pass yuh by. I'm thinkin' hard on what kinda deal we kin best make. Yuh cain't be a skinflint. Thet elk skin dress'd be the fust bargainin' chip."

Little Ned came and stood over his short partner, his big fists clenched.

Vision Seeker looked on aghast. Instead of friends the two men were acting like enemies. He was appalled. The last thing he wanted was to make trouble.

"Don't glare at me like thet," Deacon protested. "Course yuh wanta make a deal. Yuh been makin' sheep eyes at thet lass since yuh first met. It's time ta quit oglin' the gal an' ask fer her hand. Think of the good things thet little woman kin do fer yuh on the trail: set up camp, cook yer grub, keep yer bed warm, maybeso birth yuh a son . . ."

"Mind your own business," Little Ned snapped.

Vision Seeker could see the big man's face behind the heavy tan flash the color of polished pipestone. He punched things into a bag with such force he thought the seams would burst. He, too, wished the rotund trapper would keep quiet. Instead, Deacon turned to him. "Since Little Ned ain't in the mood ta deal, I'll tell yuh what. I'll bargain fer the lass fer meself."

Little Ned dropped the bag he was packing. "You old reprobate," he exploded, "you already have a wife."

"Yeah, but she's gettin' a bit long in the tooth. I'm thinkin' a young wife'd be right nice. She could hep the ol' woman -- maybeso, bear a few kids . . ."

"Taking a wife half your age, a second one at that, isn't even decent."

"Who said anythin' 'bout bein' decent?" Deacon retorted. "I'm thinkin' of me ol' age. Yuh cain't 'magine how fast it creeps up. Afore yuh know it yuh've lost yer teeth an're stove up worse'n a spavin-legged mule. Git off yer high horse an' let me hev thet dress of yers. I'll march right up ta Lone Wolf's lodge an' lay me cards on the table. I fixed up yer son, now it's time fer him ta fix me up with his daughter."

Vision Seeker was too stunned to speak. He had to put a stop to this. He turned to appeal to Little Ned. The big man was pawing through a pack for the elk skin dress. Deacon reached for the dress but Little Ned slapped his hand away and tucked the dress under his arm. Determinedly, he strode straight for Lone Wolf's lodge. In a loud voice he announced his presence. Raven Wing, herself, emerged from the tipi entrance. Little Ned placed the fancy bead and quill decorated dress in her hands. With a squeal of pleasure, Raven Wing seized the dress and darted back into the lodge pulling Little Ned after her.

Fearful of what Lone Wolf might do, Vision Seeker hurried forward only to be met by his father who stepped out of the lodge, his face wreathed in a smile. Buck Stone and Deacon, who had followed Vision Seeker, were equally astonished to see Lone Wolf raise his hand in a gesture of welcome.

"It is time we smoke the pipe of friendship," Lone Wolf said in signs. They sat in a circle much as they had when the trappers and Lone Wolf's welcoming party first met on Sun River. When the pipe made the circle and came back to Lone Wolf, he took two more puffs and passed the pipe around a second time. All the while he kept his eye on Vision Seeker who had turned the first smoke into a disaster. He breathed a sigh of relief. Second Son appeared as pleased and contented with life as did the others.

At the conclusion of the smoke, Lone Wolf stood to give a prayer of thanksgiving. He turned to lift the pipe toward Father Sun. He formed the words of a prayer but found himself thinking of the awesome dream that had launched him on the journey to buffalo country. Now, more than ever, he knew it had been a message from The Great Mysterious. The Great One had challenged him to lead his people on a second big hunt -- then tested him to make certain he had the ability to carry out this important task.

"Ah!" Lone Wolf uttered. He had stood up to the challenge. He had overcome every obstacle that had been placed in the way, and there were many. His own family had been against him. His neighbor, Weasel Face, thought him a fool, but through it all he, Lone Wolf, had prevailed.

On the hunting grounds the troubles did not cease. Starvation and the terrible snow storm nearly killed the entire party. But when things were the darkest herds of buffaloes began to arrive. Lodges overflowed with all the good things these sacred beasts brought. This change of fortunes had encouraged him to make the trip to the hairy faces' place called rendezvous. Again the Great Mysterious had tested his leadership. When the Blackfeet raided the herd, it led to the horrifying death of Toohool.

First Son also fell to weapons of an enemy, but then The Great Mysterious had relented. The Blackfeet had been defeated; the decimated herd was replenished, even increased, and Many Horses had been found, wounded but alive. No one, not even Weasel Face, could say he had not led a successful hunt.

Lone Wolf lowered the pipe. He hadn't been praying. He had been taking pride in the things he had done and the blessings he had received. He felt abashed. The Great Mystery would not approve. The Great One was certain to think of more ways to test him. What challenges might there be? It was so difficult to think. A leader had so many responsibilities it was hard to know where to begin.

Of course everything hinged on getting his people safely back to their Lapwai Valley homes. The Lone Wolf family had to set the example. That was a worry in itself. Would First Son be able to travel? His scalped, scarred head was a fearful sight. Would he be able to live with it, seeing people stare and turn away? Second Son, would he come down to earth or would he keep his head in the clouds seeing strange signs predicting misfortune? He had to warn him to keep them to himself. Grandmother, she had done well so far but could she keep up? He could not imagine life without her. Quiet Woman, ah, she always would be at his side. She might groan and sigh but never shirked work.

Now there was a new member of the family, the hairy face, Little Ned. He might be a special problem, one he had not dealt with before. The big trapper had a mind of his own and so did Raven Wing. Would they settle down in the long lodge? What of their children, if they had any? What would they be -- neither Nimpau nor hairy face, or would they be both?

A raspy, haranguing voice jerked Lone Wolf out of his reverie. It was Weasel Face. Lone Wolf groaned. He would have to deal with that annoying squint-eyed family all the way home. He cleaned the pipe and placed it in its bag. He raised his hand in the sign of farewell. The trappers acknowledged the gesture and reluctantly turned away. They hated to part with their partner, Little Ned. He had been with them since Buck Stone's trapping brigade had been formed.

"Yuh s'pose he an' thet Raven Wing'll make out?" Deacon worriedly asked.

"Of course, they'll do fine," Buck Stone answered. But he, too, could not help but wonder what kind of life the big trapper and his Nimpau mate would lead, but that was another story for another time. Perhaps when they met again he would find out what happened and add it to his journal of Indian lore.

THE LONE WOLF CLAN

HISTORICAL NOTE

The Nimpau (Nez Perce) are real people. The explorers, Lewis and Clark, reported they were the most honest and honorable of all Indian tribes. The Nez Perce were renowned horse breeders, creating the Appaloosa, a hardy, beautiful animal coveted by horsemen everywhere.

The Bear Lake rendezvous actually took place as did the battle with the Blackfeet. In the encounter a number of losses were suffered on both sides.

The Lone Wolf clan and their meeting with the hairy faces is fictional but the Nez Perce frequently trekked up the Kooskooskie (Clearwater River) to hunt buffalo in much the same manner as described.

The great Chinook fishing and trading camps, the rivers: Kimooenim (Snake), Great River (Columbia), Bitterroot, Sun, Blackfoot, Hellgate Pass, and other geographical features are truly represented. The authors can vouch for the hot springs of Lolo Pass where they spent a glorious weekend swimming in what perhaps was Toohool's former pool.

###

For readers interested in further adventures of the Lone Wolf Clan order RAVEN WING, sequel to THE LONE WOLF CLAN.

ABOUT THE AUTHORS

Bonnie Jo Hunt (*Wicahpi Win* - Star Woman) is Lakota (Standing Rock Sioux) and the great-great granddaughter of both Chief Francis Mad Bear, prominent Teton Lakota leader, and Major James McLaughlin, Indian agent and Chief Inspector for the Bureau of Indian Affairs. Early in life Bonnie Jo set her heart on helping others. In 1980 she founded Artists of Indian America, Inc. (AIA), a nonprofit organization established to stimulate cultural and social improvement among American Indian youth. To record and preserve her native heritage, in 1997 Bonnie Jo launched Mad Bear Press which publishes American history dealing with life on the western frontier. These publications include the Lone Wolf Clan series: *The Lone Wolf Clan, Raven Wing, The Last Rendezvous, Cayuse Country, Land Without A Country, Death On The Umatilla, A Difficult Passage* and *The Cry Of The Coyote.*

#

Lawrence J. Hunt, a former university professor, works actively with Artists of Indian America, Inc. In addition to coauthoring the Lone Wolf Clan historical series, he has coauthored an international textbook (Harrap: London) and published four mystery novels (Funk and Wagnalls), one of which, *Secret Of The Haunted Crags*, received the Edgar Allan Poe Award from Mystery Writers of America.

- an historical series in the style of Storyteller depicting the role American Indians played in the "Making of the West."

THE LONE WOLF CLAN

A wolf once grew old and lost his grip, but his mind does't change in his sleep also.

by

BONNIE JO HUNT & LAWRENCE J. HUNT

A LONE WOLF CLAN BOOK

THE CRY OF THE COYOTE

by
Bonnie Jo Hunt &
Lawrence J. Hunt

The antelope are gone, the buffalo wallows are empty. Only the cry of the coyote can be heard.

A LONE WOLF CLAN BOOK

A DIFFICULT PASSAGE
(A forgotten tale of the Oregon Trail)

White people with hair on their faces will come from the rising sun. You people must be careful.

by

Bonnie Jo Hunt & Lawrence J. Hunt

A Lone Wolf Clan Book

Lone Wolf Clan Book Sequence

The Lone Wolf Clan
An awesome vision launches the Lone Wolf Clan on a journey that changes their lives forever.

Raven Wing
A tale of love and spiritual seeking embroiled in a clash of cultures.

The Last Rendezvous
A tale of high adventure and tragedy in the final days when mountain men reigned supreme.

Cayuse Country
A flood of emigrants cross the "Big Open" threatening to overwhelm the Cayuse homeland.

Land Without A Country
It was a great land coveted by many but held by none. Who would have the courage to claim it as theirs?

Death On The Umatilla
Whitman Mission murderers are at large; a volunteer army attempts to bring them to justice.

A Difficult Passage
Whitman Mission murderers remain at large; a Regiment of Mounted Riflemen is ordered to bring them in.

Cry Of The Coyote
The antelope are gone; the buffalo wallows are empty. Only the cry of the coyote can be heard.

TAKE THE BEAR OUT OF MY HEART, AND TAKE THY FORM OFF MY DOOR! QUOTH THE RAVEN, NEVERMORE.

RAVEN WING

BY

BONNIE JO HUNT
&
LAWRENCE J. HUNT

A Lone Wolf Clan Book

DEATH ON THE UMATILLA

Strange is a law of the mortals who ... passed the door of Darkness through, not one returns to tell us of the road which in distance we must travel too. Omar Khayyam

Bonnie Jo Hunt and Lawrence J. Hunt

A Lone Wolf Clan Book

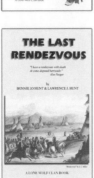

THE LAST RENDEZVOUS

"I have a rendezvous with death At some disputed barricade." Alan Seeger

by

BONNIE JO HUNT & LAWRENCE J. HUNT

A LONE WOLF CLAN BOOK

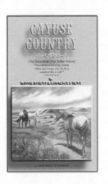

CAYUSE COUNTRY

(The Destruction of an Indian Nation)

You command all of my country, where was I to go, was I to be a wanderer like a wolf?

by

BONNIE JO HUNT & LAWRENCE J. HUNT

A LONE WOLF CLAN BOOK

LAND WITHOUT A COUNTRY

by

BONNIE JO HUNT & LAWRENCE J. HUNT

A Lone Wolf Clan Book